LOST IN THE RED HILLS OF MARS

LOST IN THE RED HILLS OF MARS

◆ ◆ ◆

Jackie Hunter

Bayada Publishing House, LLC

Illustrated by Carlorozy Clemente

ISBN-13: 9780692922606
ISBN-10: 0692922601
Library of Congress Control Number: 2017913369
BAYADA Publishing House, LLC, Richmond, VA

Printed in the United States

For Thomas and Antonio, who love a great story.

ACKNOWLEDGMENTS

◆ ◆ ◆

I WOULD LIKE TO ACKNOWLEDGE my seventeen-year-old granddaughter, Alexis Stackhouse—genius, actress and director, and future screenwriter and film producer—for her work as my final editor. You, Alexis, have helped me give a youthful voice to old wisdom. I am truly blessed to have you in my life and will be forever grateful for the hours and dedication you put into editing this novel.

I would also like to recognize Greg Smith, founder of Agile Writers of Richmond, Virginia. You cannot find a kinder, more creative, and more talented man than Greg. With his Heroes Journey techniques, he has helped me and countless others to complete our stories.

CONTENTS

CHAPTER 1

NO MORE BOOSTERS

◆ ◆ ◆

CELINE WAS PERCHED ON THE side of her bunk, playing an old flute. She impatiently watched her mom as she braided her thick honey-brown hair into a single ropelike braid. All of the females in the Martian colony, except Celine, wore their hair in this single carefree braid. Celine sighed deeply as she stretched, accidently loosening her grip on the flute: her father's precious wooden flute. She watched it fall in slow motion, flipping over and over before it crashed on top of the bunk bed beneath her—the one her mom and dad used to share—and bounced on the metal floor. Startled by the noise, her mom peered down at the flute, then looked back up at Celine.

"What's the matter with you? You know that flute has been in your dad's family for hundreds of years. It's priceless, Celine. Put it away." She returned to braiding her hair, which flowed over her shoulders and down to her waist. "You realize you can't even find artifacts made out wood anymore, right?" she muttered.

"I know that, Mom," Celine answered as she made her way down from the top bunk onto the cold floor. She carefully picked up the flute, examined it, and blew it softly. A sad melody proceeded. "It's OK. I didn't break it," she said to her mom who was still preoccupied with finishing her braid.

"I never can see myself well in this thing," her mom said, referring to the family's polished metal mirror.

Celine placed the flute into the middle drawer beneath her parents' bunk: the one her father used to keep his two jumpsuits in. Only the gray indoor one remained. It was soft and warm like hers, but darker and much larger. She touched it lightly before closing the drawer. She closed her eyes and sighed.

"Mom," she said as she stood up from the drawers. Her mother squinted as she looked into the metal mirror, ignoring Celine's comment. "Mother," Celine continued. Still no response. "Abbie Voltaire," Celine shouted.

"What, Celine?" she replied without looking up.

"Can we talk?"

Abbie turned to look at her daughter. Celine was standing only three feet from her in their cramped quarters.

"I'm not getting the Brain Booster on my birthday this year," Celine started. "It was…different…last time."

"Oh?" Abbie said with disinterest as she turned back to her mirror, twirled her long braid into a figure eight and tucked the end under. "Celine, we've had this conversation before. I haven't changed my mind." Abbie squeezed her hands together as if she was about to pray. "You don't always get what you want. You know. I don't."

Abbie pushed her small stool back from the family's dresser and stood up. "Oh, goodness. Look at me," she said with irritation in her voice. She pulled honey-brown hairs from her gray jumpsuit. "There. I guess that looks a little better." Finally, she gave Celine her full attention. "I am going to work. Make sure you finish your history lecture. Call me if you need me."

She then pushed the button on the wall next to the door. The door silently slid open, and a barrage of voices rushed in. Abbie stepped into the corridor, turned back, and with a pouty smile, blew Celine a kiss. Celine didn't smile back. The door slid closed, and the room was quiet again.

She flopped down on to the bottom bunk and threw her head back on to the folded gray blanket that she saw her mom often use as a pillow. She stared at the bare walls.

"Celine, are you up?" a female voice asked. The voice was void of emotion.

Celine bounced up, almost banging her head on the upper bunk. "Yes, Uji."

"Jeez, can you not startle me?"

"Negative. I am an Artificial Intelligence Hologram…You have not logged any hours on your lessons."

"I have not had breakfast yet." Celine sounded eerily similar to her AI. "Uji, did you know Alex Rittenhouse is coming to Mars?"

Celine wrapped her arms around her chest and batted her long dark lashes.

"The boy who is taking up thirty thousand photo files on my memory grid? Yes."

Celine studied her five feet tall, ninety-pound frame in the metal mirror. She pouted, squinted her eyes, and analyzed her face at different angles. "Not bad," she muttered. "Oh yeah, that's him, Uji. He's the best-looking boy on Earth, and he's coming to Mars." Celine twirled around once, almost banging her knee on the stool. "I'm taking my shower early this week."

"Shower activated," Uji said. Then the hologram disappeared.

Celine snatched her red goggles from her drawer beneath her parents' bunk and placed them over her eyes. Then she centered herself, still clothed, beneath a round light embedded in the metallic ceiling.

"Blue-light shower," she commanded. Instantly, she was bathed in waves of blue light. She rubbed her hands together as if washing them with the water she, herself, had never experienced.

She then rubbed her hands across her face and through her short dark curly hair.

"Wen'de ya ho," she hummed. This was an ancient Cherokee morning song her father had taught her, meaning "I am the Great Spirit." Something about the song gave her comfort.

Within minutes, she was free of all harmful and odor-producing microbes as well as negative thoughts in regard to her upcoming thirteenth birthday. Her body's electric frequency increased to a normal sixty-eight megahertz. Her skin, hair, and her only set of indoor clothing were refreshed, as was her mood.

The shower of blue lights faded along with the humming noise it made. Celine finished her routine by finger combing hair. *Alex is coming!* She checked her reflection in the mirror where her petite frame was not only streaked but slightly distorted. "Perfect!" she said, and she smoothed her gray jumpsuit.

Celine pressed the lock on the door to the small compartment. From a panel next to the door, a monitor activated and connected with the chip embedded under the skin of her left forearm. If she had been sick, for example, the door would not have opened. However, the door unsealed, and Celine stepped into the hall. Instantly her quiet world became completely disorderly. Some colonists were busy in the hall, and she could hear the chatter from the others in the commons.

The commons, the largest and busiest area in the Compound, was always full of people. It was also the only room in the Compound that made Celine feel like she wasn't living underground. The images of windows were so realistic that she felt as though she were looking out on the Martian terrain on a bright summer day.

She stepped into the commons but waited in the corridor for a moment in order to allow her eyes to adjust to the light. She was greeted with indifference. Everyone appeared too busy to notice her.

Spotting one of her neighbors, she greeted him warmly. "Good day, Mr. Kone."

Mr. Kone pressed his hands together in prayer and nodded. "And so it is. Good day, little one."

"Thank you for letting me help in the community garden this week."

"My pleasure," he replied. "A growing child like you deserves some fresh vegetables every now and then."

"Well, you know me—I love having first dibs on fresh vegetables." Celine chuckled then pressed her hands together and nodded. "Good day!"

"And so it is." Mr. Kone nodded and sashayed through the crowd toward the exit that led to the enclosed community garden.

Celine watched him as he exited. She liked Mr. Kone. He was the only colonist, other than her parents (occasionally), who seemed to have time for her. She strode toward the food dispenser. There she noticed Morg, her mom's fiancé, sitting at one of the tables. His heavy head hung low, and his face was inches from his food box. She could hear him slurping his meal. She greeted him with a perfunctory smile. He acknowledged her with a quick head bow and continued eating.

Celine then made her way to one of the two 3-D food printers.

"Breakfast in a box," she said to indicate her choice. Her breakfast, two piles of warm mush, was squirted into a small plastic box.

"You have two rations left for the day," the voice from the printer said in a quite motherly fashion.

Celine lifted the box to her nose. "Mmm, smells good." She stuck her index finger into the yellow mush and then licked it. "And a perfect consistency!"

After retrieving a spoon and napkin, she found a vacant table where she placed her food box then sat on the cold bench beneath it. Morg, who had finished his meal, came over and sat next to her as she took her first spoonful. Celine drew back a few centimeters.

"We tried so hard to find your dad," Morg said. "We found his assistant."

"Yes, I heard." Celine mumbled as she inspected her spoon. "Ms. Armbruster said part of his body was chewed away."

"Ms. Armbruster talks too much..." Morg responded, annoyed.

Celine slurped her meal and stared at the artificial window in front of her. "Well, is it true?"

"He died because of the cold weather. Some kind of scavenger gnawed at him."

"Oh," Celine said and continued to eat.

"You know we never found your father's gear," he continued.

Celine let her spoon plop into her half-eaten meal.

"Dad's gear wasn't found?"

"Nope...Neither was his assistant's. But there's probably no way that he could have survived in those hills. He didn't have enough O2 pills to last a month. How long has your dad been missing again?"

Celine didn't respond. She didn't hear anything after realizing her father's gear hadn't been found. *Morg and his crew haven't found Dad's gear because Dad has it! He's still alive!* She had renewed hope that her father was out there somewhere. She had to tell her grandma. She quickly slurped the rest of her breakfast and headed out. "See you later, Morg. I've got to go."

"Good day," she heard him say as she rushed to the entrance through the corridor.

Down the hall she raced, almost running into her mom's best friend.

"Sorry, Hannah," Celine yelled.

"Good day," she heard Hannah say.

"And so it is," Celine called back, but she continued running until she arrived home. She pushed the green button, and the door to her small quarters slid open. She rushed in, plopped down in front of the family's desk and snapped on the computer.

"Enisi," she said, but to Celine's disappointment, Uji appeared instead.

"Celine, you must complete your school lessons. You may call your Enisi when there is relevant school data in your files."

"I can finish my history assignment in twenty minutes. Can't you at least start the call?"

"When you are finished, I will call her," Uji said then vanished.

Celine sucked her teeth, but she took out a small tablet from her drawer. She clicked on her avatar, a reddish-brown Cherokee girl with two long braids. Then Celine began listening to her pre-recorded history lesson from Earth.

Celine completed her assignment thirty minutes later, and Uji reappeared.

"You may call now," Uji said and, once again, evaporated.

"Call Enisi," Celine said. "Now what to do for twenty minutes?"

Uji reappeared. "You can complete your Innovative thinking assignment."

Celine rolled her eyes. She jumped onto the floor next to her dad's drawer and opened it. She pulled out his wooden flute.

"Or I can play Dad's flute," she said.

"You may," Uji said, peering over Celine's shoulder.

Celine wrapped her nimble fingers around the flute and pressed it gently to her lips and blew.

Uji smiled.

For twenty minutes, Celine poured her heart into creating music. It calmed her and reminded her of how much her dad enjoyed hearing her play it. Suddenly, her concert was interrupted by grandmother's voice.

"Harmony unto you, Granddaughter," her grandmother said.

Uji disappeared. The A.I. always knew when to give Celine her privacy.

"Harmony unto you, Enisi," Celine said.

Enisi had long, feathery silver hair and deep, dark eyes. Her full nose sat in the middle of a cracked and weathered copper-colored face, untouched by stem regeneration. She appeared soft and feminine in her bright red cotton-like dress with its embroidered yellow-and-blue birds, but she was much stronger than she appeared. She was a chief and spiritual healer. Many members of her community came to her for advice regarding both the living and the dead. To her granddaughter, however, she was Enisi: her father's mom and the only grandmother she had ever known.

Celine placed her flute gently on her parents' bunk.

"You play nicely," Enisi said. "You remind me of your father when you play it."

"Thank you."

"Your call was unexpected. Is there any news about your dad? Have they found him?"

Celine swallowed. "They've found his assistant."

"Mr. Takei? How is he?"

"He's dead, Enisi. But they can't find his gear. And Dad's gear is missing too. That means something…Doesn't it? Dad must have it. He must have found a way to survive."

"Slow down, my child," Enisi said gently. Her dark eyes were a sea of calm.

"Enisi, Mom is going to marry Morg." Celine said it in one breath and then began to hyperventilate as tears rolled down her cheeks.

"Mr. Francis Morg? The chief protector?" Enisi lifted a single eyebrow.

"Yes!" Celine continued sobbing. "I don't like Morg, Grandma. I don't think he's really trying to find my dad."

Enisi sat straight up and placed her folded hands into her lap. Her eyes could not hide her concern. Finally she spoke, "Do not worry about things you cannot control. I will see what I can do at this end." She rubbed her wrinkled hands together and then said, "Are you aware that Mr. Rittenhouse, the colony's CEO, will be arriving on Mars for an inspection."

"Yes! And his son is coming too!" Celine said as she wiped a tear.

"Well, he's actually coming to get coordinates for an ore deposit. The coordinates were lost with your father," Enisi said. "If you have the opportunity, let Mr. Rittenhouse know you think your father is missing, not dead. Let me know what he says. Remain strong, Celine."

"I will, Grandma," Celine said.

Suddenly the computer screen went white.

"Those darn solar flares! I didn't even get a chance to say goodbye…"

Uji reappeared. "Celine, you have remaining lessons that must be logged in today."

"All right, I guess I'll get started," Celine said and picked up her tablet.

After logging four hours of school lessons, Celine was ready for some physical activity in the exercise room. She pressed the door lock, expecting the door to slide open. It didn't. She stood there, momentarily stunned. Then she pressed her thumb against the lock—this time even harder. Nothing.

Thoughts about disease and quarantines flooded her head. She was afraid to put her thumb on the lock again. "This can't be happening to me." Celine could feel her heart pounding and her throat getting dry. Every molecule in her body was on high alert. "Uji?" she said with a quiver in her voice.

Uji appeared. Its eyes looked straight ahead as if looking through Celine.

"Uji, open the door, please," Celine said in a pleading tone.

"You are ill," it replied, sounding abnormally machine-like. "You are very ill."

CHAPTER 2

WHAT'S IN THE METAL MIRROR

◆ ◆ ◆

CELINE DROPPED HER HANDS TO her sides and pinched her shoulders back. "I don't feel sick."

Uji did not respond. Instead, it flashed on and off like lights during a fire drill.

"I'm checking my vitals," she said as she touched the palm-size screen on the panel next to the door.

Numbers appeared on the screen. Celine squinted and leaned in closer.

"My temperature is thirty-seven degrees Celsius." She double-checked the monitor. "All of my vitals are normal…Uji, I am not sick!" Uji continued to be unresponsive, and its image flickered as if it were in an emotional panic.

Celine directed her attention to the locked door and began pounding on it.

"Help! Somebody, please help me!" She stopped pounding and listened for any sound outside.

"I can't hear a thing," she said in disappointment. "Uji, I'm not ill. You have to let me out of here."

The hologram faded away.

Celine rushed to her computer, and the screen lit up. "Call Mom," she said.

After a moment, Celine heard Uji's voice. "She did not answer."

"Call her again," Celine said. After a few moments, Uji's voice repeated. "She did not answer."

Celine flopped down onto the lower bunk. "I am not calling Morg. I'd rather stay in here all day then call him. Where are those doctors? They should know I'm locked in here by now."

Celine popped up from the bed. "Maybe the lock is broken!"

She headed for the panel.

As she passed the polished mirror, she caught a glimpse of herself and was startled to see that her eyes were glowing yellow. She swerved back toward the door and pulled on its frame. The door would not move. "Brighter light," she commanded, and instantly the dim room was brightly lit.

Uji reappeared. "Your heart rate has increased. You are ill." Uji disappeared.

Celine could hear her heart thumping as she inched her way across the cold floor and peered into the mirror. She squinted and then leaned in toward the mirror.

"What just happened? My eyes are…" She paused and examined her eyes from different angles. "Normal?"

With her arms wrapped around her chest and stomach, she eased back onto the family stool.

"OK, maybe the monitor is right…maybe I am sick."

"I can't believe it took thirty-three hours to get here," Alex Rittenhouse, the fifteen-year-old heartthrob from Earth, told his father. "Why didn't we teleport?"

Mr. Rittenhouse glared at his son with lips held so tightly they looked like a single line.

"Boy, didn't I tell you the situation here?" he asked. "This colony has been draining our family's finances since *my* father started this project years before you were a cell in a petri dish."

Alex flinched.

"I know that it needs work," Mr. Rittenhouse continued. He leaned back into his well-padded seat. "But I'm not putting in any more credit until it starts bringing in a profit. Quality teleportation requires investment, Junior."

"Sorry I asked," Alex mumbled and then stared silently out the small porthole of his father's spaceship. Thin white clouds of ice crystals prevented him from seeing the Martian surface, yet he continued to look through the porthole, blinking his long lashes over hazel brown eyes.

Most of the passengers had gotten up from their seats and were stretching or roaming about. Alex remained seated and continued to stare out the window, but he tilted his left ear toward his father's conversation with Stan, one of his father's personal protectors.

"I can't continue to invest credits into this Martian colony," Alex heard his father say. "My investors are going to cash in their stocks and force me into bankruptcy!"

Out of the corner of his eye, Alex saw Stan nod sympathetically.

"There is a Porta down there in the Compound." Mr. Rittenhouse nodded toward one of the portholes. "But it can't transport anyone outside the Compound. And do you know how much money it would cost me to put in one of those fancy Teleportas that Junior wants?" He motioned toward Alex.

Alex shook his head as he watched his father complain.

"Dad, please," Alex said and sucked his teeth.

"Well, look who's rejoined the living," Mr. Rittenhouse said regarding Alex. "I was just telling the boys about the Porta at the Compound."

"I know. I heard you," Alex said, and he turned his head back to the porthole to stare at the white clouds below.

"So if you want to see that planet, you'll have to walk or do some climbing. The Mav is off-limits. You hear that, Junior?"

Alex continued to stare out the porthole.

"It's for the scientists when they're on their expeditions. Not for some kid to take a joy ride. Besides, there are plenty of hills down there. You could walk faster than a Mav in those hills." Mr. Rittenhouse paused to get a second wind. "Most don't look any worse than those Himalayas. You remember the Himalayas?"

"The Himalayas?" Stan asked.

"Dad, Stan didn't go with us to the Himalayas."

"That's right. He didn't. Well, we really enjoyed those mountains. Didn't we, son?" Mr. Rittenhouse turned to face his protectors. "My boy's a great climber, you know. He was a real man's man out there…not like that sissy actor he plays every day on that stupid reality show."

Alex jumped up from his seat with his fist raised.

Mr. Rittenhouse's eyes widened, and he leaned back.

"I am sick of your insults, Dad!" Alex said. "Everyone here knows I'm your clone. If there's anything wrong with me, blame yourself."

"Come here, Alex, and sit with us," said one of the Marsologists, Amirra, trying to calm him.

Mr. Rittenhouse stared at Alex's raised hand. "You need to go sit down, son," he said with calm authority.

Alex uncoiled his fist and dropped his hand to his side, but he remained standing eye-to-eye with his father. He was nearly six feet tall, almost as tall as his dad. "I don't understand you," Alex said.

Alex looked at Stan through glassy red eyes. "You like my show, don't you, Stan?"

"Yes, Alex. I like your show," Stan replied sheepishly.

"How about you, Jerry?" Alex asked the Marsologist who was sitting next to Amirra, his wife.

"Sit with us, Alex," Amirra pleaded. "This is not the right time to talk with your father about this."

"Amirra is right, Alex," Jerry said. "You're exhausted. You haven't slept in over thirty hours. Here." Jerry patted the empty seat next to him. "Sit here, have some dried chicken, and rest."

Alex bit his lip. He knew Amirra and Jerry Gregory were worried that his father would lose his temper. Reluctantly, Alex ambled over to the Gregorys' lounge area and flopped down into the seat next to Jerry. Alex swallowed, exhaled loudly, and rubbed his hands as he stared out the porthole. Though his eyes were red, he did not cry. "I'm not hungry," he mumbled.

Suddenly, the ship penetrated the planet's atmosphere, and rays of pink and violet hues radiated through the ship.

"Look at that sky!" Amirra said. "Wow! Unbelievable!"

Everyone rushed to a porthole or shifted in their seat to get a look at the Martian sky, a mixture of blues, pinks, and violets with slithers of white clouds.

"Look down there!" Jerry said, pointing to the flat, dusty Martian terrain. "That area reminds me of Death Valley. Look at that volcano! It must be Olympus Mons!"

Alex's eyes widen as he gazed at the largest volcano in the galaxy. "Amazing," he muttered.

"Yes, it is," Jerry said and smiled at Alex. "We plan to study it up close. We might even reactivate it and give this planet some warmth." Jerry studied Alex's face.

"What do you think of that?"

"That would make a great adventure story for my show," Alex said proudly.

Alex watched his father tap the personal Com he wore on his wrist and then walk toward the apex of the ship. Mr. Rittenhouse had a scowl on his face.

"Quiet! You fools!" Mr. Rittenhouse said, interrupting everyone's childish chatter. "Can't you see I have an important call?" Alex noticed his father's eyes narrow as he looked at him.

Alex's strong hands covered his mouth and chin, hiding his grin.

The bewildered passengers—the two scientists, the three personal protectors, and the ship's navigator—became as silent as dormant robots.

"Well. I knew that was coming. Dad always has a way of making others feel small," Alex mumbled, and then he chuckled quietly.

Finally the ship touched down on the dusty planet. Everyone except the navigator squeezed himself into lightweight radiation suits and then adjusted his Graviton boots to Martian gravity. After putting on their oxygen packs and helmets, and turning on their voice amplifiers, they lined up in front of the transporter. When Mr. Rittenhouse keyed in his password on the panel next to the transporter, the door slid open, and they all crammed in.

"Surface," Mr. Rittenhouse commanded once the door was shut. In a nanosecond, the transporter had dropped fifteen feet to the surface. "Door open," he said. The door slid open, and everyone, except Mr. Rittenhouse, stretched his neck to see the surface. He stood back with a wide smile on his face. "Alex," he said, "I'll let you do the honors."

Alex raised his eyebrows. "Sure," he said and stomped onto the surface, causing a puff of red dust to rise above his knees. "This stuff is like talcum powder."

"Watch it," his dad said as he stepped onto the surface followed by his entourage.

"Follow me," Mr. Rittenhouse said as he walked past Alex. "The Amin and doctors are waiting for us on the other side."

Alex stepped out of his dad's path and got in line with the other passengers.

Flat, barren lands nearly covered the Compound, which in reality was the spaceship that had brought the first hundred colonists to Mars. It had been transformed into a three-story underground working and living quarter for the colonists. Just beyond the Compound, the lands were dotted with hundreds of ash-gray boulders of hardened lava and a sprinkle of small gray rocks. In the distance, Alex could see rusty red hills.

"I wonder what it will be like to climb those hills," he said.

"Behave yourself, and you might get a chance to find out. I bought climbing gear," his father said.

Alex bit his lip. "Sure, Dad."

"Quiet, Admin is speaking," Mr. Rittenhouse said.

In his headphones, Alex could hear his cousin, Admin Sandra Rittenhouse, speaking to his father.

"Welcome to Mars, Mr. Alex Rittenhouse: the both of you," she said and then chuckled. Alex noticed she emphasized the word "you," making reference to the cloning. He frowned.

"The medical team will be waiting for you at the rear exit," Admin continued. "You'll be spending twenty-four hours in the isolation chamber. The cook—ahem—the chef will provide you with rations and distilled water."

"Rations? Did she say rations?" Alex muttered to himself with a perplexed scowl. "Dad won't tolerate that."

"I brought my own food, Sandra. You know I don't eat anything from the printer. I have all that I need on my ship. I'll have Stan bring it in, as we need it. We have enough food to last at least a year. And I have ten water bottles."

"Ten?"

"Yes, I'll give a few out as gifts."

"Gifts?"

"One is for you, Sandra."

"Thank you! I've heard about them. Do you know how they work exactly?"

"No, Sandra. All I care about is that it keeps making water."

"Dad," Alex said, interrupting his father's conversation. "I thought we would only be here for a month."

"Alex, you're not a part of this conversation," Mr. Rittenhouse said.

"I don't want to stay on this outback of a planet for a year," Alex mumbled as he followed his dad into the Compound.

Most of the colonists were in the commons when Mr. Rittenhouse's spaceship landed. Abbie Voltaire was there as well, watching the landing of the *Stellar*. A huge screen, typically used for entertainment, was providing a clear image of all the action happening outside the Compound.

Abbie watched the screen in wide-eyed amazement. "That *Stellar* is no ordinary ship. What a beauty! Look at that V shape," she said to her friend, Hannah.

Hannah nodded but didn't take her eyes off the screen. "It's beautiful," she said.

The ship glided in quietly and hovered before releasing long spidery legs onto the surface.

"I wonder what other technologies we're missing out on since we've become full-time residents of Mars?" Abbie said.

Hannah chuckled but didn't take her eyes off the screen.

Most of the hundred colonists applauded when the ship's legs touched down and the engine turned off. Abbie did not. "Nothing but the best for our CEO," she said. Her lips curled into a soft smile.

"Hush, Abbie. You're spoiling it," Hannah said.

One of the colonists yelled, "I'm first to tour it." Hannah chimed in, "Me, too."

"You are such a typical Martian," Abbie said, first rolling her eyes, then chuckling. She stopped watching the screen and began searching the commons.

"I don't see Celine," she said. "I know she wouldn't want to miss this." Abbie looked down at the personal Com on her wrist.

"Celine has called me. Twice." Abbie pushed the recall key for her quarters and was relieved to hear Celine's voice. "Celine, why aren't you in the commons?"

"Mom! Uji won't let me out of here! It says I'm ill! I tried calling you."

"Honey, I'm so sorry. I didn't notice the vibrations. I am on my way." Abbie made her way through the cluster of colonists. She waved to Hannah as she entered her corridor.

Celine stayed on the line. "Are you OK?" Abbie asked.

"I don't know! Where are the doctors? Mom, get me out of here!"

"Stay calm. I'm almost there." Abbie walked quickly to her quarters, afraid of the attention she would draw by running. *What if she's sick? What if Celine was quarantined?*

When she finally reached Celine's quarters, Abbie noticed that the door button was blinking red. She jabbed her finger at the button multiple times, but it continued blinking. The door remained shut. She spoke into her personal Com. "Celine, I can't unlock the door."

"Where are the doctors, Mom?" Celine asked impatiently.

"With Mr. Rittenhouse and his entourage. Give me a minute to call Dr. Duke, all right?"

Abbie tapped the small Com on her wrist and said, "Call Dr. Duke." She heard static. "His Com must be turned off," she muttered. She got the same results after calling Dr. Baylor. She pushed the intercom button next to the blinking red light.

"Celine, they're not answering. I'll have to go find one of the doctors. I won't take long. You'll be OK."

"Hurry, Mom. I want to get out of here."

Though she wanted to run, Abbie walked back to the commons. "If Celine is sick, only the doctors and Morg need to know it," she whispered to herself.

She looked for Morg in the crowd of excited colonists. If anyone in the crowd could help her reach a doctor, it would be him. She found her future husband standing near the Porta. She rushed over to inform him about Celine.

"I need to speak with Dr. Duke. Celine might be ill," she said in a hushed tone.

Without a word to her, Morg took his personal Com from his side pocket. It was much different from the one she wore on her wrist, larger and more complicated.

"We have a code red in cell ten," he mumbled into the Com. "Give me Dr. Baylor. The baby is ill." He listened through a hearing device implanted in his right ear.

Abbie crossed her arms.

"Dr. Baylor is on her way to her office," he said to Abbie.

"I told you I wanted Dr. Duke."

"Dr. Duke is too busy right now. Go back to your cell and wait." Then he folded his arms in front of his broad chest.

Abbie stood there for a moment with her mouth opened. Then she pressed her lips together tightly, turned her back to Morg, and stomped out of the commons. Though she was relieved that help was on the way, she was irritated with the disrespect her fiancé had just shown her.

As soon as she reached her quarters, she went straight to her intercom.

"Celine? I am here," she said. "Doctor Baylor will be contacting you soon."

"Mom, leave the intercom on."

Abbie pushed a button on the panel. "It's on, Celine. Don't worry. I'm not going anywhere."

Abbie leaned back against the wall next to her door; her arms were wrapped around her body like a supporting hug. She replayed the conversation that went on between her and Morg in the commons. "I don't understand him. He acted like he didn't even care."

Celine sat still on her bunk. "Mom, are you still there?"

"Yes."

Suddenly a holographic image of Dr. Baylor appeared in the room with Celine.

"Oh! You startled me," Celine cried.

"Celine, is the doctor with you?" Abbie asked.

"Yes, Mother."

"Ah, there you are," Dr. Baylor finally said when Celine's visual was clear in the infirmary.

Dr. Baylor's hologram was incredibly realistic, and she had short hair like most of the men on the colony as well as a muscular face.

"Come down from there," she said to Celine. "I know you can hear and see me."

"Yes, ma'am." Celine climbed down from her bunk and went straight to the hologram. She stuck her right hand through the doctor's white jumpsuit.

"Stop joking around," Dr. Baylor said. "Go get that stool, and put it next to the Uji panel."

Celine slid the heavy stool next to the panel and sat on it. "Why do I need it here?"

The doctor ignored her question. "I am taking some samples of your blood." The square-face hologram pointed to the panel. "Your medical supplies will appear shortly."

"I don't see anything."

"Give it a few minutes to transport."

Celine heard what sounded like a gush of air behind the panel; the panel slid up, and a small self-supporting stand slid out.

On the stand was a thin acrylic slide above a magnifying tube, and next to it, an indented handprint with two cuffs on it.

The hologram peered over Celine's shoulder. "Looks like everything's in order."

"Celine, I want you to trust me."

"Why are you saying that?"

"Well. I'm going to ask you to do something that might be a little uncomfortable."

"Will it hurt?"

"Only a little."

"What do I have to do?"

"See that hand print?"

"Yes." Celine rubbed her hand over the molded print.

"I need you to place your left hand over it."

Slowly, Celine placed her left hand over the plastic handprint on the stand. In a flash, a small plastic cuff enclosed her index finger, and the larger one cuffed her wrist. A tiny, pointed hollow tube rose up from the index finger of the handprint and stabbed her finger, then suctioned a drop of blood from it.

"Ow!" Celine tried to free her hand. "That hurts *a lot,* Doctor."

A tiny blue light on the stand moved back and forth three times over her pierced finger, and the cuffs released Celine's wrist.

Abbie pressed the intercom bottom when she heard Celine scream.

"What's going on, Celine?"

"This thing just stabbed my finger."

Abbie sighed. "The doctor has to get a blood sample, Celine."

"I know that, Mom. That doesn't mean it doesn't hurt." Celine held her finger close to her eyes, studying the small red mark on the tip of her finger.

"Now that wasn't so bad," Dr. Baylor said with a slight smile.

Celine gave a sarcastic, cheesy grin.

"Go to your computer, Celine. I want you to see something."

Celine slid the stool back to its place at the desk and sat on it. The computer screen lit up, and the hologram looked over her shoulder.

"You can watch me compare your blood to my pathogen file if you'd like."

"Pathogens? Won't that make you sick?" Celine asked.

"No, these are just cataloged images." Dr. Baylor paused the image of Celine's blood cells. "Coming along nicely. Have you noticed anything different about the colonists?"

"Like what?" Celine continued to watch the images of pathogens on her computer screen.

Celine turned around to face the hologram. Dr. Baylor stared into her camera; she appeared to look directly into Celine's eyes. It was a strange moment, but Dr. Baylor simply smiled and went back to searching the pathogen file.

"No match. This looks good," she said. "Everyone will be relieved to know that."

"Why did you ask me about the colonists, Doctor?"

"Well, I noticed something special in your blood cells, and…" Dr. Baylor turned her head at different angles to study Celine's eyes. "Well, it's nothing to worry about. I might call later to do a follow-up. Are you still having difficulties sleeping?"

"Yes, but Mom says it's because I'm missing my dad…"

"Click!" Celine heard the door unlock. Her mother rushed in and wrapped her arms around her.

"Mom!" Celine said and twisted away from her.

The doctor's hologram chuckled at the interaction between the mother and daughter but continued with Celine's diagnosis.

"According to your tests and vitals, your body is not making enough melatonin."

"Melatonin? What's that?" Celine asked.

Without answering her, the doctor wiped the sweat from her brow with her sleeve. "That's a relief," Dr. Baylor said. "There's no need for quarantine."

"Thank goodness," Abbie said.

"Celine will need light therapy. I'll have my assistant bring a light therapy box to your quarters. Have her use the box every day for three to four hours. During her school lessons would be ideal. We'll try that for a month—a Martian month. I will personally reevaluate her then. Do you have any questions?"

"No, Doctor," Abbie replied.

Celine waved her hand. "Um, I do."

The hologram whipped around to face Celine. "Melatonin is a happy hormone. Basically, you need more happiness," she said as she burst out into laughter.

Celine and her mother scrunched their faces.

Dr. Baylor regained her composure, but her eyes still danced. "It's very important you get well before your birthday. Wouldn't want you to miss your Brain Booster."

"Thank you, Dr. Baylor," Abbie said.

The computer screen went white, and both Celine and her mom gave a sigh of relief.

"Celine, I was so worried about you." Abbie placed her hand across her mouth as her eyes began to tear up. "I'm so happy you're OK."

"Mom…" Celine hesitated. *Do I tell her?*

"Yes, dear." Abbie looked lovingly at her daughter.

She looks so happy. I can't tell her now. "I've seen you and Dad using the light therapy box. Does it hurt?"

"No, it doesn't. I thought you knew that." Abbie paused and studied Celine's face. "You look worried. Something else on your mind?"

"No," Celine said. "Do you think Dr. Baylor seemed a little weird today?

"A little. Maybe. I don't know her that well. She hasn't had an emergency call since you were a baby. Come to think of it, she didn't come to the planet until you were born…Anyway, I'm just glad you're not sick."

"I know." Celine exhaled.

"My, what a day. Are you hungry? Have you eaten?"

"I had one meal, but I'm not hungry." Celine sat on her mom's bed.

"Are you sure? I could bring dinner after I finish work…Oh, by the way, I found a virus…"

Celine squeezed her lips together.

"…in the computer program," Abbie finished.

"Oh," Celine said with relief.

"The cold storage pantry hasn't been working properly. I don't have to tell you how serious that is. So I'll be gone awhile."

"Did you get to see Alex earlier?" Celine asked.

"Not exactly. The lights on his helmet were off…I'm sorry you didn't get a chance to see the landing."

"Me too." Celine cast her eyes down to her hands in her lap. "Do you think I'll get a chance to meet him?"

"I don't see why not."

"And Mr. Rittenhouse too?"

"Why would you want to meet him?"

"I don't know. I read that Alex is his clone. Maybe I can see what Alex will look like when he's older."

"Silly girl...I'll ask Morg to give you a clearance pass to meet them." Abbie held Celine's face and turned it side to side. "And maybe an outdoors pass. You look like you could use some sun."

Celine wrapped her arms around her mom's waist. "Thanks, Mom. If you didn't *force* me get that stupid annual Brain Booster, you'd be perfect."

Abbie pinched Celine's cheeks. "And you will be getting yours soon. Get some rest."

After the door shut behind Abbie, Celine rushed to the mirror to examine her eyes. "What did I see in the mirror earlier?"

Celine's AI reappeared. "Please repeat."

Celine hoisted the folded blanket and threw it through Uji. "You've got some nerve showing up now, Uji." The hologram disappeared.

Celine went over to the mirror and leaned into it. She used her fingers to open her eyes wider. For a second, they flashed a glowing yellow. Celine screamed and pushed back from the mirror, causing the stool to fall over.

Uji reappeared. "How may I assist you?"

"Something's happening to my eyes, Uji."

Abbie returned to the commons, where she was surprised to see Dr. Baylor talking with Morg. She went to join them, but the doctor quickly shuffled away when she noticed her coming.

"So the baby needs a light therapy?" Morg said to Abbie when she walked up to him.

"Stop calling her that. So Baylor is giving you medical reports now?" Abbie said, fuming.

Morg turned up his lips. Abbie assumed he did this in order to control his temper.

"Everyone knows we are engaged," he said. "I am sure even Dr. Baylor knows about our relationship."

"Still, she had no right to tell you."

"So how is Celine?" Morg folded his arms in front of his barrel chest.

"She's shaken. Being trapped in a cell for hours would startle anyone. The doctor said—oh, the doctor has already told you about her condition, hasn't she?" Abbie said sarcastically.

"I just wanted to know how the baby's doing," Morg replied.

"Stop calling her baby! Her name is Celine, and she's not a baby! You know she hates when you call her that."

Morg changed the conversation. "I don't think she should get her Brain Booster this birthday."

"What? Did the doctor tell you that?"

"No, but don't you agree?"

"No, I don't. You don't know my daughter! You don't know what she needs! I do."

"Lower your voice." Morg moved in closer. He appeared to be swelling with anger.

"Look, I have work to do. I'll talk with you later." Abbie rushed to the Porta, but before entering it, she turned back to look at the man she was soon to marry. He was nowhere in sight. *I don't understand him: one moment he's interested in us, and the next moment he couldn't care less. Well, off to cold storage for me. It won't be any colder than it is in here.*

Celine rushed into the corridor and ran into Morg.

"Celine, where are you going? Shouldn't you be resting?" he asked.

"I've got to find Mom," she said and continued hurriedly down the corridor and toward the commons.

Morg turned and followed her. "Well, I just saw your mom a moment ago. I'm sure she went to work in a restricted area. Do you need something? Can I help?"

Celine slowed down, giving Morg a chance to catch up. "Then I'll wait for her in the commons," she said, looking at the floor as she spoke. She entered the commons and spotted a vacant table near the Porta. She hurried over to it, sat down and buried her head into her arms on the table.

Morg followed her and sat on the bench in front of her. He reached across the table and patted her on the head.

"Celine, I have a special job for you."

Celine opened her eyes, but she did not raise her head.

"I know how much you like that Alex boy. I need you to give him a tour of the Compound tomorrow."

Celine raised her head and sat up. For a moment, she thought she saw Morg flinch, and she quickly averted her eyes.

"Also…You would tell Dr. Baylor if you noticed something strange happening to you, wouldn't you?" he said. He looked down at his fingers tapping on the table. "She would want to know that."

"Yes, I would. And thanks."

"For what?" Morg asked.

"For giving me the tour assignment." Celine shifted on the bench. "When is Mom going to finish her work?"

"I don't know. I'll go down and check on her, and I'll let her know you're waiting in the commons. OK?"

"All right." Celine closed her eyes and rested her head on the table.

Moments later, Abbie rushed into the commons with Morg by her side.

"Celine, what's the matter? Why aren't you in bed?"

Celine grabbed her mom's hand. "Mom, come on," she said and began pulling her mom toward the corridor.

"Thanks, Morg," Abbie said as she allowed Celine to lead her. "We'll talk later."

"Keep me informed," he responded and then headed toward the Porta that led to Dr. Baylor's office in the infirmary.

Once Celine and her mom entered their home, Celine burst into tears.

"Look at my eyes," she cried as she held her head up. Her water-filled eyes widened.

Abbie examined Celine's eyes and said, "Do you have an eyelash in them?"

Celine faced the mirror. "Mom, they were glowing yellow."

"Celine, these metal mirrors are horrible. I'm sure what you saw was a reflection of the light."

"Mom, it happened twice."

"Is that all? You don't need to worry about anything you see in this mirror. Believe me. I never look like myself. Now, I want you to get some rest. I heard you have the honor of taking Alex on a tour tomorrow."

"Oh, yes! Isn't that wonderful?" Celine's face suddenly brightened.

"I'm sure you don't want dark circles around those beautiful brown eyes. To bed with you," Abbie commanded, signaling the bunk.

"Whatever, Mom," Celine grumbled as she climbed into her bunk and pulled the covers over her head. Ten minutes passed, and she was asleep.

In the small isolation chamber, portable sleeping cots had been set up for Alex, the two scientists, and Mr. Rittenhouse's personal protectors. A full-size bed had been blown up for Mr. Rittenhouse.

Alex looked around the small quarters he would be sharing with his father and six others for the next twenty-four hours. See-through acrylic surrounded the room.

"There's no privacy in here...And this place smells like hot metal...Where is the bathroom?"

"Shut up, boy. Always whining."

"I'm not whining. I really do have to go." Alex responded rather forcefully.

"Sandra?" Mr. Rittenhouse called his cousin. "Admin Rittenhouse?"

Dr. Baylor answered. "Sir, she's left. May I help you with anything?"

"Sure. Show this boy to the toilet," he replied.

Dr. Baylor's face reflected no emotion, but Alex noticed a "just slapped in the face" type of look in the doctor's eyes. Alex smiled and waved at her. "Over here," he said to Dr. Baylor, who rolled her eyes at his dad.

"Over here, Alex," she said and pointed to a partitioned area in one of the corners of the isolation chamber.

Alex had thought it was a storage area. He pulled the partition back and saw a single vacuum toilet that looked like a hole in the floor. "That's it?" he said. "No sink?"

"Afraid so," she said with a smile. "I hope you and your father enjoy your stay."

The next morning, Alex, his dad, and the entourage sat at the dinning table eating a breakfast of cold cereal when a petite, reddish-brown complexioned young girl walked past the isolation chamber. She had a foolish smile on her face as she stared at Alex. She walked in next to Mr. Morg, the chief protector of the colony.

Alex raised his eyebrows and grinned at his dad. "What's that? Is that a boy?" he asked as he nodded toward Celine.

"Don't be silly. Anyone can see that puny thing's a girl," Mr. Rittenhouse said quietly. He nodded a greeting to Celine and Morg. Celine smiled, showing all thirty-two of her pearly whites. "She's giving you the tour later today."

Alex got up from the table and stepped toward the entrance door. He paused and looked back at his father and his entourage, then pushed the privacy button next to door. Instantly, the acrylic windows that surrounded the isolation room became dark, and the uninvited guests in the infirmary could no longer see them. After recuperating and clearing his mind for a moment, Alex stepped back into the open space. He was stunned to find the majority of his companions were staring at him.

"What?" he asked when he noticed the smug looks on everyone's faces. With irritation in his voice, he cried, "Leave me alone, all right? She's the ugliest girl I've ever seen."

CHAPTER 3

ENISI

CELINE HUMMED, "WEN'DE YA HO," as she worked on a Chakra school assignment. This evening she would give Alex a tour of the Compound. She worked quickly because she knew she had to meet Morg in the commons to get her tour passes.

"Incoming call from Enisi," Uji announced.

"Grandma!" Celine shouted. She paused her lecture and turned the computer Com to View so she could see her grandma's image.

Enisi was seated formally on her leather-covered chieftain's stool, another one of the family's ancient keepsakes: nothing modern was made of *real* leather.

Celine noticed her grandma's face was pinched into a forced smile, but her worried eyes could not hide the truth. Even so, her grandma exuded a regal aura.

Enisi spoke in Cherokee. "Dohiju agwajeli yotli?" (How are you child?)

"Osda, Enisi." (Fine, Grandmother.) "Except…" Celine paused. She wanted to say, "Something strange is happening to me." Instead she waited for Enisi to speak.

"I am going to tell you something that will bring you great joy," Enisi said, "but it will also cause some anxieties. Forgive me, Granddaughter, but there is no other way."

Celine held her breath and waited for her grandmother to explain.

"I had a vision this past Sunday," Enisi said.

Celine held her breath and waited for her grandmother to explain.

Celine knew that visions came from the dead. *Is she going to tell me she heard from Dad's spirit?* Tears began to well up in her eyes.

"The Great Spirit has shown me my son still lives," Enisi said. "I saw him inside the bowels of a cluster of red hills. He is not himself. I could not communicate with him."

Celine was speechless, and thoughts of her glowing eyes were lost.

"Dad's alive? Dad's alive?"

"Yes, child. I saw a great canyon next to the cluster of hills. Do you know of such a place?"

Celine's heart raced as she thought of seeing her dad. "Enisi, there are many red hills here." She sucked her teeth. "Dad could be anywhere."

Celine pushed her shoulders back and held her head proud as she stifled her tears. "I will find him, Enisi."

"You cannot do this alone, Celine. You are not ready for such a journey yet. You must prepare. You must be strong. Your dad has what he needs to live."

"Why hasn't he come home? Or called us?"

"He cannot."

"Why? I don't understand."

"Just know, little one, he would come home to you if he could."

Thoughts raced through Celine's mind. *Mom won't have to marry Morg. I won't have to take my Brain Booster.* This gave her strength.

"I haven't had a chance to speak with Mr. Rittenhouse."

"Mr. Rittenhouse has hired Mr. Morg to help him locate the Olivine ores. Somehow Mr. Morg has won Mr. Rittenhouse's trust. You cannot depend on him now."

"How do you know that?" Celine asked.

"You know I used to work in the Company. I still have friends there. They keep me in the loop," Enisi replied.

"You must get the boy, Alex, to help you. You cannot do it alone, Celine. Goliga?" (Understand?)

Celine nodded. "I'm supposed to show him around the Compound today. What do I tell him?"

"Tell him you know your dad's alive and that he has the coordinates to the Olivine ores. That is all you will need to say."

"You are right, Enisi. I *am* full of joy, but..." Celine rolled her eyes upward and exhaled. "I'm scared."

"Be strong, Celine. Never let fear lead you. I know your dad's alive, and with Alex's help, you can find him." Enisi swallowed. "Get him back home."

"Asehi, Enisi," (Yes, Grandmother.)

"Gvgeyu, nigohilvi." (Love you, Granddaughter.)

"Gvgeyu, Enisi." (Love you, Grandmother.)

The transmission ended.

Celine remained seated at her computer, feeling numb. She returned to her Chakra lecture but heard none of it. Even the warmth from her light therapy box felt chilled. After listening to the lecture a second time, Celine placed her mom's blanket on the floor and sat cross-legged on it in front of the drawer that contained her flute. Her mother had asked her to not play it, but she had to. Something about its haunting melody seemed to calm her. She lifted and held the flute as if it were sacred, then pressed it to her lips and began to gently blow into it. The melody was soft but rich, and somehow it evoked a calmness and strength.

Uji appeared and stood behind her and swayed its head side to side. Sometimes Celine wondered if Uji knew it was only an AI.

Suddenly Uji stopped swaying and said, "You have an appointment with Mr. Morg. Time to go."

Celine played one more bar, then carefully placed the flute back into its resting place.

She stood up and took a long stretch. "I can do it," she said.

"Punctuality is very important," Uji said.

Celine smiled. She turned to the desk where the family's precious mirror hung, and she studied her profile. "Nice," she said after staring into her big brown eyes. She began to pat and smooth her curly hair with her fingers.

"I honestly can't believe Morg is giving me this assignment. This is the nicest thing he's ever done for me." Celine looked at her image in the mirror. She had dark, curly hair like her father. She pouted. "But you'll never be my dad, Morg." With confidence, she stepped into the corridor and headed for the commons where Morg was waiting at a table.

"Hi, Morg," she said. "Thanks for the tour assignment."

"Sure. Your mom told me you're a big fan of his. She said you have more photos of Alex on your computer than you do of your own family." He grinned. Celine looked away.

"By the way, Dr. Baylor is also a big fan of Alex's."

"I didn't know that."

"She has some of his latest adventures if you're interested."

"Really?" Celine shifted from one foot to the other.

"Sure, I'll let her know you'd like to see them."

"Thank you."

"Here are your clearance badges for the tour. Take good care of them. They'll give you access to every place in the Compound."

"Yes, sir, I will." Celine took the badges and attached one to the magnetic strip on her chest pocket and held the other in her hand. "Oh, Mom said you have passes for us to go out on the surface."

"That's right, I do. I figured you could use some natural sunlight."

Morg's Com hummed. He tapped it and listened. "We're on our way. Let's go, Celine." They headed for the Porta. "I guess we all could use a little sunlight after spending six months underground. It's been a cold winter. Might get you well sooner. Gotta keep the baby well," Morg said playfully, gesturing toward Celine.

"Don't call me that," Celine said. "I'll be thirteen this year."

"I know," he said. "But you've gotta understand: you're the only child ever born here, so to me you'll always be the baby." He reached into his jumpsuit pocket, pulled out the two passes for visits to the surface, and handed them to Celine.

Without saying a word, she took the passes, placed them into her jumpsuit pocket, and straightened her suit.

Morg took a wrapped meat jerky stick from one of his pockets as they waited for the Porta.

"Want some?" he asked.

"No, I've already had my morning rations."

"So are you excited about having your birthday celebration?"

"I don't want to talk about that, Morg." Celine looked down at the panel. "I wish this thing would hurry up." Just then the door to the Porta opened.

Morg dropped his wrapper on the floor. That irritated Celine, but instead of confronting Morg, she stepped into the Porta before its door closed. They descended forty feet below ground where the colonists had expanded their facilities.

"Remember to take good care of your badges," Morg said.

"I won't let them out of my sight."

The door opened, and Alex and Admin were waiting by the isolation room.

"Good day, Admin," Morg said.

"And so it is." Admin nodded to Morg and then Celine.

"Good day, Alex," Morg continued. "You remember Celine? We were in the infirmary earlier today. She's taking you on a tour of the Compound."

"Good day," Alex said and nodded at Morg and then Celine.

Celine thought she saw his lips curl when he nodded at her. *He doesn't know the correct response to the greetings here.*

"I'll take my leave," Morg said to Admin Rittenhouse.

"Dismissed," she replied. She turned her attention to Alex and Celine. "Celine is the only child on this planet," she said fondly. "She's our first true Martian."

Alex's lips turned down as if he smelled something rancid.

Oh, is he already bored with the Compound? Celine thought. She had wondered if there was enough action in the Compound to keep an interplanetary traveler like Alex entertained.

Alex folded his arms in front of his chest and stared at her as if studying a specimen. Then lifted an eyebrow.

What was that all about? Celine thought. "Alex, I really am your biggest fan," she said nervously.

"Really?" His voice revealed no appreciation.

"Yes! I have thousands of images of you in my files, and I've seen all of your adventures on *Space Flick*."

"Great!" Alex responded mockingly. "Let's get this tour started." He scoffed as he strutted to the Porta, leaving Celine standing with Admin.

"Did I say something wrong?" Celine asked.

"He's had a tough morning—a little conflict with his dad," Admin replied and then laughed.

Why does Admin think that's funny?

"Maybe you can cheer him up."

"I'll try..." Celine said and then ran to the Porta to join Alex.

"Here," she said as she handed Alex his badge. "Put it on your magnetic strip. You can use it to open any door in the Compound."

"Really," he said and raised a devious eyebrow.

Something about Alex's expression made her uncomfortable. "*I,* personally, would never abuse its power," she said matter-of-factly.

Alex snapped on his badge and grinned. "Neither would I."

They entered the Porta together and arrived in the commons shortly after.

Oh, this is going to be so exciting! I'm giving Alex Rittenhouse a tour! I'll have to pinch myself. He's literally the cutest boy on Earth. I will make sure that this is the best tour of his life!

"So, the commons is the busiest place in the Compound. It's where most people work. We have our meals here and sometimes entertainment," she said proudly.

"What kind of entertainment?"

"Poetry readings, storytelling..."

"Poetry?" Alex regurgitated the word.

"We also have holographic movies." She pointed to a small marquee set close to the wall next to one of the four exits. "The winter list is still up."

Alex scrolled down the list of movies on the marquee and then turned up his nose.

"These are old."

"Oh," Celine said, feeling deflated. "Well, they're new to me," she recovered.

She pointed to one of the food printers. "This is where everyone gets their meals. We can choose anything we want."

"We brought our own food from Earth," Alex said. "Freeze dried. Much better than this synthetic crap."

"Well, I like it!"

"That's because you don't know any better. Is this it? Is there anything else to see?" Alex asked.

Celine had never met anyone so rude. In fact she had never technically "met" anyone up until this point. She racked her brain for something that might impress him. "Maybe you'd like the fitness room. It's the most fun place on the entire Compound."

"Fitness room? Let's go."

They walked down one of the four corridors that extended from the commons. Soon they arrived at the fitness room. Everyone was required to use it at least thirty minutes a day.

"It's the second-largest room in the Compound," Celine said. "I used to come here all the time to climb and swim with…" She hesitated, and memories of climbing and swimming with her father flooded her brain. "I used to come here every day with my dad."

"Climb?" Alex looked around the padded room and walked over to the manager panel.

Celine joined him. "Here are my simulations," she said and placed her thumb on the panel. "I love climbing."

"I do too." Alex grinned.

Celine smiled. She was happy that she finally found something that Alex enjoyed. "Maybe we could do some climbing together."

"Mountain climbing?"

"No. Wall."

"That's nothing. I don't wall climb. Where's the challenge in that?" he rolled his eyes, and it was clear that he was not amused. Celine, fed up, mustered up enough courage to blurt out, "Are you *always* so rude?"

"Most of the time," he replied and then chuckled.

Celine opened her mouth but was speechless. She rushed out the fitness room, through the commons, and to her quarters. She then flopped on her parents' bunk.

"He's horrible!" Celine wailed.

Uji appeared. "He's horrible?"

"Yes, Alex is the most obnoxious boy I have ever met."

"You have never met a boy."

"Well, he's still obnoxious! I'm deleting every single picture of him from my files." Celine flopped down at her desk, ready to delete all photos and videos of Alex, when the buzzer to her quarters rang.

"Enter," she said, expecting to see one of the colonists. Instead, in walked Alex.

"So, this is where you live?" he said, eyeing their cozy quarters from the doorway.

"Yes, this is it," Celine said. She gritted her teeth and flared her nostrils.

"Small," he said.

"What do you want?"

"Look, I'm sorry. When I am at home, it's just Dad, the guys, and me. We mess around a lot. You're just too sensitive." The words tumbled out.

"I'm not sensitive! You were rude to me…And I was your number-one fan." Celine bit her lip. She was determined not to cry.

Alex's mouth remained parted to continue his critique of Celine's behavior, but he said nothing.

Celine thought he looked uncomfortable. They locked eyes for a moment before he looked away.

"I will accept your apology," she said softly.

"Thanks," Alex said, turning to leave.

"What's 'messing around'?"

Alex chuckled. "It means to joke around."

"Oh. I see. Strange." She smiled.

"You live here with your parents?"

"Just Mom and me." Celine swallowed. She wished her dad was there to give Alex a piece of his mind. "My dad was lost in a sandstorm right before winter."

"I'm sorry. That's tough."

"Yeah. I miss him."

"Sometimes I wish mine would disappear."

"I don't understand that."

"Sometimes, he...Never mind." Alex appeared to be in deep thought. "How did it *happen* exactly?"

Celine studied Alex's face. He seemed melancholy, and he appeared to have a faint haze of blue outlining his body. She glanced at herself in the mirror and was relieved to see her eyes were normal.

"Celine?"

She looked up at Alex, snapping out of her hypnosis, and she could no longer see the blue haze around him. "Oh, sorry," she said quickly. "Um, all right...Where do I begin?" she whispered. "Dad and Mr. Takei, dad's assistant, had been out gathering samples of rocks in the Aureum Region. It's about thirty kilometers away. They were on their way back home when the storm came up. Dad called Mom on his Com. I could hear him shouting over the winds. He said it was a small storm, nothing to worry about: a little lightning and a few dust devils." Celine paused to moisten her lips. "Dad said that he and Mr. Takei had found shelter...But then there was static, and his Com signal died." Celine swallowed. "That was the last time I heard my dad's voice."

Celine stared into space. "Well," she continued. "Turns out the 'small storm' actually developed into this insane sandstorm covering the entire planet."

"I've learned about those," Alex said referring to the sandstorm.

"Yeah..." Celine responded, slightly annoyed that he chose to respond to the most irrelevant part of the story. "Anyway. I could hear the winds howling and the sand swishing overhead against the top of the Compound. No one could go looking for them or take them oxygen or water." Celine cleared her throat. "We lost our power and were in complete darkness for hours. The maintenance crew finally got everything working again after a few hours, but it was tough. The storm lasted for days, and when it finally stopped, the exits were covered with sand. We had to dig for hours just to leave this place. Then Morg and his crew went out to search for..." Celine's voice faded, but she was determined to finish the story. "My dad's body. No one expected them to survive, especially since no one truly knew whether or not they had shelter."

"You don't have to tell me anymore if you don'—" Alex said.

Celine noticed he sounded slightly choked up. "I want to," she interrupted. "I need to talk about it actually." Celine continued. "They couldn't pick up his life signature or Mr. Takei's. After searching for two days, they found Mr. Takei's body...He was a kind man. They found him near a cave, but there were no signs of my dad."

"Sorry, Celine…That's awful."

For a moment, they were both dead silent. Then Celine spoke. "My dad is an awesome person. He's one of smartest people I know."

"You said 'is.'"

"Yesterday my grandma called me from Earth."

"Yeah?"

"Enisi—my grandma—is a spiritualist. Do you know what that is?"

"I think so. Someone who speaks to spirits, right?"

"Yeah, kind of like that. Anyway, Enisi had a vision about my dad."

"She saw your dad's spirit?"

"No, the opposite."

Alex's eyes widened. "Get to the point."

"She had a vision. Enisi saw my dad inside a cave beneath some red hills. She said he's alive, but he needs my help."

Alex ran his hands through his hair. "I don't get it. I thought you said your dad was dead."

"They never found his body, but I never believed he was dead. And now Enisi confirmed that he's alive." Celine paused to gauge Alex's reaction. "Alex…I need your help to find him."

"Sure."

"You will?" Celine responded eagerly; she didn't pick up on his sarcasm.

"I hardly know you, and you want me to help you? And what about Mr. Morg? Isn't that his job? Why don't you ask him to help you?"

"I don't trust Morg. He doesn't want my dad found." Celine rubbed her hands together nervously. "He wants to marry my mom."

"Oh, that's right. Your mom and him are engaged," He chuckled. "I heard Ms. Armbruster talking about them." Alex left the doorway and sat next to Celine. "Even if I were to help you, you've got another problem on your hands. My father thinks the world of Mr. Morg."

"I know. See why I need your help?"

"Why mine? Isn't there someone else you could ask?"

"Everyone thinks Dad is dead. They think I'm just a kid who can't face the fact that my dad's gone."

"Just a kid." Alex repeated. "I know the feeling," he muttered. "This seems dangerous: just the two of us looking for your dad on the surface. *We* might get caught in a sandstorm, Celine."

Then Celine remembered Enisi's message and said, "My dad has something your dad wants."

"Oh yeah, Martian Girl? And what might that be?" Alex sounded irritated, but it was clear that he was intrigued.

Celine resisted the urge to show her discontent with the name "Martian Girl." "He has the coordinates to the Olivine ores that your dad wants."

"The what? Why would my dad want olive oils?" Alex laughed. "You've got to be joking. This is all a big joke, right? Not funny, Celine," Alex said as he got up to leave.

"I didn't say olive oils, you idiot!" *And he's the one who's supposed to help me find my dad?* "I said Ol-iv-ine ores! It will make your dad super rich!"

Alex removed his hand from the door lock. "And how do you know your dad even has those coordinates?"

Celine could see that mentioning the coordinates had piqued Alex's interest. "He told my mom before he was lost in the storm that he had found the 'mother lode.' I think that's why he and Mr. Takei were really out there."

"Who else knows besides your mom?"

"Everyone knows. Dr. Baylor tried tracing Dad's life signature, but it disappeared right after he said he had found shelter."

"You know, even if I were to help you find some cave, your dad might be dead."

Celine stepped back from Alex as if he had punched her. "He's alive! I know he is!"

Alex sucked his teeth and exhaled. "I'll think about it," he said as he exited.

The next day, after getting a few hours of light therapy and completing a math assignment, Celine decided that she wanted to go for a swim in the exercise room. She had not yet heard anything from Alex, but she recalled how his eyes lit up at her mention of the ores. *He's going to help me. I know it!* She put her tablet in her drawer and checked her eyes in the mirror.

"Perfect," she said. "I'm leaving for a swim, Uji."

Uji appeared.

"Perfection is an impossibility," Uji said.

Celine decided to have some fun with her AI.

"Uji, are you perfect?"

"Mathematically, I am perfect."

"How is that possible? You said perfection is an impossibility."

Uji was silent for a moment as if calculating. "Perfection is based on opinions of the thinker."

"Can you think, Uji?"

More silence. "Perfection is based on the calculations of the calculator."

"Well, by my calculations, I look perfect. See you later."

"Wait. You have not finished your school assignments."

"I'm taking a break," Celine said as she stepped into the corridor and headed to the exercise room.

Celine went directly to the electronic manager in the exercise room. There were several different simulations, but her favorites were obviously wall climbing and swimming. She typed in the number code for a swim.

The vertical wind tunnel, artificial gravity, and image provider came on as she completed the code. Instantly a pool of blue waves appeared. She dove in. Supported by the winds from the tunnel beneath the room, she began mimicking swimming motions. To her, this was swimming, like the kind she had seen on her computer. However, her dad had told her it felt more like skydiving without ever hitting the ground. *Doesn't matter to me. I love it!*

Alex pondered Celine's request. *Everyone thinks that just because I have an adventure show, I'm really that character. Hate to tell her, but everything on that show is staged. Sure, I can climb a mountain and swim miles in the ocean, but there's never any real danger. The cameramen are there, the studio's protectors help me if I need it, and the scene is always scoped out before I set foot on it. But honestly, I have to do this. It's the only way I can prove myself to Dad. Get him to shut his mouth. I've got to get my hands on those coordinates.*

Once Alex finalized his decision, he felt happier than he had in a long time.

He imagined a conversation with his dad: "I'll show you what I can do, old man. I'll get those coordinates for the oil ores while Morg leads you around in circles." Alex's lips turned up in a self-satisfied smile. *Right now though, I'm gonna have some fun!*

Alex called Stan on his personal Com. "Hey, Stan, where's my climbing gear?"

"It's on the *Stellar*," Stan answered from the commons. "Give me a few minutes. I'll get it together and bring it to you. Uh, where should I bring it?"

"I'm heading to the exercise room. Bring it there."

After looking through nearly half of the ten backpacks filled with clothing and games, Alex found his mountain-climbing-simulation chip.

Alex left Admin's quarters where he and his dad were staying during their visit. After a few perfunctory smiles and salutations, he arrived at the exercise room. The In Use button was lit, so he peeked through the window. He could hear the wind tunnel and saw Celine swimming in the waves of air. *Pretty good swimmer*, he thought, genuinely impressed.

Celine noticed him watching her and stepped out of the pool of wind and waves; she was completely dry. She walked over to the manager panel on the wall and turned off the simulation.

Alex stepped into the room. "Are you done?" he asked.

"Yep, I did four laps."

"Four laps? That's impressive." For a moment Alex stood there, wondering what to say next.

"I see you have a simulation," Celine said. "May I see it?" She took it from his hand before he could answer.

"It's a climb simulation," Alex said.

"I love climbing. I'm really good at it."

"So you're a *real* climber?"

"I have a chip already programed if you want to use it."

"Mountain climbing?"

"No, wall climbing. Remember?"

"No, thanks. I told you I need a little more challenge than that," he said.

Celine frowned.

"Wall climbing is challenging too," he said, attempting to be more considerate, "but I just prefer mountain climbing."

"Oh. Is it really all that different?"

"Two different beasts. Look, anyway," Alex started nervously. "I've been thinking about the conversation we had…You know, the one about your dad."

"Yes?" Celine said. Her eyes brightened, making Alex's heart beat a little faster.

Ignoring the heart flutters, he said, "I have a proposition for you. If you can learn how to climb—mountain climb, that is—I'll help you find him."

"You will?" Celine asked with stars in her eyes and her hands held as if in prayer. She shrieked with joy. "You won't be sorry, Alex. Thank you."

To Alex, Celine almost sounded as if she was singing rather than speaking. He smiled. Something about the tone of voice made him feel warm inside, but he came back to his senses just in time to step away from her, dodging a hug. "I have some extra gear on my ship if you'd like to try it."

Celine continued smiling.

"Look, will you wipe that stupid smile off your face before I change my mind?" He regretted his words as soon as he said them, and he noticed the crestfallen look on Celine's face. *Too sensitive. How am I going to tolerate her?* He was relieved to see Stan peeking at them through the door. "Sorry," he said to Celine who was now standing with her hands on her hips and a frown on her face.

He dashed to the door to get his equipment from Stan. "Would you go back to the *Stellar* and get another climber's backpack? And put a small climber's suit in the pack for Celine."

"Are you sure that's all you need?" Stan asked. "I've got other things to do."

"What, Stan? What do you have to do?" Alex asked. He was not about to let Stan embarrass him in front of a girl, even if she was an ugly one.

Stan replied, "Yes, sir, Mr. Rittenhouse. I will return with the backpack immediately."

"That will be all, Stan," Alex said. He laughed to himself, and then he turned to see if Celine was watching. To his disappointment, she had missed the entire episode; she was too busy looking at the gear in the backpack that he had placed on the floor.

"What's this?" she said, pulling a bag of carabineers from the backpack.

"Hey!" Alex darted across the room to Celine. "This is safety gear! Don't touch it!"

Celine sat wide-eyed next to the backpack.

Alex noticed she wasn't holding the simulation chip she had taken from him moments ago; a rope was wrapped around her hand instead. "Didn't I just hand you my chip?"

Celine stuttered, gave a nervous smile, then shrugged her shoulders.

I can't believe this. "Where is the chip, Celine?"

She dropped the rope and began searching the backpack.

Alex watched her frantically searching for it. He then noticed the chip lying on the floor next to the backpack. *Let's see how long it takes her to notice it.* He rubbed his chin where one single hair had grown.

After pulling everything out of the backpack and lifting the pack to shake it, Celine finally saw the chip lying on the floor. "Oh! Here it is," she exclaimed, carefully picking it up from the floor, "exactly where I left it." Then she sheepishly handed it to Alex.

He snatched the chip from her, strode angrily over to the panel and shoved it into the electronic manager. *I don't know if this going to work. She's too...* Alex searched his thoughts for a word to best describe Celine and concluded she was indescribable. He turned to observe her as the air in the room became cold and thin. "How are you feeling?" Alex asked deviously. Then he noticed Stan waiting at the door.

"Come in, Stan," he said. "You're a good man."

"Thanks, Mr. Rittenhouse." Stan smirked. "Mighty cold in here," he said as he looked over at Celine who had wrapped her arms around herself and was shivering.

"That will be all, Stan."

Stan gestured with his left hand, about to speak. Alex raised an eyebrow and watched Stan's hand drop to his side.

"Have a good day," Stan said.

"I always do," Alex replied. He set the backpack on the floor next to Celine.

"This backpack is for you, but don't touch it," he said. Then he opened it and removed an insulated hooded faux jumpsuit. "Put this on," he said, handing the clothing to Celine.

Shivering, Celine stepped into the suit and zipped it closed. "Woah...This feels amazing. I've never felt anything so warm."

"And just in time," Alex said as tiny white flakes of imitation snow began to fall and he slipped into an identical white jumpsuit. "Normally, these are red," he said, referring to the suits, "but I heard you colonists wear white here."

"Yes, and gray. Most people wear gray."

"So I've noticed."

"Wow, this is so beautiful," she said as the snow began to fill the room and cover rows and rows of spiraling hills and mountain-like shapes.

"Don't you get snow here?"

"All winter. But we never go to the surface during winter. I've never been in it." Then she held her chest and exhaled loudly. "I can't breathe, Alex."

"Hold on. I can make some adjustments," Alex said and keyed in *3010* on the electronic manager.

Celine stood behind him, gasping for air. "Hurry," she wheezed.

Alex increased the oxygen level to 20 percent per cubic meter of air. "How's that?" he asked as he studied Celine's face. "You're alive," he said with a chuckle when he noticed that she was OK.

"That wasn't funny. I'm not sure I even want to do this simulation anymore."

"Don't be such a baby. You can handle it. You want me to help you find your dad, don't you?" Alex could see Celine was struggling with her decision. "Tell you what I'll do. There will be no more surprises. I promise. If something weird is gonna happen, I'll tell you ahead of time. All right?"

"OK," Celine said hesitantly.

"Let's sit on the floor, and I'll show you what's in the packs. Here's where you'll keep your first-aid supplies," he said, pulling a white electronic box with a red cross on it from a side pocket on the larger backpack.

"Look, it has refrigeration for your stem cream. And here," he pointed to a grayish bulb at the other end of the container, "is blue light sanitizer."

"Let me see it," she said.

Alex handed her the box. "It's standard: tweezers, ointments, absorbing cloths."

"And a scalpel?" she asked as she opened the box and saw the small cutting tool.

"Why would I need something like this?" She examined it. "It's so...*primitive*."

"Look, it saved Stan's life once. He was bitten by a poisonous snake when we were climbing in this place called Virginia."

"I know Virginia. Grandma lives there. That's my dad's hometown."

"It's not a town. Anyways, Stan was bitten by a snake, and Dad had to use the scalpel to cut a small hole in his leg and drain the poison."

"Oh." Celine turned up her nose and set the box on the floor. "There are no snakes around here."

"Doesn't matter. It's now part of the safety kit, and we're keeping it."

Alex pulled out a flat rope that had buckles on it. "Next, we have a safety harness."

"Oh yeah, I know what that is! I've seen you use it on your show."

"Yeah...So, I'll show you how to put it on correctly." He pulled a harness from her pack and handed it to her.

"Watch me first. You step into it like you would a jumpsuit. See?" he said, as he stepped into his harness. Celine mimicked him. "Now tighten it so you don't slip out. The harness is your safety net." Celine then adjusted some buckles and pulled on her harness. "Good job," he said, extremely impressed with the manner with which Celine quickly and skillfully tightened her equipment.

Next, he showed her how to attach the belaying device to her harness. "This part is extremely important because if you fall, which you probably will, I can use the belaying device to slow you down."

"What do I use to slow *you* down if *you* fall?"

"I'll have to attach us to a wall or a boulder or something," he replied nervously. "But I won't fall."

He fed the thin but strong rope he had taken from her pack through the belaying device attached to his and Celine's harnesses. "We're literally attached at the hip."

Celine smiled. "I guess so," she muttered.

"OK, let me unfasten this thing before you get some dumb ideas. Here are your boots," he said as he took a pair of folded boots from her bag.

"They're ugly...Do we have to wear them?"

"These are Gravo-ton boots," Alex said grandly and placed one in her hand.

"They're still ugly. They look like they belong on a low-task robot or something."

"Doesn't matter. They might save your life."

"Really? Wait...I've heard about these actually. You can adjust the air pressure in them, right?"

"Yes, you can adjust it to where it feels like you're walking with Earth's gravitational pull. Or Mars, or Lunar—whatever you need."

"Show me."

"Fine. Here's the pressure button." Alex pointed to a red button in the arch of the sole of one of the boots.

"I remember this," Celine said as she examined the boots. "You used it in that episode when you were playing football on Lunar. After the coach fixed your boots, they kept you from flying all over the place," Celine pressed a hand over her mouth to stifle her laughter.

Alex remembered that embarrassment. It was his first time on Earth's moon, and he was playing as a guest with the Lunar Dusters. He had missed the informational meeting with the coaches and didn't know the correct adjustments for his boots. At the game, he found himself over jumping and skipping when he attempted to walk. *Why did she have to bring that up?*

"Yeah, sure," Alex said. "Put the boots on. I want you to see how they feel."

Alex unfolded the larger pair of boots, slipped his feet into them, and shimmied them up to his knees. Then he tapped each gravity adjustment button beneath his arches and pushed the buttons three times to adjust for Mars's gravitational pull.

"They don't look different," Celine said as she ran her fingers across the tops of his boots. "Still terribly ugly."

"But they feel different. Put them on now." He handed Celine the smaller pair and pushed the buttons on the bottoms of her boots. "Stand up," he commanded, "and walk around."

Alex watched as Celine stood up. He snickered to himself.

"I can't move. Feels like my feet are literally glued to the ground."

Alex bit his lip to choke back the laughter as he watched Celine try desperately to move her feet. "What's wrong, Celine?"

"I can't move my feet."

Alex's stomach was tight from holding back the laughter. *That'll teach you to make fun of me, Martian Girl.*

"Is something wrong with my settings? You have them set for Jupiter's gravity, don't you?"

"Yep!" he said between bouts of ear-piercing laughter. Alex couldn't contain it any longer. "Fine, I'll set it for Martian gravity." He yanked one of Celine's feet back as if he were shoeing a horse.

"Hey!" Celine said as she almost lost her balance.

"Stop whining," Alex snapped. Then he carelessly dropped her left foot and pulled up the other. Celine held her balance. "How's that?" he asked after he dropped her right foot.

Celine pranced around like a galloping pony.

"OK, don't overdo it." *What an idiot*, he thought as he reached down and scooped up the smaller backpack with one hand.

"Gee, that looks heavy," Celine said as she pranced back to Alex.

"It is," he said. He began placing it on Celine's back as soon as she settled next to him. "Slip your arms through this," he said, shoving her arm through one of the straps.

"How am I supposed to climb with this heavy thing on my back?" she asked.

"It contains your gear: everything you'll need to survive in the mountains. So deal with it." Alex stuck out his chest and held his head high with authority. "You'll also need rappelling gloves," he said, "and a small helmet—Hey, what do you think you're doing?"

Before Alex could say another word, Celine had unfastened her backpack and allowed it to slide down her arms and onto the floor. "It's too heavy," she whined.

"You need to get used to the weight."

"Not today, Alex," she said and began removing gear from her overstuffed pack.

Alex was furious. "Do you want my help or not?"

"Of course. Why would you even ask that?"

"Then do what I tell you," he said. "All of these things," he said, pointing to the gear Celine had spread across the ground and then waving his arms over his head in frustration, "are needed to survive the hills. I'm not taking you to the red hills and then carrying you over the mountains."

"You make it seem so easy on your show."

"Well, it's not easy. It's hard work, and if you're not prepared, you could literally die. Do you understand?"

"We need *all* of this?" Celine said as she looked at the gear on the floor.

"Yeah, and possibly more. So what are you going to do?" Alex waved his pointed finger in Celine's face.

Celine sighed and began gathering her gear into a small pile and shoving it back into her backpack.

"Stop!" Alex said impatiently. "Everything has a special place." He sat on the floor next to her and began putting the small metal gadgets into the inside pockets. He rolled a rope and placed it next to him. "All done," he said when they had finished repacking, and he once again helped her put on her backpack.

He picked up the coiled rope and said, "Let me attach this to your harness." He fastened the rope onto a shiny carabineer that hung from Celine's harness, then pulled on it to check for slack. "That's tight enough. Wouldn't want you falling through," he said. Then he fastened the other end of the rope to the belaying tool that was attached to his harness.

"First, we are climbing to the top of this small hill," he told Celine. "That should be easy enough. Ready?"

Celine nodded nervously.

The hill was covered in what appeared to be hard-packed snow, and moving wheels behind the simulation screen gave the illusion of a never-ending climb.

Alex led the way, and Celine came up behind him. "You're a pretty good climber," he said when he noticed how agile she was and how quickly she followed him.

After Alex had pulled Celine to a ridge, where they briefly rested, he was ready to ascend to the next one. He screwed an ice screw into the hillside, and it made a realistic crunch. Then he rammed the pointy aluminum crampons positioned over his boots into the ice like he was stabbing the hill with his toes. After he belayed the rope around the edge of the higher ridge, he pulled himself up. Then he maneuvered and pulled on the rope line until Celine was pulled up by his side. He was in the zone, feeling as though he'd already climbed hundreds of feet.

He thought Celine was moving along nicely—that is, until they reached the third ridge. When he pulled her up next to him, she appeared spacy, preoccupied in thought. "Focus," he demanded. But Celine didn't appear to hear him. "What's wrong with you?" For a moment he thought he saw a yellow glow coming from her eyes, but she closed them so quickly he wasn't certain. "Open your eyes, dude. Have you lost your mind?"

"I'm fine, thanks for asking," she muttered sarcastically without looking at him, clearly agitated.

"Well, we'll finish this hill and call it quits, all right?" Alex threw the rope over the next ledge and began slowly pulling himself up. Suddenly, he felt himself being pulled back. Celine had slipped and was pulling him down with her.

"Stop! You're going to pull me off the hill!" Alex yelled. Quickly he pulled his cutter from a carabineer attached to his harness and then cut the tether that attached him to Celine. She fell with a thump to the padded floor.

"That's it!" he said when he was finally able to steady himself. "I can't help you. You'd get one of us killed. Mission aborted."

Alex was so shaken that he hardly noticed Celine paid him no attention. She didn't even look at him but kicked off her boots.

"Watch it!" Alex shouted as one boot narrowly missed his face. He watched as she scrambled to her feet and unfastened her backpack and harness, allowing them to fall to the floor. Then she stepped out of the climbing suit and bolted from the room not even looking back or apologizing. "Celine, hold on!" he called and bolted to the door after her. But when he opened it and looked down the corridors, she was gone.

Celine ran down the hall and did not stop until she was safe in her quarters. As she had ran past her neighbors, she could see hazy glows of different colors surrounding each of them.

He saw my eyes, Celine thought as she remembered the expression on Alex's face. *That's what scared him. Now he's not going to help me. I'm right back where I started. I have no one to help me find Dad.*

She was exhausted. She flopped into the chair next to her computer, and her motion-sensitive computer came on instantly. "Restart last call," she said into her Com, and a signal was sent through space to her grandmother's com. Celine studied her face in the metal mirror, examining her eyes from every angle, while she waited for the call to go through. *They're not glowing now...Maybe Alex didn't see them.*

Twenty minutes later, her Uji chimed, "Incoming Com," and her grandmother's concerned face appeared on the computer screen.

"Celine, how are you?" she said.

"Something's wrong with me, Enisi. I'm changing." Celine took a deep breath. "Into an alien or something..."

Enisi's eyes widened. "Why do you say that, child?"

"I don't know how to explain it, Enisi. I just know I am changing."

For a moment, Enisi did not say anything. She rubbed her wrinkled chin and appeared to be in deep thought. Then she said, "Do you see mirages? Faint images around others?"

"Yes, Enisi. Like colored outlines around their bodies. It happened today when I was climbing with Alex. I had to run out of the exercise room. I left him standing there, calling my name. I don't understand what's happening to me. I'm scared. I don't know what to do. If I tell Mom, she'll tell Dr. Baylor. And I can't stand her. Of course *Morg* likes her." She scoffed.

Enisi listened quietly, almost as if she were in a trance. Then she locked eyes with Celine for what appeared to be moments, and Celine felt as if a surge of energy had rushed over her from head to toe.

"Oh!" Celine startled after twenty minutes and then batted her eyes. "That was strange," she muttered.

Celine did not know Enisi's spirit had traveled through time and space. When Enisi's spirit reached Celine, it hovered above her before commingling with Celine's spirit until it could comprehend Celine's vibrational tone. Then Enisi's spirit returned to her motionless body on Earth.

"Are you OK, Enisi?" Celine asked when she noticed her grandmother's lifeless eyes.

Enisi closed her eyes, and when she opened them, she appeared refreshed, happy almost. "You are like your grandfather," Enisi said.

"How am I like him, Enisi? The only thing Dad ever said is he worked for the military, but he didn't want to."

"That is true. The military misused his talents. That is why you must tell no one about your changes."

"Not even Mom?" Celine swallowed.

"Your mother knows you are changing, but she does not understand the ways of our family. Tell no one." Enisi continued in Cherokee. "Skina gesvi ganayegi!"

Celine understood the warning: "To tell others would be dangerous."

Few people knew Cherokee. Celine's dad had taught her. His mother had taught him. To speak in Cherokee was to speak in code.

"It can only be discussed in person," Enisi said. "I can say no more about it."

"Mom is making me take my Brain Booster, but I don't want the shots anymore." Celine continued the conversation in Cherokee.

"You do not have to. I have not, nor has your father," Enisi said.

"Mom said Dad did."

"I am his mother. I know the truth. You do not need a Brain Booster to increase your intelligence."

"Can you tell Mom that?"

"I have told her, child. It is not her ways. You are Waya! Do not be afraid of being Waya."

"I'm not. I'm proud to be of the wolf clan." Celine chuckled, lifting her head high, holding her shoulders back as her father had taught her. "I am afraid of what's happening to me though."

"You will understand the meaning of my words in due time. Let us not speak of it now."

Celine's eyes widened. She had never seen fear in her grandmother, but it was there. Enisi's chin was held high, but her lips trembled and her eyes were tightly shut. When she reopened them, her quiet strength had returned. "We must not be afraid," Enisi said. "We are Waya. You must decide if you want to be less. Your dad will help you understand. I cannot. There are too many eyes. Too many ears."

The monitor screen went white.

"Solar flares! Not again!" Celine cried out. She tried several times, without success, to reconnect with her grandma. "Oh what's the use? She already said she can't help me. I have to find Dad. But how can I get Alex to help me now?"

Back in the exercise room, Alex thought, *Celine's a weirdo. She looked at me like she saw a ghost and then closed her eyes. Who in their right mind closes their eyes while climbing?* Alex shook his head as he put the last bit of climbing gear into his backpack.

If she wants my help, she's got to be able to handle herself out there. Alex sucked his teeth. *And I thought she was doing so well. What caused the holdup? Maybe the air was too thin. I tried to do too much, too soon. We're going back to square one. I am teaching her to climb. I'll help her get up her strength, and then we're going to find those coordinates.*

To Celine's surprise, Alex came to her cell. He waited next to the intercom for her to let him in. She glanced at herself in the mirror. "Come in," she said softly.

Alex stepped into the doorway. "How are you?"

"I'm better. Thanks."

"I'm sorry," they both said in unison.

"Why are you sorry? I almost got you killed," Celine said.

"I'm sorry for putting you through…" Alex appeared to be searching for the right words. "For putting you through…"

"The entire thing?" Celine finished for him. "And you cut me loose!"

"You closed your eyes! What kind of idiot closes their eyes while climbing?"

Celine squeezed her lips together. She knew Alex was right, but she wasn't ready to concede.

"Maybe the simulation was too difficult for you. I mean, it was for experienced climbers. I have a beginner's version," Alex said.

Celine was surprised. *Experienced climbers? I didn't do too badly after all.*

"You were saying you're sorry," Alex continued.

"If we had been on the surface, would you have cut me loose?"

Alex rubbed the few hairs on his chin.

"I honestly don't know," he whispered.

Celine studied his pained face. "I'm sorry, Alex. If this had been a real climb, I could have gotten both of us killed."

"Yeah, I know. What were you thinking?"

"I'm dealing with stuff, all right? But I know what I have to do now." Celine emphasized the word "have." *I have to learn how to control the Waya.*

Every day for weeks, Alex and Celine trained in the exercise room. She had convinced him to continue using the experienced climbers' version, and she had not had another episode since their first climb.

Together they climbed miles of hills until their legs ached; she noticed her body becoming more muscular and toned. She was able to pull herself up to the ridges right next to Alex. And she could tell, though he never said it, that Alex was pleased with her progress. Finally, one day after a grueling session, he said, "You're ready. "You've become a real mountaineer."

With one hand, she slung her backpack to the floor. Her toned arms were drenched in sweat. She ran her fingers through her soggy hair, slid down to the floor next to her backpack, and buried her head into it. She didn't know if she wanted to laugh or cry. She squeezed her eyes together tightly. "At last," she mumbled. Then she looked up at Alex. "So, you're helping me find my dad?"

"I am."

Celine held her hand over her lips and began crying and laughing simultaneously.

"There is one small problem."

"Oh?" she asked, but at this point a "small problem" could not crush her happiness.

"I need you to do one more thing first."

Celine waited patiently for Alex to speak.

"We need the code to your dad's life signal. Do you know who keeps it?"

"Morg has it."

"Morg?"

"Yes. Dr. Baylor gave it to him when he was out looking for my dad."

"Did you call me, Celine? Is everything OK?" Morg poked his huge head through the doorway. "I thought I heard my name."

"Morg! Yes! We're fine," Celine said startled, nearly choking on her words.

"It sounded like you were crying." Morg's eyes held Alex's for a moment.

"I was laughing so hard. Alex is just *so* funny, I couldn't help myself."

Morg raised an eyebrow. "You kids sure have been using this exercise room a lot. Remember there are other folks who want to use it too."

"Absolutely, Mr. Morg," Alex said. "We were just leaving."

"Let's go to your quarters," Alex told Celine after Morg closed the door.

The two of them raced through the commons, down the corridor to cell 10. "Do you think he heard us?" Celine said after she locked the door to her quarters.

"Hard to tell. We're just gonna have to start being a little more careful."

"I was *so* loud, Alex…"

"Yeah, you were, but we can't do anything about it now. Anyway, Morg has your dad's code?"

"Yes, Dr. Baylor gave it to him."

Alex mulled over an idea for a moment, then said, "You'll have to get it. Get the code, and we can find your dad. Simple. I'll use my Navi to get his exact location."

"No one has a Navi for Mars."

"OK, but I do. Well…My dad does. I can get it though. You just need to get that code, and we'll have everything we need to find him."

CHAPTER 4

BRAIN WAVES

WHEN CELINE WANTED TO TAKE short breaks between school lessons, she'd play her dad's flute. For some reason, it made her feel at ease. She had heard that teenagers on Earth listened to music created from their brain waves. Perhaps the vibrations of the Cherokee melodies were similar to those of her own brain waves. Regardless, the buzzer suddenly interrupted her music.

"Enter," she said, expecting her visitor to be Alex. They had trained together for weeks and seen each other daily.

Alex stepped in wearing a set of white indoor wear. "School lessons again?" he inquired.

"No, but don't you ever have any?" she replied. "Nice jumpsuit by the way. You wear a different one every day...How many do you have?"

"Hundreds actually, but I only brought ten. And no, I don't have school assignments when I am on vacation. Don't you ever get free-range play?"

"Free-range?"

"It's when—Ah, forget it. Do you still have the copies of the clearance badge?"

"Yes." Celine laid down the flue and then muted Uji.

"Well, today you get a chance to use it."

"What do you mean?" she asked, feeling hesitant about using the forged security badge that Alex had copied on Admin Rittenhouse's 3-D printer. The badges they used during the initial tour had expired, but Alex had updated them. "Having clearance to go anywhere might come in handy," he had said.

"Morg is taking my dad and his entourage to view Olympus Mons. They'll be gone all day. This is your chance to get into Morg's computer and get your dad's life signature code."

"I don't know if I can do it. Just because my mom's a computer expert doesn't automatically mean I am."

"You said you could."

"What if I get caught?" Celine exhaled. Then she noticed the frown on Alex's face. "Fine, I'll do it." She said it quickly, not allowing herself the chance to change her mind. "I can't believe I'm doing this. What would my mom say if she knew I was hacking into Morg's computer?"

"I taught you well?"

"That's not funny, Alex."

"You're always so serious," Alex groaned. "You've been around grown-ups too much."

"You're going to get me in trouble."

"That's what friends are for. Now hurry and get those badges."

Celine opened her dad's drawer and reached under his indoor wear where she had hidden the badges. *I'm doing this for you, Dad.* She took a deep breath. "Let's go. I'll go down the suites corridor. You come later and wait for me near the marquee. Use your Com to let me know if you see a protector coming my way. Morg's suite number is two."

"Good idea," Alex said. "Why didn't I think of that?"

Celine grimaced.

She went through the commons and saw that everyone was busy as usual. No one paid her any attention as she headed down the corridor of suites where Morg lived. His suite was at the end of the hall across from Admin's. After what seemed like an eternity, she was finally standing in front of his door. *Is this really happening?* She checked around to make sure she was alone in the corridor, and then she eased the security badge from her right sleeve and waved it once in front of the lock. "Shhh," she whispered as the door slid open. She slipped inside and stood motionless like a robot without an energy pack, not daring to even take a breath until she heard the door slide closed behind her. She breathed heavily like she was just learning to climb a tall hill in the exercise room. Her eyes began frantically searching the room for the computer. She had seen it on Morg's desk when she and her mom had visited, but it was gone. *Where is it?* Celine dug her fingernails into her palms. "It's got to be in here," she whispered.

Suddenly she heard Alex speaking to Theodore, Morg's crewman, outside the suite.

"I lost my Personal Com," Alex said. "Can you help me find it?"

"Sure. Let me drop off Morg's computer first."

Celine could hear Alex making small talk with Theodore, obviously loud enough for her to hear. *Where can I hide? Right! The toilet area, the only place with a door!* Celine tiptoed quickly to Morg's private toilet area; its sliding door was open. She stepped into the compact area, shut the door, and held her breath.

Theodore entered the quarters just as Celine slid the door closed. He paused, as if he had heard something.

Celine was thankful when she realized Alex was rushing Theodore to leave Morg's suite. "Theodore! Let's go. I need my Personal Com. I'm expecting a call from my dad," he said.

"You're just like your dad—impatient," Theodore mumbled as he laid Morg's computer on his desk and left hurriedly.

Celine slid down to the floor. Her knees were like water gel, and her lungs ached. She held back the tears. *For you, Dad.* With trembling hands, she willed herself to slide the door back and peer out. Morg's suite was empty and quiet. *That was close. I've got to work fast.*

She rushed to the chair in front of Morg's computer. As soon as she sat down, the screen lit up to a password prompt. "What would Morg possibly use as a password?" Celine whispered. She swiped across the empty password box. "I am sure it's left a data phantom."

She pulled up her mom's website, entered her mom's password and clicked on the tools to began her search for the Phantom Inspector, an application her mom jokingly called the PI for *Privacy Invasion*. Celine smirked. She pasted the copied invisible password into the tool.

"Darn it." *I can read the numbers 3, 6, 4, 5, and the sign #, and the letter M clearly, but what are these characters?* "Is this an *O* or a zero?"

she mumbled. "I'm going with *O.* She typed in the letter *O* with her tensed index finger. If she put in a wrong letter or number, the computer would shut down immediately, and she'd have to wait thirty minutes to try again. Time was of the essence. *Great. The screen is still active.* She directed her attention to the lower-case *L—* *or is it a number 1? If I were Morg, what would I choose?* "Well, Morg would think he's number one, no doubt." She typed the number 1, and the screen remained active. *Great, but is this last letter a* T, *or is it a plus? T for tall, perhaps? Morg's seriously tall, six feet six. Or could it be a plus? He always wants more—so greedy.*

Celine held her finger over the letter *T* and then the plus sign. She held her breath as she tapped the plus sign that represented greed. She blinked to moisten her dry eyes. She wiped her clammy hands on her pants.

"Welcome, Morg." The feminine voice on his computer announced, startling Celine and nearly making her knock the computer shut. *It worked!* She held back a laugh. She had actually figured out the password.

Her nimble fingers began the search through Morg's Roster files. She typed in her dad's name, but it was not among the lists of colonists. She then came across a file labeled "Complications." She opened it. *There's Dad's code. Mr. Taikei's. Hannah's? Mom's? That doesn't make sense. Why would Morg consider Hannah and Mom "complications?"*

She rubbed her forearm. She couldn't feel the chip that had been under her skin since birth. *Morg will know I've been here. I better not stay here too long. Focus. I need to do what I came here for.* She inserted her Memchip into Morg's computer and downloaded her dad's life code. She also quickly added her mom's and Hannah's. "Just in case," Alex would say.

"Download complete," blurted the feminine voice on the computer.

"Quiet," Celine whispered. Then she threw her hand over her mouth and looked around to make sure she was still alone.

She removed the Memchip and placed it in her jumpsuit pocket.

Then she saw a file labeled "Military." Everyone on the colony knew Morg had served time in the military. She clicked on it, and the file went into Hide Mode. *I don't have enough time to figure out how to get into it. Besides, I have what I came for.*

Now that she had completed the task she set out to do, thoughts flooded her brain of what she might tell Morg if he were to ask about her unauthorized visit to his suite. She had a strong feeling he would ask.

She practiced her mocked conversation with Morg over and over in her head like an actress.

Why was I in your suite? Alex couldn't find his Personal Com, and I was looking for it.

How did I get in? Oh, I just used the security badge you gave me! I thought it would be expired, but it worked. You want it back? Sorry, I don't have it. I put it in the disposal in the commons.

Yes. That'll work.

She logged out of Morg's computer, pushed the door lock to exit and ran right into Theodore.

"What were you doing in Morg's suite, Celine?"

For a moment she froze, and then, like a recording, she began spilling out the lines she had rehearsed moments ago. "I was looking for Alex's Personal Com."

"I was just helping Alex search for it. Did you find it?" he asked.

"No, sir," she replied, being overly polite, as she continued walking away toward the commons. When she was finally out of view, she took off running.

Alex was waiting for Celine next to the movie marquee. He could see she was shaken.

"What happened? I tried to call you," Alex said.

"No, you didn't. It was so quiet in there, I would have heard it."

"Celine, I called, and you didn't answer."

"Let me see your Com." She snatched up Alex's arm to look at his Personal Com, then dropped his wrist, letting his arm flop to his side.

"Do you see a Personal Com on my arm? No! That's because I don't have one! You were calling my home. Why didn't you call Morg's Com in suite two, like I *told* you?"

"Chill, Celine. You should have made it clearer. Besides I kept Theodore away from Morg's quarters. Maybe you should have worked faster."

"Seriously, Alex," Celine cried. "Theodore is going to log my encounter with him in his report and tell Morg. I know he will ask me about it."

"Don't worry about it. We'll figure out what to do before Morg returns."

"You said 'we.'"

"We're in this together now."

"Thanks." Celine beamed and reached to hug Alex, but he stepped back out of her reach.

"Got the code?" he asked.

"Yes! Got it!" Theodore had flustered Celine so badly that she had forgotten how excited she was to have her dad's life signature code in her possession. Now the excitement was back, and she was ready to continue their plans.

"Let's go, Alex. I want to see what that Navi can do."

Celine and Alex headed back to Admin's quarters. Celine avoided the other colonists, fearing they would read her guilt in her body language. She had never invaded someone's privacy. Colonists don't do that. But she had to push the envelope if she was going to find her dad.

Alex had set up his own computer in Admin's guest room; the two entered and closed the door. He downloaded Mr. Red Cloud's code from Celine's Memchip on to his computer, which was connected to his Navi.

"I'm not getting a location," he said as he looked at the map on his computer screen. Alex checked the locator's preferences. "What the heck? Why would someone turn off the locator?" Alex corrected the system with the locator's code, and a beeping dot appeared on the screen.

"Wait, I see it! There! He's there!" Celine pointed to the blinking blue dot on the map. It was the Red Hills in the Chaos Region. *Don't worry, Dad. We're coming to save you!* "Hurry, Alex." Celine stood over Alex, wringing her hands as he downloaded the location from his computer to his Navi.

Then suddenly, exactly what she was afraid of happened—the blinking dot disappeared. *Could Morg have intercepted Dad's signal? Had some wild animal attacked him?* Celine's stomach was in knots. "Oh no. It's gone." Her throat was so tight that she could barely get the words out.

Alex checked his Navi. It was flat and rectangular like a primitive cell phone, small enough to fit in the palm of his hand.

"Celine, I have it. I got the coordinates before the signature disappeared."

"Are you sure?" The idea that her father's location was so easily obtained seemed impossible.

"The Locator Satellite is on, but we're not getting the signal now. I have no idea why. But according to the Navi, he's about one hundred seven kilometers from here."

"Jeez, I thought he'd be a lot closer."

Alex recalculated the distance on the Navi. "It's accurate. Besides it's all we have. That will have to be good enough. We need to pack our gear. I'll put aside enough food to last a week."

"A week? You think we'll be on the surface for a week?" Celine had never spent a night on the surface, and she wasn't comfortable with that idea.

"What's wrong? You didn't think we could find your dad in a day and get back before nightfall, did you?"

"I guess I hadn't thought about it…" Celine said nervously. "I've never spent a night on the surface."

"We'll have my body-heat tent."

"Mr. Albolino had a body-heat tent, and his collapsed. He almost died. His skin was gray like a boulder, and he had ice in his eyelashes!" Celine shivered. "Can you imagine? His eyes were almost frozen!"

"Calm down, Celine. My tent's not going to collapse."

"You can't guarantee that."

"Celine, we'll be fine. This tent is one of the best on the market—it's out of this world, for that matter." Alex chucked.

Celine did not find Alex's jokes funny.

"Why are you so paranoid?" Alex shook his head. "How many kilometers do you think you could cover in a day? I can cover about forty-eight kilometers. If you can keep up with that, we'll reach him in three days."

"Oh, you and your dad were in the Iron Man Competition on Earth when you did that, right? I saw that episode." Celine giggled.

"Celine." Alex folded his arms across his chest, cocked his head to one side, and gave Celine a stern look.

"Sure, I can do it." She'd agree to anything at this point.

"Great! I'll get the climbing gear and tent. You gather the food and water," Alex said. Alex seemed to have had second thoughts. "I'll bring some food too…and a Travel Bottle." The Travel Bottle was one of the latest water bottle innovations. It had a small, powerful battery that could send an electric current through gases taken from the surroundings and create a bottle of water a day. "We won't have to worry about running out of water."

"I'll bring some water gel packs just in ca—"

"Fine, whatever. What about O2 pills? Do you have any?"

"I'd thought we'd take oxygen canisters."

"No, I hate those things. They're heavy and will slow us down. I only carry them if it's absolutely necessary."

"I have two O2 pills in my drawer with my outdoor wear."

"Can you get more from the infirmary?"

"I don't want to go to the infirmary. How would I explain myself?"

"You're right." Alex rubbed his chin for a moment. "I'll get some from Dad's entourage's supply. They have so many; they won't miss them. Besides Dad paid credits for them."

Celine only half-listened to Alex's rambling. She couldn't believe she was finally going to search for her dad. She didn't like the idea of staying on the surface after sunset, but she knew it was something she had to do. Every time it crossed her mind, she covered her eyes with her palms until she could feel the warmth radiating from them, reassuring her that she would not let her eyes get cold enough to freeze.

"Alex, there're a few things I need to tell you before we leave." Celine hesitated. She hadn't told Alex that her dad's assistant had been found dead with parts of his body chewed away. She didn't want to spook him with stories of wild animals. She knew they were out there, but she had never seen them. *They're probably just scavengers anyway.*

"What?" Alex leaned in to listen.

Celine hesitated. "Oh, it's nothing. You already know I've never spent a night on the surface. I'm nervous."

"Well, neither have I, but I won't let anything happen to us. Trust me, I wouldn't go out there if I didn't think it was safe."

Just as I thought. I'd better keep all of my secrets to myself. Even so, she felt guilty she had not told him about the wild animals, or the strange things that had been happening to her.

"You're taking your ray gun with you?" Celine asked.

"Of course I am. Why wouldn't I? Is there something you're not telling me?"

Her mom had told her that only giving half of the truth is practically telling a lie. But she had also told her that sometimes the victory outweighs the means. Celine decided to cling to the latter. "You know all that you need to know for now."

Alex sucked his teeth. "We have everything we need but the right time."

"I could pretend to show you my rock collection. That would take hours, and no one would know we had left."

"No, we need something bigger than that, and besides, we need to take out the drone."

"And how are you going to do that? The drone won't let you get near it. When I was younger, it was my playmate. But if I ever got close enough to touch it, it would—"

"I know about drones," Alex interrupted. "I'll think of something."

Celine returned to her quarters to find her mom waiting for her.

"Morg has been helping me plan your birthday celebration," Abbie said.

"Mom. If I hear that name again, I *will* play Dad's flute nonstop for twenty-four hours!" Please! Celine's response came out much sharper than she had intended.

Abbie opened her mouth in surprise and then chuckled. "Dr. Baylor wants to know if you want your Brain Booster before or after your birthday celebration."

"Mom, you know how I feel about that," Celine said. "Actually, I'd rather not have it at all. And why isn't Dr. Duke giving me my injection?"

Abbie's mouth formed the word "Morg" and then closed. "I think Dr. Baylor would be better for you."

Celine frowned. *Why is Mom listening to Morg?* "Mom, why would you…" Celine noticed a small red mark on her mother's wrist. "What's that?"

"Oh, honey. I forgot to tell you. Dr. Baylor gave me a new implant for tension headaches. Where is your Memchip? Dr. Baylor said I should put my new code in it."

"You had surgery without even mentioning it to me?"

"It was minor. I'm wearing it for a week, so I didn't want you to worry. Now hand me your Memchip."

Mom would never have a procedure done without telling me first. And when did we start putting codes in Memchips? Celine patted her pocket flat so the imprint of her Memchip would not show.

"Mom, I left it in Admin's quarters. Alex was giving me new photos of him."

"You and Alex have been spending an awful lot of time together, and you usually wouldn't be so irresponsible as to leave your Memchip somewhere. Maybe you need to cut back on all the time you spend with him."

"Mom, no! You can't do that," she whimpered.

"You really like him?"

"Yes! I do! Plus, he's the only friend I've ever had. Mom, please."

Her mom raised a brow. "The two of you spend a lot of time together, Celine."

"It's not like I have other friends my age," Celine retaliated.

"Well, you get that Memchip from him first thing in the morning."

"Yes, Mother." Celine knew she would have to leave the Compound to find her dad soon. *Morg knows we have information about Dad, and he's trying to stop us. But how does he know?*

"You're not neglecting your studies?" Abbie interrupted Celine's thoughts.

"No, Mother. I am on level fifteen in every single lesson."

"Good. But I'll be watching you two more closely. I don't want you getting into situations you shouldn't be." Abbie pinched Celine's cheeks as if she were a chubby-cheeked baby.

Mom would never do that. Celine backed away from her and reached for her tablet on her desk.

"Look, Mom," she said and handed her the tablet.

Abbie started at it, dumbfounded.

"It's the stack of books," Celine said.

Abbie clicked the icon of the stack of books.

"See, Mom. All of my assignments are current." *Why hasn't she checked with Uji?*

Abbie looked at her competed assignments. "Ocean Colony Design Project? Sounds exciting."

Celine reached for the tablet. "Mom, you helped me with this last week."

Abbie sat at her desk. "I seem to be forgetting a lot lately." Then, like a humanoid on cue, she smiled and said, "Getting back to your celebration. We're having the cook bring out some vegetables from the garden. He's making your favorite: tomato bisque."

"Great. I can't wait." *I know we've had this conversation before, a week ago to be exact.*

Abbie rambled. "I haven't been feeling well. Tension headaches. Dr. Baylor thought I should wear this for a few days." She patted the implant in her arm. "That was a week ago, I think. That's odd. I really should know."

"Do you know if Hannah's gotten one?"

"What, dear?"

"A new implant?"

"I don't know. Is that something I should know?"

"Mom, may I spend the night at Hannah's? I'll bring the Memchip to you early in the morning."

"Of course, dear. Hannah would like that. See you in the morning." Abbie gave Celine a hug.

Abbie was having a rough week. She had been a little spacey, and Mr. Rittenhouse had questioned her competency. She had been trying to remove a complex computer virus that had infected the cold storage area. Having Mr. Rittenhouse peering over her shoulder didn't help the matter either. *I can understand why he's so concerned about cold storage. After all, his stem cells are in there too. But I've got this under control. At least, I think I do. I'll have Madison double-check it tomorrow.*

She rubbed the red spot on her forearm. *I'll ask for some stem cream tomorrow.*

"Oh dear, how could I have forgotten? Hannah got her new implant the same day I did. Can't remember anything." She rolled over in her bed. "Goodnight, Celine. Lights out."

Meanwhile in cold storage, an unattended computer flashed on, creating a surge in the cooling system. In the walls of cold storage, an electric fire began smoldering.

CHAPTER 5

MY RADIATION SUIT!

BONG! BONG! AN ALARM SOUNDED in the early morning, waking everyone just as the sun rose.

"Celine, get up! The fire alarm just sounded!" Hannah yelled.

"Huh? Why do we have a fire drill so early?" Celine croaked groggily as she slowly climbed down from the bunk above Hannah's small bed.

"My radiation suit! It's in my drawer at home!"

"Go get it! I'll meet you outside!" Hannah quickly climbed into her suit as Celine ran home.

Celine pushed through the crowd as colonists headed to their assigned exits. She slipped into her quarters. Her mom wasn't there. She was glad she didn't have to face her. She rushed to her drawer where she kept her outdoor wear and found a lightweight radiation suit lying within. On top of it lay her dad's flute. Celine gently set it aside and then slipped into her suit. Comforting to her body like fine mesh, it covered her from head to toe and would undoubtedly protect her from the sun's radiation. She pushed the small button on her right sleeve to activate the suit's electromagnetic field. She could feel the hairs on the back of her neck and arms rise, which was her sign that the suit was activated.

Celine then reached for a small foil packet in the bottom of the drawer and carefully unwrapped it, revealing a tiny blue pill; she placed it beneath her tongue, all the while staring at the flute. *I could never forgive myself if something happened to it.* Suddenly, Celine felt her lungs shut down. *The O2 pill is working.* Now, she wouldn't need to turn on the oxygen synthesizer on her mask for at least twenty-four hours. Next, she grabbed her helmet and fastened its strap beneath her chin. The red facemask on the helmet made the room appear red: just like the Martian surface before a thunderstorm. Finally, she grabbed the flute. "I'm not losing you," she whispered as she pulled the instrument to her chest. Celine dashed into the corridor and through the commons, gripping her dad's flute tightly as she dodged the fleeing colonists.

As Celine exited the Compound, she saw her mom in her oxygen mask, heading toward the smoke and carrying a sonic fire extinguisher.

In the brisk, dry morning air, the colonists huddled together. As usual, the early morning gales blew forcibly, like the strong winds exuded by Earth's oceans. The gales blew away precious body heat and left Celine wishing she had grabbed her gray blanket. Just last night, the temperature was thirty-eight degrees below zero, but the sunrise had quickly raised the temperature to just above freezing. *By noon, it would be a comfortable ten degrees Celsius,* Celine thought. Fantasizing about the warmer temperatures to come, however, did not ease her discomfort.

Celine wove her way toward the center of the crowd where she knew she would find both warmth and Hannah. Hannah had been Celine's assigned caretaker since she was an infant, and she also happened to be her mom's personal assistant and best friend.

"Stay close." Hannah hesitated. "...baby. We can keep each other warm."

"Don't tell me you forgot my name, Hannah," Celine joked through shivers.

Hannah smiled.

Inside the Compound, the fire was quickly contained with bass sound waves from the fire extinguisher but not before the toxic fumes had done serious damage to an electrical engineer's lungs. Madison, who had found the fire, was brought to the surface wrapped in a gray blanket and laid at the feet of his jittery wife.

Celine noticed heat rising above everyone—everyone except Madison. She blinked. *It's happening again.* She could see halos around the colonists. She wondered if her eyes where glowing, but since no one near her seemed alarmed, she assumed her eyes appeared normal. Slowly, she made her way toward Madison to get a better look. Then she heard something she'd never heard before—a sickening yet sorrowful moan from Madison's wife. Celine froze in her tracks, and Hannah grabbed her by the arm.

"No, don't go," Hannah whispered. Her eyes were wide with despondence.

Everyone was silent for a moment. Then, like a noisy beehive, the colonists began talking all at once. Celine listened for bits of conversations.

"Madison is dead."

"How is that possible?"

"His lungs were damaged from the toxic fumes."

"I know that, but why didn't one of the doctors treat him with his stem cells?"

"The fire was in the cold storage."

"That's awful."

"I know. The stems were damaged."

"All of them?"

"Yes, all of them. The fumes got to them. Some even burned in the fire."

Whispers of damaged stems and Madison's death spread from one colonist to the next like a wave of despair. Celine noticed Alex's dad waving his hands to get everyone's attention.

"Everyone stay calm," Mr. Rittenhouse called. "We won't be able to bring Madison back, but we knew there would be dangers and challenges when we took on the mission to make this planet a livable place. This is not the end of our mission. Yes, Madison is dead, but his dream lives on. *Our* dream lives on."

"What about the stems?" someone in the crowd shouted, and a chorus of colonists echoed the question. *Yes, what about the stems?* Celine thought. *Mine are gone forever.*

Mr. Rittenhouse raised his hands again to quiet the crowd.

"Look, I'll send Dr. Duke back to Earth to supervise the recollection of your stems. We still have your birthplaces on file."

"Not Dr. Duke," Celine muttered. "Send Dr. Baylor."

"What did you say?" Hannah hissed into Celine's ear.

To Celine's surprise, Hannah's voice sounded menacing. "I like Dr. Duke. I don't want him to leave. Why can't Dr. Baylor leave?"

"Be quiet," Hannah snapped in a hushed tone.

"My ship can make the trip back to Earth in thirty-three hours," Mr. Rittenhouse continued. "Stan," he shouted to one of his personal protectors. "Go to the *Stellar* and contact the Company. Tell my vice president, Mr. Adeboye, about this situation. He'll get the intervention started."

"Yes, sir, Mr. Rittenhouse," Stan said.

Celine noticed the big smile on Stan's face, and she envied him for the warmth he was about to experience going into the *Stellar* to fulfill Mr. Rittenhouse's orders.

Mr. Rittenhouse continued his lecture to the colonists. "I will contact the World Authority to collect the stems from your birthplaces and have them sent to my company's cold storage. That should take no longer than a week."

"Martian time or Earth time?" Mr. Armbruster yelled. "A Martian week is *fourteen* Earth days!"

"I know that," Mr. Rittenhouse barked back. "Earth time. Any other questions?"

No one else spoke, and then suddenly someone in the crowd yelled, "Thank you, Mr. Rittenhouse!"

Another chimed, "We'll have to be extremely careful for the next few days, but I think we can manage."

A chorus of agreement moved through the crowd until everyone was on board with Mr. Rittenhouse's plan. The colonists formed a circle around him.

Dr. Baylor, who had been speaking with Madison's wife, squeezed past Celine in order to stand directly next to Mr. Rittenhouse. "If anyone gets hurt, I still have photon therapy," Dr. Baylor announced to the colonists. The colonists dispersed so quickly that one would have thought Dr. Baylor had been holding a photon injector in her hand.

"That thing is painful," said Mrs. Armbruster. "No one wants that."

"It's all I have now. So stay well," Dr. Baylor replied. To Celine, Dr. Baylor appeared to smile.

Then Celine noticed Mr. Rittenhouse taking Alex aside to speak with him. She could tell by the expression on Alex's face it was not good news.

"Alex, I am sending you back to Earth with Dr. Duke," Mr. Rittenhouse told his son.

"Dad, I'm finally getting used to this place. Why do I have to go home now?"

"This Compound is not as safe as I had envisioned. I want you home with your uncle until I return."

"But, Dad, I—"

"You're going back to Earth," Mr. Rittenhouse snarled.

Alex groaned. "Is it safe to go back into the Compound to get my things?"

"Not yet. We're waiting for Ms. Voltaire to give the all clear. What's taking her so long?

Alex scanned the crowd for Celine. "Dad, there's Celine. I need to go over and tell her goodbye."

"Fine, don't stay too long. I'll need to send the ship back to Earth shortly."

Celine stood next to Hannah pondering about the damaged stems. Unlike the other colonists, she was born on Mars, so she wouldn't have any stem cells on Earth. *I suppose I'll have to be extremely careful for the rest of my life,* she thought. *Oh, here comes Alex.* Her tight lips turned into a warm smile.

"Hey, Hannah. Can I give Celine a quick tour of the ship while we're waiting for the all clear?" Alex asked.

"Fine. Celine, do you—"

"Yes, I do," Celine replied before Hannah could complete her question. *This is odd,* Celine thought. *Hannah would never allow me to leave her sight in a time like this.* Nonetheless, Celine quickly joined Alex, and they headed to the *Stellar.* As soon as they were inside the spaceship, Alex said, "This is the time to make our move. The drone is down. All systems are offline until the electrical engineers can finish their inspections, and they're short one. No disrespect to Madison."

"We can't leave yet. There's something wrong with Mom," Celine said.

"We have to, Celine. My dad's sending me back to Earth."

"What?" Celine felt as though she had just been punched in the stomach. "He can't do that!"

"Well, he's going to if we don't take action now, Celine."

"What about the stem cells? You can't put yourself in danger without your stems."

"Dad's already said they'd be replenished in a few days."

"Why don't we wait for yours before we leave?"

"Celine, my dad is sending me back to Earth *today*! I doubt he'd let me come back. We have to leave now!"

Celine moaned. "I had plans to call my grandmother and tell her about my mom…"

"She's millions of kilometers away. She can't help you."

Alex is right. How can Enisi help me now? "Alex, I'm scared. Bad things are happening to the people I love. I don't know why. I don't know who I can trust anymore."

"You can trust me. And you can trust your dad. Let's go find him."

"I guess you're right…" Celine took deep breaths. *Dad will know what to do. I have to believe that. Mom and Hannah will be OK until I can get Dad back here. Everything will be OK when Dad's home.* Celine gently closed her eyes and prayed, *Great Spirit, keep my mother and Hannah safe until we can bring Dad home, and keep Dad safe until we can get to him.* Then she opened her eyes and softly said, "All right, I'm ready now."

Alex raised an eyebrow, then bolted to his dad's sleeping area and took two armbands from a dresser drawer.

"Put this on your left forearm," he told Celine. "It will mute your life signature."

"And why would we want to do that?"

"So we won't be followed, you idiot. You said Morg doesn't want your dad found. You think he's going to be happy when he finds out we're out looking for him? We don't need him trailing us."

"Grandma was right. You're going to be a *huge* help."

"Yeah, whatever. Let's get out of here."

Celine and Alex hurried from the ship to the west side of the Compound where their packs had been hidden behind her rock collection. *Dad and I started this rock collection,* Celine thought.

"Hurry," Alex said, snapping Celine out of her thoughts. "We need to leave before someone realizes we're missing."

"Sure." Celine slung her backpack over her shoulders.

While the colonists waited on the east side of the Compound in the morning sun, the teens finished gathering their gear and quietly slipped away. Leaving the safety of the colony behind, they headed for the Red Hills.

Meanwhile, the medical wing had been cleared for reentry, and Dr. Duke was preparing for his trip to Earth to oversee the stem cell collections. He passed Abbie on the way to the *Stellar*.

"I'd love to go with you," she said. "And take Celine with me..."

"Well, I'd love to have the company of two beautiful women," he said warmly. They both smiled.

"Celine's stem cells are in my hometown," she reminded the doctor.

"I know. It was very wise of you and Averill to send them to Earth with Captain McAndrew. You ever communicate with the captain since he brought in our first shipment?"

"No. I've heard he's taking shipments to the moon now."

"He's a good man."

"He is. I miss him," Abbie said. "He always told stories about the latest happenings on Earth."

Abbie's eyes glazed over.

"Is there anything you'd like me to pick up for your family?"

"No. Thank you, Thomas. I just wish Celine could see Earth."

"Maybe one day."

CHAPTER 6

DEATH VALLEY?

◆ ◆ ◆

CELINE AND ALEX BEGAN THEIR trek under a violet-gray sky with wisps of thin white clouds floating high above them.

So much like Death Valley, Alex thought. *Gotta remember that those clouds are not made of water; they're frozen carbon dioxide crystals. Without my O2 pills, I'd be gasping for air…* He looked back at Celine and wondered if he had made the right decision. *She doesn't look as pathetic as she did the first time we met, but she's still no Alex Rittenhouse.*

"How ya doing back there, Martian Girl?" he called back. He knew Celine didn't like being called that, but he didn't care. He watched her look at the Compound, totally ignoring his comment.

"It seems so small in the distance," she mumbled.

"Hey, Martian Girl—Focus."

"Shut up, Water Boy," Celine yelled. She chuckled at her cleverness. "You live in an ocean on Earth, right? So I'm calling you, Water Boy."

Alex burst out in laughter. "So now I have a pet name?" he called back, attempting to restrain his amusement. "Well, I've been called worse. Actually, I think I like it." He grinned at Celine as she struggled to catch up. *Looks like she's skipping.* He chuckled. Then he looked back at her as she awkwardly scrambled to keep up, and he noticed what appeared to be a yellowish glare coming through the red facemask of her helmet. *Must be the glare from the sun,* he thought.

When Mr. Rittenhouse and the captain went on board the *Stellar*, Mr. Rittenhouse expected to see Celine on the ship with Alex. He had seen them board but had not seen them leave. He was considering sending Celine and her mother to Earth and having them return to Mars with Dr. Duke once the stems had been collected. Primarily though, he wanted to have some truth serum slipped into Abbie's food or drink. *I know there was a transmission between her and Red Cloud. She might have the coordinates to the ores and be planning to sell them once all of the commotion over them dies down. I can't have another company coming here and staking a claim over my ores.*

I am certain Alex would get a big kick out of showing off our home and Earth's oceans. He's been spending a lot of time with that little Martian girl. Mr. Rittenhouse smiled as he envisioned his fabulous home and the expressions on every visitor's face upon seeing it; one side of his home gave a panoramic view of the ocean's wildlife and flora. He was so proud of it. *Alex says the girl is fascinated with Earth's oceans. Swims every day in that little entertainment room. Won't she be surprised when she sees what a real ocean looks like?*

Mr. Rittenhouse strode over to his intercom. "Alex, come up to the saloon. I need to speak with you." He waited an impatient second for a response, then told the captain to search the ship. "Should never leave teenagers alone," Mr. Rittenhouse mumbled. "Stan!" he yelled as he burst into Stan's bedchamber. "Get up, you lazy fool. Where's Alex?"

Stan rubbed the sleep from his eyes. "Sorry, Mr. Rittenhouse. Can you repeat that?"

"Get up, and earn your keep. Antonio went downstairs to look for Alex. Assist him."

"They're not in here, Mr. Rittenhouse," bleeped Antonio's voice on the intercom.

"Mr. Rittenhouse, the *Stellar* has cameras in every room," Stan said.

"I know that. What's your point?"

Stan smirked.

"Get to the point! You idiot!" Mr. Rittenhouse yelled.

"Yes, sir," Stan snapped back. "Sir, we might learn where the children are if we watch today's video."

"Well, get to it. Notify me when you've found something." He turned to the captain who was waiting patiently in the doorway.

"Go check the Compound. Tell Alex to get his things and return to the *Stellar* immediately. I told that boy he would be leaving for Earth soon. What's wrong with young people these days? Don't they ever listen?"

Moments later, Stan had found footage of Alex and Celine. "Sir, there's something you need to see."

Mr. Rittenhouse took Stan's seat at the desk in the saloon. Together they watched the recording with full audio and visual.

"I don't understand how that girl could have talked Alex into helping her search for her father. Everyone knows he's dead…" Mr. Rittenhouse groaned and rolled his eyes. He then turned to Stan, who was standing behind him. "None of the condoms are missing, are they?" Stan's mouth froze wide open, but no words came out. "You're right. Cancel that thought, Stan."

"What could Alex possibly gain by helping her?" Mr. Rittenhouse mumbled.

"He likes her, sir," Stan said with trepidation.

"She's not his type. There's something in it for him. I know my boy just as well as I know myself." As the recording of Celine and Alex continued, Mr. Rittenhouse saw Alex and Celine putting on the armbands to muffle their life signatures. Mr. Rittenhouse grimaced.

"You imbeciles! No!" he moaned at the screen.

"Can I do something for you, sir?" Stan asked.

"Yes. Call Morg." He shook his head in disgust. "And call that girl's mother."

"I have no idea why Alex would be helping Celine," Abbie told Mr. Rittenhouse during her interrogation. "Maybe he wants to help a friend in need."

"I know my son too well to agree with such a simplistic deduction."

The captain interrupted their conversation. "Sir, one of the body-heat tent is gone. Some dried meat and berries, a water bottle, and two weeks' worth of rations are also missing."

Mr. Rittenhouse opened his mouth to say something but found himself in a rare position: he was speechless.

"Sir," the captain continued, "they also have some climbing gear."

That was the final straw. Mr. Rittenhouse couldn't believe his son had taken climbing gear, especially knowing the stems were damaged.

"Get Dr. Duke. And I want you and those stems back here yesterday!" he shouted to the captain.

"Understood, sir," the captain replied and nearly trotted from the salon.

Hours passed as Mr. Rittenhouse and Abbie waited in silence in Admin's quarters for Morg's call. They expected the teens to be found and brought safely back to the Compound before nightfall. They grew wary when they heard nothing by the time the sun faded into the horizon.

Morg had remained at Olympus Mons with the Marsologists when Mr. Rittenhouse and his personal protectors had returned to the Compound days ago. The scientists had gathered data from the volcano while Morg stood guard. Wild, doglike animals had been seen in the area.

He was disappointed when the Marsologists' data showed that Olympus Mons was too large of a volcano for a controlled reactivation. *That means we've got to trek miles away to a smaller volcano in the Chaos Region. Commander's not going to like that.*

"Most of the volcanoes in the Chaos are lopsided," Morg said.

"We know that, Morg," said Jerry, one of the Marsologists.

Morg could sense the irritation among the scientists, regardless; he had no intentions of taking *anyone* to the Chaos Region. In fact, it was his sworn duty to keep all colonists, even nosy visiting scientists, away from it. He had killed to keep the secrets of the region hidden, and though he didn't enjoy it, he would do it again if he had to.

"I know Mars better than anyone on this planet," Morg continued. He noticed a surprised glare from Amirra, Jerry's wife and fellow scientist.

"Morg, do you have another volcano in mind?" Amirra said.

"Albor Tholus would work better, and it's not far."

"You think so?" Amirra said.

"Yes. It's kind of difficult to get to the volcanoes in the Chaos, and most of them look like they've collapsed. I don't think you could activate them."

"Morg, I think we might have underestimated you," Amirra admitted after a thoughtful pause.

Morg smiled at the two Marsologists. *Most people tend underestimate me.* He chuckled silently.

Amirra turned to Jerry and said, "Honey, why don't we take a look at it?"

"We'll take a look at it," Jerry said hesitantly. "We'll run the numbers."

Pretty smart fellers, Morg thought. *Don't want you to see anything that might get you folks killed.*

Morg and the Marsologists were packing their equipment and gear when Morg received a call from Theodore, his second-in-command. He informed Morg of the fire in the cold storage area that had damaged the stems. Morg was shocked that Madison had died and had since been cremated. Never had he heard of someone so young dying of such injuries—murdered, yes, but even that was rare.

With Morg's encouragement, the Marsologists readily agreed that they should head back to the Compound until Dr. Duke returned with the stems.

Morg received a second call; he was not in the slightest expecting to hear from Mr. Rittenhouse's captain.

"Celine and Alex are missing. It appears they are looking for Celine's father."

"Her father? And why do you believe that?"

"We know, sir. We have recordings of them discussing their plans."

"What exactly were their plans?"

"To find Celine's father, sir."

"But he's…" Morg stopped himself. "Did they say where they were headed? Did they have any gear? Does Celine's mother know about this? Speak up, man. You've given me nothing to go on."

"Sir, here is Ms. Voltaire."

"Morg, I'm in shock. Celine and Alex are gone."

"Where? Did anyone see them leave?" asked Morg.

"Madison's widow saw them leave, but she thought they were the Marsologists. They were headed west toward the Red Hills."

"I'll find them, dear. Don't worry. Tell Mr. Rittenhouse to not worry. I'll bring them back safe and sound." Morg ended the call and then called Theodore.

"Does everything fall apart under your watch?" Morg snapped at Theodore. "Get a team together! I'll send these scientists back to the Compound and meet you at these coordinates: fifty longitude, thirty latitude at thirteen hundred hours."

Heading toward the hills means they are probably going to the Chaos Region. I should have flooded that area when I had the chance, Morg thought. He slid some explosives out from Amirra's pack and placed them with his own things. *Why would Alex help Celine search for her dad? That's going to make finding them a little more difficult; that boy has more gadgets than an electronic warehouse...I've got to get those kids back to the Compound before they find out too much.*

CHAPTER 7

RED HAZE

THERE ARE NO HIGHWAYS, MIDWAYS, or skyways here—only the two of us in the middle of this wide-open desert. So quiet...Not even the sound of a chirping insect can be heard. It reminds me of Death Valley, but at least in the valley I'd see a trapdoor spider running for cover, or perhaps a sidewinder sliding sideways to get out of my way. Nothing's here to distract me from the monotony, nothing but a constant haze of fine red dust.

Alex, who was overtaken by boredom, began to sing, "A hundred creepy buzzards on a limb of a dead tree, a hundred creepy buzzards on a dead tree, one flew away, and the rest slid down, now ninety-nine creepy buzzards on a leafless dead tree…" He sang loudly, completely unaware that he sang to the tune of an ancient beer bottle song.

"What's that song?" Celine asked.

"Something to kill time," Alex answered half-heartedly.

"Catchy." Celine joined in the song, "Ninety-nine creepy buzzards on a limb of a dead tree, ninety-nine creepy buzzards on a dead tree, one flew away, and the rest slid down, now ninety-eight creepy buzzards on a leafless dead tree." Celine wasn't so sure of the song's meaning, but she enjoyed the tune. They marched toward the Red Hills in time to its beat.

Alex stopped singing once they reached the top of a small hill. He took his binoculars from a side pocket on his backpack and studied the terrain. "Not many places to hide if we needed to—a few boulders here and there. A person could get seriously lost out here without the right equipment. So glad we have the Na—"

"Shh. Listen. Do you hear something?" Celine turned her head toward a sound.

"No. What it is?" Alex waited for her to speak.

"Sounds like something's moving beneath us."

"That's just the sound of rocks crushing beneath our boots, Celine."

"No, I'm positive I heard something else."

"Or not—it was probably a delayed echo."

"Oh, I hadn't thought of that." A gush of cool air lifted the red dust and swirled it around them.

"Alex, we'd better set camp soon…the cold will come."

"We still have a few hours of light. We can do a few extra miles."

"No!" Celine could feel the winds pushing her gently. "Can't you feel the gales? Night will fall soon, and the cold will come." This would be Celine's first night on the surface, and she was anxious. She grabbed Alex by the arm and shook it. "The cold will come quickly! We could freeze!"

"OK, OK, I get it! The *cold* will come. I never figured you'd be so afraid of everything." He looked through his binoculars. "There's a boulder about a kilometer west."

"I see it," Celine mumbled back.

Alex tilted his head to the side, as if examining the rock in the distance. He then sharply whipped his head back at Celine. "We'll set camp there," he said.

This time Celine led the route, running toward the boulder. Running with her heavy backpack was more challenging than she had anticipated. Nevertheless, she was ready to set camp. After less than ten minutes of running, she finally flopped down on the ground next to the boulder and slid her backpack from her achy shoulders.

"In a hurry?" Alex asked when he finally reached the boulder moments later. "Relax, Martian Girl. I've got you covered," he said as he took the tent covering from his backpack.

"Get it? Covered, cover." He roared with laughter. "This is *gold*, Martian Girl. Get a sense of humor."

Celine rolled her eyes. "You're not funny, Alex. The cold will come. And it will come quickly."

Alex smirked. He gave Celine one end of the covering, and they stretched and pinned it to the ground. They did it quickly, as the evening gale winds increased. Fortunately though, they were stationing themselves on the west side of the boulder where it was relatively warm from the evening sun. Alex pulled out a tube of rods from his pack and began pulling one rod out of the other until it was a four-foot pole in his hand. After locking it in place, he screwed it into the center of the tent's floor. They placed their packs next to the pole to prevent their gear from freezing solid in the night air. Then they sat next to their packs in the center of the floor, back to back. Alex pushed a small button on the pole, and like a large clear umbrella, the tent rose from the pole, engulfing them in a plastic bubble that would prevent body heat from escaping. Celine breathed a sigh of relief. She hoped they would stay comfortable no matter how low the temperature outside dropped.

"Are you comfy, Martian Girl?" He asked as he took off his helmet.

"Couldn't be better, Water Boy." Celine took off her helmet and boots.

"Yeah, well we covered sixteen kilometers less than planned."

"It's my fault, it's it?" Celine said, looking down at her tired feet.

"You did all right," Alex said in a big brotherly fashion. Then he teased, "Maybe I made a mistake in thinking you were ready for this trek."

"I couldn't help it that my feet were tied," Celine said.

"Didn't you just say you were comfy? After we eat, why don't you change your boots to a lighter gravity setting?"

"If I do that, I'd probably find myself skipping instead of walking. Or one of the gales could blow me away...I have better control like this. I'll get use to it." Celine mustered a smile.

"Try not to think about it," he added. "We need to make up the distance tomorrow." He took a second look through his binoculars. "There's nothing out there. No drones, no search party…"

Celine looked back in the direction of the Compound. She could see two bright orange auras a few kilometers below the hill. Though she was having trouble seeing small details, she could tell they were Morg's crewmen, neither one was large enough to be Morg though.

"They're out there," she said.

"Well, if there's a search party out there, they'll need to set up camp pretty soon if they don't want to freeze to death," he said in a shaky voice.

The two sat in silence for a minute.

"We'll break camp early tomorrow at sunrise—after the cold's gone."

Celine turned her back to Alex and watched the search party set up camp next to a boulder on the side of the hill. *Do I tell Alex my vision is better than his* with *binoculars? How would I even explain that?* She looked over her shoulder at Alex as he opened a food packet.

"Hungry?" he asked as he handed her a meal pack.

"Thanks," Celine responded softly. Her body was covered in dry sweat, and the air within the tent was hot and stuffy. She felt unclean and was less than thrilled to eat her first meal on the surface in these conditions. Nonetheless, she was hungry and ate quietly. The meal was like nothing she'd every tasted: dried bird (Alex called it chicken jerky), dried berries, and nuts. She might have genuinely enjoyed the food, had it not been for the floating dust particles that had settled on top of it.

"Happy birthday by the way," Alex said warmly.

My birthday. "Oh. I hadn't thought about it."

Celine's thoughts had been consumed with adjusting to the surface and hiding whatever was going on with her eyes.

"I wonder what my mom is doing right now. I hope she and Hannah are OK."

"I'm sure they're fine."

"If they're not?" Celine shifted nervously.

"Then we'll get my dad to deal with it when we get back to the colony…Don't worry. He's pretty good at fixing things." Alex looked up at the star filled sky and the two lopsided moons. "This is stunning. I wonder if the past universes were as nice as this one."

"I don't think so. My grandmother says everything is more beautiful today than it was in the past."

Alex smiled and nodded in satisfaction. He turned to Celine, and the two briefly locked eyes. Slightly flustered by the intimacy of the moment, Alex reverted the subject back to his father. "I am sure my dad has sent out a search party; they're probably reporting back to him as we speak. He doesn't like to get his hands dirty." Alex looked down at his hands crossed in his lap; for a moment, Celine thought he looked rather sad.

Here she was spending her birthday with the hottest boy from Earth, and neither one of them was in a party spirit.

What if I transform into something? What if I hurt Alex? Celine watched him as he chewed his dried chicken. *How could I forgive myself? I have to tell him what's going on, but what can I say? I don't even know what's happening to me—or why.*

"What's wrong, birthday girl? You look kind of down."

"I am OK. Just tired." Then Celine noticed a pair of eyes watching them in the distance. She could see the heat rising from its body in a red haze shaped like a crouching wolf.

"There's something out there," she whispered.

Alex crouched; his eyes search the perimeter as he eased his ray gun from his backpack.

"Where? I don't see anything," he whispered.

"It's gone."

"Are you sure it wasn't a shadow?"

"What difference does it make? It wouldn't have been a shadow of a walking boulder."

"Well, what did it look like?"

"A wolf." At that moment, a lonesome howl in the distance pervaded the silence.

Alex's eyes widened. "That's not a wolf." He gulped. "I've never heard anything like that."

"What are we going to do?"

"Well we're not going back to the Compound until I have those coordinates."

"I don't want to go back. I'm afraid to go back without Dad."

"Afraid of what?"

"I don't know. I just don't feel safe there anymore."

"But you feel safe out *here*?"

Celine bit her lower lip. "I'm scared, Alex. I don't know where I'm safe."

"Look, just calm down. I'll take the first watch."

Celine sighed deeply then rolled over to her left side and closed her eyes. After a few minutes, she rolled onto her back and began looking at the night sky.

"Can't sleep?" Alex asked.

"No." Celine stared at the night sky. "Hey, see that blue dot?"

"Earth?"

"I've never seen it any other way. Funny, isn't it. I'm the human who's never been to Earth…What's it like?"

"Some parts look like Mars. But then there are forest and grass-lands and—"

"Do you think I would like it there?" Celine interjected.

"I don't know. You might. But I think the key is just trying to have fun wherever you go. Earth, the moon, Mars…Just enjoy yourself."

Celine smiled.

"You're welcome to visit me whenever you want," Alex said sheepishly.

"Really? Thanks. Do you still have your pet seal, Flipper?"

"You know about Flipper?"

"I've watched all of your shows, Alex…"

Alex chuckled. "Flipper would be happy to meet you."

"Now that would be a *real* birthday celebration!" Celine said. They both laughed.

"Get some rest, Martian Girl. We have a long day ahead of us."

In the underground tunnels, Morg was still on the go. He would rest when the job was completed. Unlike the Martian surface, the tunnels were warm, receiving heat from the planet's hot inner core.

The commander had agreed with him; the tunnels must be flooded. He knew exactly where to detonate the explosives to release the underground river. "I am going to miss these tunnels," he said aloud as he thought about how he had used them frequently while others traveled on the harsh surface.

"Tough, Red Cloud," he said referring to Celine's father. "You should have never found these tunnels. If you're still alive, you won't be for long. Once the flood comes, only the glowworms will know the secrets of the caves, and they're not talking."

CHAPTER 8

SMOKY

THE NEXT MORNING, CELINE AND Alex awoke to find their tent glistening and completely covered in frost. Celine panicked. It appeared they were losing body heat through the tent. Smoky gas from the frozen carbon dioxide rose from the tent's cover like smoke from a campfire.

"Don't touch it!" she said when she saw Alex putting a finger on the icy tent cover.

Alex held his finger in midair. The blue aura around him became dull.

"Your fingers might stick to it. Put on your gloves."

Alex shoved his hands into his gloves in silence. Celine noticed his aura becoming red.

"Anything else you need to tell me before we get out of here?" Alex said.

Celine was enthralled with the color change of Alex's aura; she paid little attention to the change in his voice.

Alex moved from his reclining position to sit up and began massaging his temple. "My head is pounding." He coughed to clear his throat. "Hey, what's going on with my voice?" The words spewed from his lips an octave higher; though it did not sound quite like a Helium voice, it was obviously not as low as usual.

"Yes, your voice will change," Celine said with a smirk, her voice at a higher pitch as well. "I was wondering when that would happen," she chuckled as she noticed herself surrounded by the usual orange aura. She wished she could tell Alex about the colors that surrounded them.

"What do you mean?" Alex asked. His voice continued to crack.

"Well, when you've been on the surface for a few hours, you get a Martian voice. Didn't you know that?"

Alex shook his head. "This is not funny!"

"Don't worry, Water Boy; you'll get your voice back." Celine paused for dramatic effect. "When we return to the Compound." Celine could hardly contain her laughter.

"Seriously, it's not that funny!" Alex squawked. That made her laugh even harder.

"And that awful headache, it'll go away in a few hours… Hopefully," she teased.

"Welcome to the Martian experience, Water Boy."

"I've changed my mind. I'm going back to the Compound."

Celine stopped laughing. "Alex, you wouldn't."

"Got you." Alex teased. Celine joined him in laughter.

" All jokes aside. Is there anything else I should know about Mars?"

Celine paused. *Should I tell him about me?*

"No. No more secrets, Alex…" She could not look at him.

"What's causing this headache?"

"Have you ever been on the O2 for more than twenty-four hours?" Celine noticed his confusion. "On Mars?" she added.

"Ah, well, no." Alex stifled a laugh. *This voice…Wonder how Dad would sound.*

"Well, headaches are usually the side effects."

"So does that mean I'll have to use an oxygen canister? I only have one."

"No. The headache will probably go away." Celine noticed the smoked had stopped. "We can take down the tent now." She slid her foot into one of her boots.

"You'll be fine," she continued. "I remember when I was ten; the Carbon Dioxide Extractor needed repairs, so we had to take O2 pills for a week. Practically everyone complained of headaches the first day."

Alex looked at her with his head cocked to one side.

"I thought I would be leading this expedition," he said. "You might come in handy after all."

"Oh? The Water Boy leads the Martian Girl on Mars? Interesting notion."

"You're just so naive." Alex put on his boots and then his gloves.

Celine ignored his rude comment and slipped a hand into one of her gloves. She looked back into the distance where she had last seen the search party. "Wait, where are they?"

Alex whipped his head in the same direction.

"Who? Or should I say what?"

"The search party. They're gone." Celine squinted as she search the perimeters.

"Why would they leave so quickly?"

"I never saw them."

Celine picked up her helmet. "Something's not right." Celine noticed a large ball of light forming in the sky.

Alex quickly fastened on his helmet and pushed the voice amplifier button. "What's happening?"

"We need to find shelter. I think a storm is coming."

Alex looked up at the sky and saw large balls of flashing light. Then he heard what sounded like a giant hand scratching a huge balloon.

"Over there," Celine called as she pointed toward a group of boulders. "We can wait it out over there."

They moved as quickly as they could toward the boulders. The scratching sounds were getting louder. All of a sudden, one of the large balls of light headed down toward the planet's surface. Celine could see it smash into the ground, burning a round hole about the size of her helmet into it.

"Under here," she cried. She heard Alex mumble, but there was no time for questions.

"Wait up, Martian Girl," he called, but Celine didn't stop until she had slid down a slope and was huddled beneath one of the boulders.

Seconds later, Alex slid down the slope to join her.

They both listened in silence as the storm moved further away.

"I think it's safe to get out now," Celine said. She noticed Alex's wide eyes had gone dark.

"Sure," he said as if had just awakened from a trace. He took his binoculars from his backpack and looked in the direction of the storm. "The crazy weather here hadn't even crossed my mind."

"Mine neither." Celine brushed red dust from her uniform.

Suddenly the Navi began to beep.

Alex stared at the Navi screen. "Look, we're getting another signature."

Celine looked at the new beeping red dot on the Navi. "What does that mean?"

"It might be your dad moving around."

"You told me my dad was in the Red Hills. Right?"

"Yes, and I have his coordinates. But I haven't seen his signal since we left the Compound."

"So, technically, you don't know where he is?" Celine stacked her arms in front of her chest.

"Not exactly. But if he's alive, he might be moving about. Right? This is a good sign."

Celine threw up her hands. "Oh, great, now the truth comes out: after we've been caught in a storm and nearly frozen, you don't actually know where my dad is. Well, since we're being truthful here: I failed to tell you that Dad's dead assistant was found with parts of his body gnawed away!"

"Is that supposed to scare me? Only scavengers eat dead things, and last time I checked, I looked pretty alive."

"That's not funny, Alex." Celine pouted.

"Wasn't supposed to be."

"Well, suppose the signature you're getting is actually *inside* the belly of the thing that chewed on Mr. Taiki."

"Look, the signal is only a few meters out of the way. If it's nothing, we won't lose much time. If you are afraid, you can wait here. I'm going."

Celine shook her head. "I don't think we should separate. That animal—whatever it was—was watching us last night. You heard it."

"Sure." Alex unzipped his backpack and removed his ray gun. He attached it to a fastener on his radiation suit. His body was tensed. Celine heard him mumble something that sounded like "It better get out of my way." He looked back over his shoulder. "Follow me," he said, and Celine obeyed. After walking several meters through the red dust, Celine spotted something shiny in the distance. It appeared to be one of the capsules she had seen in a spacecraft graveyard in the Gold Plains. Silvery and covered in red dust, the pod was large enough to hold a big animal.

"I see something out there," Celine said.

"Where?" Alex cupped his gloved hand against his helmet to block the sun's glare.

"It's shiny. Do you see it?"

"I'm not sure. Could be a glare." Alex took out his binoculars and looked in the direction where Celine had pointed. He squinted. "Are you wearing binocular contacts? That thing has to be at least a kilometer away."

Celine dodged his question. "You see it? It's an old space capsule."

"I know what it is. Some governments sent dozens of them here."

"Well, yes, but I didn't know there was space junk on *this* side of the planet."

"I've got to get a closer look at it."

"I don't think we should get too close. Sometimes wild animals have been seen lurking around those things."

"You think you know everything," Alex said as he continued walking toward the capsule.

"Wait up." Celine skipped to catch up. She looked for signs of heat or auras coming from the capsule but saw none. Her eyes scanned the surface around the pod for signs of life. Nothing.

As they got closer, Alex stopped and moved the setting on his ray gun to high. He slowed his pace, and Celine caught up. Together they approached the capsule.

The capsule's exterior was scorched. Its blackened sides peeked through layers of red dust. It was windowless but well lit by the sunlight that shone through its small opened door. The simplistic control panel contained two push buttons. *Simple enough for a dog or monkey to operate.*

"The signal's coming from inside," Alex said.

"I'm not going in there."

Alex stopped in the doorway. Two small seats were attached to a corroded floor.

"I don't see anything in there. The chip must be behind one of the seats." Alex crawled in.

Suddenly a furry mole-like critter dashed for the door. It had long teeth hanging in front of what appeared to be its mouth, and there was no visible sign of eyes. It almost glided across the floor right into Celine. They both screamed.

"What was that?" Alex yelled.

"I don't know." Celine responded, still shaken up. "I think it's a Martian rat."

The animal burrowed into the ground, and dirt fell into the hole behind it, leaving no trace.

"How have I never heard of them? This should have been the news story of the century! Life found on Mars! In the form of a fat rat." Alex snickered. "Ah, disgusting. Here's what it's been gnawing on." Alex pointed to Mr. Takei's severed arm. Celine cringed.

"Listen. Do you hear that? Sounds like something moving underground." Alex ran past Celine. As she stepped backward, her foot slipped into a rusted hole in the capsule, and she fell on one knee.

"Ow! Watch it!" she cried. Carefully she twisted her foot loose and examined her pants leg for any damage. "I'm OK," she sighed. She then turned toward the cooing sound and faced hundreds of the mole-like critters crawling toward her.

Alex saw them too and pointed his ray gun at them.

"No! Don't!" Celine said. She could see a yellow hue around each of the critters' bodies. "They're friendly. They wont hurt me."

The sea of reddish-brown fur stopped a few meters away from Alex and Celine. The creatures appeared to be studying them, although they had no visible eyes.

Alex kept his ray gun pointed in their direction as he beckoned Celine from the capsule.

The teens backed away from the animals, keeping their eyes on them. The critters moved forward each time Alex and Celine took a step back. Then Celine noticed a muddy red hue around one of the larger animals in the middle of the group. Slowly the red hue spread from one animal to the next. As it did, the animals began to chatter and squeal. Suddenly all of the animals were engulfed by red hues, and they seemed extremely agitated. "This is not good…"

Celine could hardly speak the words before the red hue spread around Alex as well, and he shot into the crowd, striking several of the animals at once. The animals began hissing and spitting; their saliva seemed to burn right into the surface of the planet.

"Did you see that?" Celine asked.

Alex didn't answer, but she could tell by the fear in his eyes that he had. He began shooting wildly at the critters that were closest to them, but they continued to advance as they slithered over their stunned comrades.

Celine closed her eyes and began to pray and meditate. As she did, her orange aura became yellow, then white; then it expanded into the animal's auras. The creatures began to slow. Celine opened her eyes. Her aura was glowing white and spreading from one animal to the next, changing their auras to a light pink. They cooed as their auras changed. Then they burrowed their way into the ground, pulling their stunned comrades with them and leaving without a trace.

Did I do that? Celine thought.

"Let's get out of here," Alex said.

"I couldn't agree more." Celine looked up at sky. The sun seemed to shine brighter.

Kilometers away, underground in the Chaos Region, Morg was heading deeper into the warm tunnels. He noticed the glowworms on the ceiling were dimming their bioelectric lights, making it more difficult to tell where he was going. *What's happening? They've never done this before.* He remembered the first time he encountered them. In a sense, they reminded him of small electric eels, but their power never gave out. They always provided bright light throughout the tunnels. Today, however, they were behaving differently. They were leaning in toward him as he walked past but then recoiling as if he smelled funny. *Maybe they can sense their days are numbered.* Just as the thought crossed his mind, the glowworms stopped glowing, leaving him in total darkness. He turned on his flashlight, but the light was swallowed up by the darkness. He didn't feel sure-footed anymore. *Should have brought a miner's light.* He fumbled around in the darkness until he could see light that led toward a tunnel exit, not exactly where he wanted to go, but he was relieved to head out of the darkness. He had never paid much attention to the low-life glowworms. They had always provided constant light. The idea that they could sense him (and his intentions) had never occurred to him.

He took out his Com to call his crew and find out their progress in regard to locating the children.

"Do you have the kids?" Morg asked Theodore.

"We've seen evidence of their campsite, but they appear to be heading away from the Red Hills, eastward now. We lost some time heading southward. We were chased by a pack of those wild wolflike creatures. You know, the descendants of those dogs that were sent here during the first missions…"

"Yah, yah." Morg felt impatient with his second-in-command, who always answered a question with more rhetoric than needed.

"Stay on their trail. We need to get those kids back to the Compound safely.

Keep me informed of your progress. Call me if they head westward again. I don't want them anywhere near the Chaos Region. Plus, the longer they're on the surface, the greater the chance of something bad happening to them. I don't won't them getting lost like Celine's father. Abbie would be devastated."

"Understood, sir," Theodore replied.

The call ended. And Morg didn't hear his second-in-command complain.

"He's obnoxious. Why is he the lead protector of the colony? Why is it so important to keep everyone from the Chaos Region?" Theodore said to his fellow crewman.

Morg called the Compound to let Mr. Rittenhouse and Abbie know that the children had survived the night and were heading eastward, to an area that was less dangerous than the Chaos Region.

Then he made the dreaded call to his commander.

"I haven't flooded the tunnels. The glowworms put me in total darkness. It was eerie. I had to get out of there," he told his commander. "I don't think the children are going to the Chaos Region. Perhaps we won't need to destroy the tunnels after all."

Ignoring Morg's recommendations, the commander responded, "I'll send back up. Lay low. Don't leave the site until the mission is completed. Understood?"

"Understood," Morg said. He flopped down near the entrance.

"Yes, I understand. I've got to go back into that creepy tunnel. Who knows what those creatures might do." The thought of those glowworms was so eerie, it made his skin crawl.

CHAPTER 9

SCORCHED

CELINE SAID A PRAYER FOR the stunned critters. *Poor things. They didn't know what hit them.* Then she rushed to catch up with Alex as they headed westward.

"Thanks, Alex. You saved my life."

Alex bit his lip. "Yep, I did. So why did you pray for those critters? They could have made a meal of us."

"It's what my father would have done."

"My dad would have scorched the entire colony." Alex lifted his chest in pride.

Celine walked silently beside him. She was beginning to understand why Alex's aura shifted from red and blue.

"We need to hurry and find my dad so we can get back to the Compound."

"Agreed. This venture is too real."

"Did you get any information from the chip? Did it tell you where Mr. Taiki had traveled?"

"I didn't have time to collect any data, and I have no plans of going back there. At least not with you."

"Oh, Alex," Celine moaned. She walked ahead of him.

"Hey, earlier, when you made those animals calm—how'd you do it?" Alex called out as Celine marched ahead.

"I didn't do anything!" Celine called back, continuing ahead. "Oh, Dad," she whimpered. "Where are you? Please give us some sign."

Celine and Alex continued their journey westward. When they reached their old campsite, Celine could see the remnants of heat signatures from Morg's men.

"They've been here," she said.

"What do you mean? Who's been here?"

"Morg's crew."

"How do you know that? I don't see anything."

Celine studied the area carefully to find something tangible that Alex could see. She saw a heel print that was made from a boot, larger than hers and Alex's.

"Do you see that huge heel print? There." She pointed to the print next to Alex's foot. "You're almost standing on it."

Alex crouched down to study the number in the center of the heel print.

"Size twelve. You're right. This wasn't here before." Still crouching, Alex surveyed the area. "Where are they?"

"They're gone. Probably have been for hours," she said as she pretended to examine the heel print for clues.

"Well, let's get out of here before they come back." Alex said. "I want those coordinates. I *need* those coordinates. And I'm not letting Morg or his men get in my way." He placed his right hand on the ray gun hanging from its clip.

"You wouldn't dare shoot them," she scoffed.

Alex looked down at his ray gun.

Celine could see a muddy red hue, almost brown, surrounding his body. She quickly looked away. "Or maybe you would…"

"Let's go, Martian Girl," Alex said as he took a few steps and looked back to see if Celine was following.

"Right behind you, Water Boy. Watch where you're walking. I wouldn't want you to step on one of those furry critters. It might spit and burn a hole in your boots."

"That's not funny." He stopped to study the terrain.

Celine caught up and walked past him. "Follow me, Water Boy."

"Gladly. Keep in mind I made the fat one screech," he chuckled. "That'll teach those Martian rats."

Celine changed the subject.

"Look at that," she said. She pointed to kilometers of rippled terrain.

"That's going to be difficult to navigate."

"I know. And my feet are already tied."

They hiked over rocky soil and stopped to rest next to boulders, keeping themselves out of sight from any perceived dangers. After taking a sip of water from the water bottle, they continued their trek toward the rugged terrain.

"Hey, careful," Alex called out. "It's pretty uneven up here. You could easily twist an ankle. This whole area looks like it could have been underwater at one point."

"How can you tell?" Celine didn't see anything unusual about the land.

"Look at these grooves. See how they're all carved in the same direction."

"Yes…" She tilted her head.

"It's like a dead river bed," Alex said with authority.

"Hey, look over there. The hills!" Celine waved her arms over her head as if she were doing a victory dance. She could see shadowy brown openings leading into the hills.

"Do you see that?" she asked. She pointed toward the hills. "Those dark brown shadowy areas."

Alex took out his binoculars and looked in the direction Celine had pointed.

"Might be caves," she said.

"I think you're right," he replied. "You can see that far away?"

"Well, um…Lucky guess."

"Amazing." Alex continued to study the area through his binoculars.

"Do you see that crater?" he asked.

Celine reached for Alex's binoculars even though she didn't need them.

"It's like Enisi said—red hills next to a crater. It's enormous."

"We can either go around it to get to those hills, or we can cross it. It's about ten kilometers across."

Celine listened patiently.

"If we go around the crater," Alex continued, "it will take us nearly two days to reach the hills, but probably seven hours if we cross it."

"Well, that settles it. Let's go across the crater."

"Let me finish, Celine. If we were to go across the crater, we'd have to do some serious climbing. Are you ready for that?"

"Sure, I can do it."

"It will be dangerous. Looks like a thousand-meter vertical drop."

Celine swallowed. "Have you ever done a descent that deep?" she asked.

"A few times. But this is Mars, and Mars is full of surprises."

"Well, I trust you, Alex. We can do it…together."

"OK. Let's rock and roll."

"Huh?"

The teens continued their trek. They walked over hard rocks and around boulders, moving upward to the edge of the crater. When they arrived, Alex slipped off his backpack. Celine eased toward the edge and looked down. Then she looked across to the other side of the crater, where she and Alex needed to go.

"Magnificent. It's really beautiful, but scary."

"Now is not the time to be scared." Alex had already taken out his harness and was stepping into it.

"It seems so different than the hills we practiced on."

"Yep. Take off your backpack and get out your gear."

Celine bit her lip, then took a deep breath. "You're right. No time to be scared now."

Celine eased off her backpack, took out her harness, and stepped into it.

"Make sure it's tight. Wouldn't want you to—" Alex stopped himself.

"Wouldn't want you to fall through. I know." Celine finished his sentence for him. Once they were both secured in their harnesses, Celine sat on the ridge while Alex hammered in an anchor.

"There are no ledges."

"That won't be a problem. We'll just lean back on the rope when we need a rest. I doubt if we will need to rest."

He attached the anchored cord to his and her belaying plates, along with a shock absorber, in case one of them fell.

Celine looked up to the coral-colored sky and began to pray:

> Wakan Tanka, Great Mystery,
> teach me how to trust
> my heart,
> my mind,
> my intuition,
> my inner knowing,
> the senses of my body,
> the blessings of my spirit.
> Teach me to trust these things
> so that I may enter my Sacred Space
> and love beyond my fear,
> and thus Walk in Balance
> with the passing of each glorious Sun.

This was a prayer her Enisi had taught her to calm her spirit. After her prayer, Celine thought about the training Alex had given her at the Compound. She remembered how Alex would press his feet into the side of a hill and lean back to test his weight against the anchor's support before pushing off. He would take small hops back to a ledge and then wait for her. But she did not see any ledges, not even a plant—only the rippled rocky sides of the cliff's wall.

Alex had been waiting quietly for Celine as she prayed. "Celine, are you ready?"

"Yes." Although her lips trembled as she spoke, she held her chin up.

"I'll go down first. I'll descend about seven meters, and you'll follow. We'll do it just like we practiced. You can rest on the crater's wall by pressing your feet against it and leaning back on the harness. Got it?"

"OK. Let's do it."

Celine watched Alex as he hopped backward over the cliff. After descending about seven meters down, he waved to her to start her descent. She was nervous; her heart pounded loudly. Wall climbing was one of her favorite sports, and Alex had taught her to mountain climb. This vertical drop, however, was nothing like what she had practiced on at the Compound. Not to mention that if things went wrong at the Compound, she merely had to say: "End program."

She eased over the wall and took her first jump backward. As the rope tensed, she steadied herself and pressed her feet against the wall. *OK, one down and hundreds to go.* Over and over, she pushed off and hopped back until she was dangling next to Alex.

Each time she joined him, he would hammer another anchor into the wall of the crater. It seemed as though he was always ready to push off and descend another seven meters the moment she stationed herself.

Everything was going swimmingly. They were ten meters from the bottom when Celine jumped from the belaying station. She felt her rope twist and tangle around her boot. She heard a loud pop and saw her anchor fling past her. She was jerked hard and began falling, slamming several times into the crater wall. For a moment she felt like gravity had no hold on her. She felt like she was floating instead of falling, but the fact of the matter was that she was free-falling, and all she could see was the bottom of the crater coming toward her unbelievably fast.

Then she felt an abrupt jerk and found herself dangling and sweating profusely, her heart racing faster than ever before. She could hear Alex calling down to her, asking if she was OK. She couldn't say a word. She wanted to scream but was too exhausted to even whimper.

Alex was next to her in a matter of minutes. "How are you, Martian Girl?"

"OK," she whispered. "You won't cut me loose. Will you?"

"Shut up!"

She took notice of her body. "I think I scraped my knee, and my feet hurt, but everything else is OK. I'll be fine. I'll put some cream on it tonight." She remembered the small container of stem cream she had placed in her backpack before the fire at the Compound.

"From here on down, I'll need you to descend first. Do you think you can do that?"

"I guess I have to," she said.

"I am going to hold your dead rope and ease you down slowly. You can use your hands and your feet to push away from the wall—but no hopping. Can you do it?" he asked firmly.

"Yes, I can do it."

Alex retied her cord into a figure eight through her belaying plate. He rechecked her harness by pulling on it. "Ready?" he asked.

"Yes, I'm ready," she confirmed with a surprising burst of energy. Though she had no idea where this energy was coming from, she was grateful.

"I need you to lean back and start taking small steps backward. No hops.

You're going to walk this baby down. Got it? Don't look back. Keep your eyes on me. That ought to be easy enough." He smiled, but his eyes could not hide his concern.

Celine looked at him as she slowly walked backward. He had never looked more handsome. He began feeding her more of the rope.

After what felt like an eternity, Alex said, "Look back, Celine."

She didn't want to look back, but she turned her head to find she was a mere two meters from the bottom of the crater. She continued her slow descent until her feet touched the ground.

She slid down into a seated position and leaned back against the crater wall.

Alex started his descent. Within a few moments, he was standing beside her.

"You're sure you're OK? No broken bones?"

"No, I just banged my knee. I'll look at it tonight once we've camped."

"Get up. Let me see you walk," he commanded.

Celine got up, took a few steps, and began running toward the other side of the crater. She had fallen from the side of a cliff and survived. She was exhilarated.

Alex ran after her. "You Martian fool!" he shouted jokingly. "Wait for me."

Hours later they arrived on the other side of the crater's floor. The other side of the canyon was almost level: smooth like an asteroid had slid across its landscape, leaving sloping ridges for a manageable climb.

"It looks like an easy climb, but I don't think we could reach the top before nightfall," said Alex.

"And my knee really hurts." Celine limped. All of sudden, she whipped her head back toward a humming noise.

"The drone!" they said in unison.

"How did it find us?" Alex said, perplexed.

"My armband!" Celine shouted. She patted her arm for her band. It was twisted and nearly wrapped around her elbow. She fumbled with the arm of her suit and finally eased the band up her arm and over her forearm, successfully covering her signature chip. But the drone continued to hover above them. It relayed their coordinates back to the Compound where Stan manned the search computer. He sent the coordinates to Morg, hastily deleted them, and continued his interrupted exercise program.

Alex unzipped his backpack and began searching for his ray gun.

"It's in the side pocket!" Celine shouted.

Alex reached into the side pocket of his pack, pulled out his ray gun, and began firing at the drone. He hit one of its wings, and it dove to the ground and landed.

"It's too late. They know where we are."

CHAPTER 10

INFLAMED CLOUDS

◆ ◆ ◆

"Can't we set camp on the other side of the canyon?" Celine rubbed her gloved hands together.

"Celine, we won't have enough time to find a new campsite. It's not like we can set this tent anywhere." Alex scanned the area.

"I know that, but Morg has our coordinates now."

"We need flat level land, or the tent won't seal properly... Here." Alex pointed to the level land next to the sloping wall. "Next to this wall is perfect. Besides, look at those clouds."

Celine looked over her shoulder at the darkening red sky and inflamed clouds that surrounded glowing balls of light.

"Lightning," she said, woefully.

A ball of light was discharged and followed by a sound reminiscent of something scratching the surface of a supersize balloon—but amplified a hundred times.

"Well, that settles it. We will have to stay put. We'll leave at sunrise...if the storm is gone."

Celine was not going to argue with that. Even on Mars, lightning was something to take seriously.

"Sunrise it is," she said. She unfastened her backpack.

That night, Celine watched the balls of light discharged in the distance. *How can Alex sleep through this noise?*

She took her flute from her backpack. *Thank goodness it wasn't damaged.* She pressed it to her lips and began playing. She missed Uji peering over her shoulder and swaying to the music. And she missed her mom and wondered if she and Hannah were OK.

"What are you playing? It's beautiful." Alex rolled over to face her and listen to the music.

Celine continued to play. The storm moved further away, and she could hear a little scratching in the distance. She doubted Alex could hear it at all.

"My father taught me. I don't know what it's called. Maybe his father taught him."

"He means a lot to you...your father?"

"He's my world." Celine became silent. "He's the smartest person I know."

"My father wants me to run the family's business." Alex smirked.

"You say it like there's something wrong with that."

"I like what I do. I have the most popular show in the world. I'm a natural at acting."

"So I've noticed. Can't you do both?"

"Not to his standards." Alex shifted his position and looked out at the star-filled sky. "The stars appear larger here, even larger than on Earth's mountains on a cloudless night."

Sensing that Alex didn't want to talk about his relationship with his dad, Celine continued the conversation about the Martian sky. "This is the only sky I know, and I don't know it very well."

Screech! Suddenly, a ball of fire streaked across the sky. Celine jumped. Alex reached for her flute. Celine clutched it. "Careful. That's priceless."

"I don't know why you brought it." Alex said. He removed his hand from the flute and shook his head. "I don't understand you, Martian Girl."

Celine ignored him and carefully wrapped her flute in its cloth and placed it in the center of her pack. "I brought it out during the fire." *I don't understand myself.* Celine looked up at the quiet sky. "I think the storm's moved on. I hope it bypasses the Compound."

Alex studied the night sky. His knees were bent and cramped.

"Do you like Mars now?" Celine asked.

"I haven't decided. It's too unpredictable."

"Yes, it can be that way, sometimes. So is life."

"What could you possibly know about life? You've spent your entire life living in a can on Mars."

Celine wanted to say, "Don't talk about my home like that." She didn't because she was tired of sparring with Alex.

"I call it the way I see it."

"That's enough! The problem is you don't see it. I've had a wonderful life, a happy one, until my dad went missing. I want my old life back."

Alex's eyes widened. "Well, if it's what you want, I hope you get it."

Celine smiled. She lay on her back next to Alex. "Thank you," she said softly.

Alex continued to observe the night sky. "You've got to see Earth."

"And Lunar," Celine said cheerfully to change the solemn mood.

"You can bypass that. It's just a step up from Mars." Alex smiled. "But Earth. There're hundreds of worlds on Earth. There are the ocean dwellers. And the desert dwellers that live in enclosed cool cities. There're…" Alex swallowed. "Now you've got me homesick."

"Tell me more." Celine clapped her hands together.

"It's getting late. I'll tell you more when we are in the safety of the Compound. We need rest. I've got a nagging feeling we're going to be glad we've gotten some." Alex rolled over on his side. "Good night."

"Good night, Alex. I'm sorry I yelled at you."

"Sleep."

Celine turned on to her side to get as comfortable as possible. That night she dreamed of her grandmother. "Listen to your inner voice," her grandmother said.

Celine awakened in the dawn. Alex was still sleeping. *I have been listening to my inner voice.*

Alex awakened. "You're awake early," he said.

"I was dreaming about my grandmother."

"She hasn't changed her mind about the red hills, has she?" Alex grinned.

Celine sat up slowly. "Oh my goodness." She rubbed her knee.

"Moving a little slowly this morning, huh?" Alex asked. Then he chuckled.

"Like I was run over by a herd of buffalo," she said. "My knee is so sore."

Alex raised his eyebrows in surprise. "Amusing," he mumbled. "What could a Martian Girl know about buffalo? Even I know little about them." He smirked. "Buffalo? I take that as you're not feeling like running today?"

"I feel awful." Celine stretched her arms over her head but was careful to not touch the frost-covered tent.

"Well, what am I going to do with you?"

"We've come too far to turn back," she said.

"Who said anything about turning back? I was thinking about leaving you here," he joked.

She felt too sore to verbally joust with Alex. So she moved slowly into a seated position and crossed her legs in front of her. She tried to relax her shoulders as she rested her hands on her knees. With her eyes closed, she began chanting.

"Hey, yeh yeh Aka lotahey…"

"What do you think you're doing?"

"Chanting," she said, her eyes still closed. "It will make me feel better. Hey, yeh yeh…"

"Nonsense!"

Celine's eyes snapped open. "My father taught me how to do this! You should try it!"

"No way am I sitting like a pretzel and making a fool of myself."

"Suit yourself. What's a pretzel?"

"Twisted bread snack on Earth."

"Bread?"

"Pray, please."

"Dad said the vibrations from chanting synchronizes with God Vibrations and heals us."

"Really."

"You have to believe in the medicine of the chant and visualize yourself healthy."

"So I can get rid of this headache?"

"You might."

Alex folded his legs in a half-lotus position.

"I am curious. I've done many things but never anything like this."

"Now close your eyes and repeat after me," Celine said. "Visualize yourself healthy."

"Hey yeh yeh…." Alex opened his eyes. "I don't feel any better."

Celine rolled her eyes under closed lids.

"How long do I need to say this 'Hey yeh yeh' stuff?"

"At least two hundreds times."

Instantly, Alex opened his eyes. "You're joking?"

Celine didn't answer, but continued her chants. "Hey yeh…"

"Celine, we don't have time for this. Remember the drone."

Celine eyes popped open, and she squeezed her lips together tightly. "How could I have forgotten the drone?" She bent over and rubbed her sore feet. "I am so achy. What can I do to get rid of this pain?"

"Get up, and help me put this tent away. Start moving. That's all I know."

Celine wanted to continue her chants. Chanting had made her feel extremely relaxed when she was at the Compound; it made her feel closer to her dad. Her dad chanted each morning and had taught her how. But she and Alex needed to move on. She didn't want Morg and his crew to find her and take her back to the Compound with unfulfilled dreams. She couldn't let a sore knee slow her down. She rolled up the right pants leg of her suit. Her swollen knee was blue. Then she took her first-aid kit from her pack and removed the small container of her stem cream. Using her pinky, she removed a tiny bit of the cream and rubbed it into her bruised knee. Immediately, the color improved, and the swelling began to go down.

"Come on; get moving," Alex said. He had already put on his boots.

"Your command is my wish, Captain Water Boy," she said. She dressed and was ready to help.

Alex chuckled. "You have a lot to learn," he said. Then he started breaking down and packing away their tent's top.

Celine grabbed an end of the tent's floor and folded it. "So do you," she said.

After they were all packed, Alex, using long strides, headed toward the hill. "Bring up the rear, Martian Girl."

"Bringing up the rear, Water Boy." Celine ran to catch up.

The teens used their climbing gear once, in an area that would have been a dead end for nonclimbers. When they reached the top of the canyon and looked ahead at the landscape, it was easy to understand why the area was called *Chaos*. To the west was a maze of hills and valleys. Some of the hills were lopsided, as if they had collapsed like deflated balloons. To the north were tall hills with wave-cut strandlines cutting into their slopes, giving them a rainbowlike appearance of different shades of rusty reds and pinks.

"They're beautiful!" Celine said. She waved her arms over her head.

"Yes, they are," Alex agreed. He sat his backpack on the ground and took out his binoculars.

"Look at the gullies." Celine pointed at a hodgepodge of lopsided hills and deep gullies, waterworn ravines of rusty red rock.

"Niagara Falls." Alex muttered. "Without the water. Unbelievable!"

There were so many different landscapes. It was chaotic. They stood on loose sedimentary rocks and sand, not hard and dense rock like the area on the other side of the canyon. *Useless for anchoring a climb,* Celine noticed.

"I didn't know Mars had trees," Alex said, pointing to the dark brown areas cascading down the sides of some of the sand dunes in the distance.

"That's dark sand, not trees. We think it was darkened by volcanic ash."

"I see." Alex spied a volcano through his binoculars, past the sand dunes. "This is something to behold. Breathtaking. The only thing I can think of that compares to it is the Grand Canyon back on Earth." Alex took out his data recorder and began recording images of the different landscapes.

"One day, I plan to see the Grand Canyon," Celine said.

"I'm sure you will." Alex pointed his data recorder toward a lopsided hill.

As they walked, squeaking noises came from the rocks and sand beneath their feet.

"This sounds like we're walking on broken glass," Alex said. "It would be difficult for anything to sneak up on us. That's a plus."

"True, but anything could hear us coming. That might not be a plus."

As they continued, creating their own path toward the hills in the west, Celine could feel something vibrating beneath her, sounds of continuous movement. It sounded like nothing she had ever heard. Layers of rock and sand muffled the sound.

"Stop, Alex. Listen. Do you hear that noise?" *Please hear it, Alex.*

Alex stopped. He bent down, getting his ear closer to the ground.

"Sounds like moving water!" He shouted, his eyes wide in disbelief "It can't be water. Can it?" Alex entered the coordinates into his Navi. "Water would be more valuable to the Company than any ore."

"Maybe it's lava," Celine said. "You saw those volcanoes."

"No, lava would be hissing and popping and moving slowly. This is way too fast to be lava." Alex paused and studied Celine. "You were walking when you heard that. How did you do that?"

"I don't know." Celine didn't want to elaborate. "Let's go. You have the coordinates." Celine walked westward toward the ledge.

"Come back here, Celine!" Alex ran after her. "And you can see better than I can with these binoculars. Don't deny it." Alex stopped a few meters from her.

Celine noticed Alex's heel was too close to the ledge.

"Alex, watch out! You're going to fall!"

Alex's left heel slid, and he fell to his knees. Just as he slid, Celine caught him by an arm. She fell back on her bottom and dug her heels into the rocks.

"Don't move," Alex said. "OK. I'm going to turn around so I can sit next to you."

Celine released his arm. She could hear some of the rocks fall to the crater floor.

Once he was seated next to Celine, he said, "Use your hands behind you to push away from the edge." They both did. When they were no longer in danger, they sat there silently.

"I've been wanting to tell you about me..." Celine was winded.

"Not now." Alex stood up and reached down to take Celine's gloved hand to help her up. He took out his Navi and appeared to be studying the map and comparing it to what he saw.

He began to walk toward the red hills. He looked back at Celine. "Bring up the rear, Martian Girl."

"Bringing up the rear, Water Boy." Celine was relieved that she didn't have to explain her strange abilities to Alex—at least, not yet.

Alex looked back at Celine and grimaced.

Spirit, please don't let my eyes glow now, Celine thought.

The teens walked silently for three kilometers.

"Your dad's signature is coming from that area," Alex said. He pointed toward a rusty red, lopsided hill. "I think we can reach it hours before night falls."

"Wait. I saw something flash in that dark opening." She pointed to a different hill. *I also saw a heat signature for a moment, and then it stepped back into the cave. Dad, let that be you.*

"You have vision like no one else I know. So lead the way." They turned and headed in the direction of the flash, about a half day's trek, no serious climbing.

As Morg waited impatiently for his backup at the entrance to the tunnels, he felt the vibration of his Com. "Now what? I gave my coordinates. What's the holdup?" he said, thinking it was the commander. When he checked the Com, he saw a message from the Compound that said the drone had located Celine and the boy and had delivered their coordinates. Morg studied the coordinates. "How did they get this close to the Chaos? Surely my men can catch two wandering teens." Calling his crew, he found out that the men had spotted Celine and Alex as they climbed the sloping side of the crater. This meant that the pair could reach the tunnels within the day. Morg stepped out of the cave's entrance. He stayed in the shadows of the cave to avoid detection as he searched the area for the teens.

They were out there. He could see them clearly. *Heavy backpacks—looks like they're going camping.* He laughed. *Real troopers. That little girl has really taken to this planet. Not like her mother.* He was impressed. *One day she'll become a superior soldier.*

They're heading westward. Most of those caves lead to dead ends. A few of them, like the one her dad hid in, lead to the tunnels. But those tunnels won't be there for long. "Where's my backup?"

Morg stepped back into the cave and placed his shiny binoculars in his bag. He fished out a piece of synthetic meat jerky from his ration box and devoured it.

As Morg chewed his third piece of jerky, he thought about how the tunnels had been very useful to him. When others had traveled on the surface, he had travelled alone in the comfort of the tunnels. It was never cold down there. He thought the planet's hot liquid core might have had something to do with that, but he was no scientist. *I'm going to miss those tunnels. Real sorry the commander thinks it's more important to keep the tunnels a secret than to let me enjoy their comforts.*

He stepped outside the cave to call Theodore. In between bites of jerky, Morg berated him, "Can you explain to me how a couple of kids can get so far ahead of you?"

"Sir?"

"Where are you?"

"We are about two days away from the Chaos Region." Neither of Morg's men considered themselves good enough climbers to climb the canyon wall to save the day.

"We don't have any stem cream, so we're taking the route around the canyon."

"I have the children in my view," Morg said. "I'll bring them in. You cowards can return to the Compound. I'll bring the children in."

It was not like Theodore to disobey an order, but he thought Morg was hiding something in the Chaos Region.

"Morg, you're not coming in clearly. What did you say?" Theodore turned off his Com signal.

Morg called him back but only got static noise. "Darn solar flares," he said. "Those darn kids are going to ruin everything."

CHAPTER 11

MEAT JERKY WRAPPERS

◆ ◆ ◆

Morg munched his fourth meat jerky. *Nothing much ever happens on this outback planet*, he thought, so his greatest source of joy came from his food. His pleasure was interrupted by a steady humming sound. To untrained ears, the humming sounded like a constant flow of air moving through an opening in a cave. Morg, however, recognized the sound as that of his backups. They were wearing Angel Wings, the military's name for a small box that contained a small electric rotary engine and large flexible angel-like append-ages. It was a one-man flying machine.

The two soldiers had flown over six hundred kilometers, ten meters above the ground at speeds of two hundred kilometers per hour. Morg had attempted to use the Angel Wings once, but he found them too difficult to control. He reassured himself by claiming only a lower ranking soldier could possibly build up the kind of core muscles necessary to maneuver them. *Officers like me don't need to use them.*

The soldiers were cloaked in the best camouflage available: metallic fabric that reflected the environment around them. They were practically invisible to untrained eyes.

"I am here," Morg called as he stepped out of the shadows. Two humanoids deactivated their cloaks and alighted next to him. Neither said anything. They stood at attention, like GI Joes: strong, handsome faces and lifeless eyes.

Morg didn't care much for humanoids. They looked and moved like the perfect military man, but there was nothing human about them. They were single-minded, emotionless killing machines. Morg gave Humanoid One the coordinates to the river.

As they entered the cave, Morg made his way between the sol-diers for protection. The glowworms remained lightless, but the darkness presented no problem whatsoever for the humanoids. Morg walked in the middle of them like a prisoner; they neither spoke nor replied to any comments he made. Though Morg was a big man, nearly two meters tall and 114 kilograms of almost perfect muscle, he looked puny next to the humanoids. Each stood two and a half meters, and their weight was changeable. Humanoids could weigh what they needed to weigh to get the job done. Humanoid One led the way to the designated site. The other trailed Morg, sandwiching him in to keep him safe. Nonetheless, he didn't feel safe around them. He didn't trust these machines to make decisions. *You never know what they may perceive as a threat to the mission.* They were created to serve as soldiers and nothing more. Hundreds of them sat dormant at the base, like ancient Chinese Terracotta Warriors on Earth, waiting either to be activated in an emergency to fight and protect humanity or to do the bidding of the commander who held their wake-up codes. The mission for these two humanoids was to escort Morg to the location near the river that would release the water through the tunnels, covering everything the military wanted to hide.

Morg had to walk quickly in order to keep up with the nameless robot in front of him and to prevent the one behind him from trampling the back of his heels. When they finally arrived at the river's mouth, Morg quickly set the explosives as the humanoids stood guard.

In twelve hours, his favorite place on planet Mars, the tunnels, would be underwater. He would utilize them one last time to take him westward where he had last seen the children. Certainly there was enough time for him to find them and get them far away from the Chaos Region. He would return them safely to the Compound. He would be Abbie's hero.

Morg used the maxi beam enhancer: a powerful searchlight the humanoid had given him while setting the explosives. The lava tubes had never been brighter. He stepped jauntily through the lava tubes heading westward toward the children. He smirked as he walked. *I can't wait to see the look on their little faces when I tell them about the volcano that's going to blow its top. They'll have no choice but to return with me. Wonder what that idiotic crew of mine is doing?* He started to call them on his Com but decided he'd wait until he was out of the lava tubes.

After a relatively short trek across rocky terrain, the teens arrived at the cave where Celine had seen the flash of light. No one was there, but Celine could tell someone had been. There were four meat jerky wrappers at the entrance of the cave. Celine's thoughts began to race. *I know only one person who eats this much and has the audacity to leave his trash behind.*

"Morg's been here," she mumbled. She picked up the four wrappers and angrily stuffed them in a pocket on her backpack. "Greedy slob…I can't believe I brought us to Morg!" she cried.

"You messed up big time. I knew we should have followed the Navi." Alex looked across the rocky terrain they had just covered. "I'm not letting Morg get in the way of my plans." He patted the pocket on his backpack where he kept his ray gun. The gun was set on high.

The evening gale winds began to blow gently.

"It'll be dark soon," Celine said.

Suddenly a barrage of red dust began to pummel them.

"It might be safer to set camp inside this cave. It's way too windy out here."

"What about Morg?"

"Don't worry about him. If he finds us, he'll be sorry!"

Celine opened her eyes in surprise. *Is this how people behave on Earth?*

"You would actually hurt him?"

"Let's go!" Alex shouted over the howling winds. He shoved Celine into the cavern.

With barely enough light from the cave's entrance, they were able to find their gena-lights. Alex turned his on first and began searching the contents of his backpack for his data recorder.

"It's in there," Celine said as she pointed to an outer pocket. "You didn't answer my question."

"I know."

"Well, answer me."

"I don't know why I even bother telling you anything."

"I don't like him—" Celine looked around the cavern for heat signatures but saw none. "But I could never hurt him."

"Look at the readings on this recorder." Alex's face showed excitement. He appeared to have not heard Celine's concerns. "We have oxygen! We don't need to take O2 pills in here."

He began to unfasten his helmet.

Celine touched his gloved hand. "Not yet. Collect more data first."

"If you insist."

Celine stepped deeper into the cave. She shined her bright light onto the cave's wall.

Alex followed with his light dangling from a carabineer attached to his suit, leaving his hands free to record data from the cave. "It's six degrees Celsius in here."

"That makes sense—I thought it felt unusually warm in here."

"And there's oxygen and nitrogen."

"No carbon dioxide?"

"There's a lot, about four hundred ppm, but I've recorded that much in some of the cities on Earth. Solar radiation is low. That's to be expected."

"So it's safe here?"

"It seems that way."

Both teens unfastened their helmets and attached them to their backpacks.

Celine stood in the center of the cavern turning around in circles, looking up and down at its features. The cavern walls appeared white, like limestone, and the ceiling was rounded out like a planetarium and dripped with blankets of red and pink stalagmites.

"Amazing. I never knew anything like this existed on Mars." Alex said.

Celine titled her head to the side. "I've never seen anything like this either."

Alex pointed to a lava tube that extended from the dome-shaped cavern. "There's running water in there."

"Wait! Look at this." Celine pointed to three sets of distinct footprints leading in the direction of the sounds. "This must be Morg's. See the boot size number?" Celine could also see the heat signature rising from the print. "Fresh print," she mumbled. "These four." She looked at the deep prints showing tread marks but giving off no heat. "They're Humanoids."

"Humanoids? Are you positive? Why would there be soldiers on Mars?"

"I don't know why, but Morg definitely has some with him."

"Seriously?" Alex appeared shaken. He searched the cavern.

"Yes, he does," Celine said dreadfully.

"Well, Celine, I think we need to find a place to hi——." Alex dry-heaved, interrupting his sentence. "I am not feeling well."

Celine could feel the muscles in her stomach knot up. "I'm not either." Alex didn't need to tell Celine he was sick, for she had watched the unusually high amount of heat rising from his body.

"I see a place where we might be safe. Over there," she said and pointed to a small opening in the shadows, close to the floor.

"That looks like some kind of animal den," Alex said. "Use your X-ray vision to see what's in there," he joked.

"I don't have X-ray vision." Celine wondered if she had done the right thing in sharing so much about herself with Alex. She studied the den's opening but saw no heat escaping from its tiny entrance "But I *can* tell there's nothing's in there," she said.

"Oh, you can?" Alex bowed. "After you, Madame Martian Girl."

Celine pushed her backpack through the small cave's opening. She listened for movement and heard none. On her hands and knees, she cautiously crawled through the small opening. There was no source of light, but she was amazed that she could see as if it were daylight. "Come in, Alex. It looks safe. There are no signs of animals."

Alex shoved his backpack through to Celine. "I can't see anything. It's way too dark in there." He began to crawl through the opening.

"Ah!" Celine shouted.

"Ouch!" Alex butted the back of his head as he stood up to back away from the entrance.

"Oh, are you OK?" Celine felt guilty that she had frightened Alex.

"I'm fine." He rubbed his sore head.

"I'm sorry—I shouldn't have done that."

"Yeah, you're right…I butted my head, but I didn't draw blood. And wait, there's barely any room in here!"

Alex crawled and twisted his arms though the opening. Celine helped pull him into the den.

"I think I snagged my suit." Alex turned his back to Celine. "Check my back. Do you see any tears?"

She shined her light on Alex's suit even though she didn't need the light. Alex had dust on his face and in his hair. "A small snag. It doesn't look like it'll break."

"Good," he said. "All right, this place is not bad. There's enough room to spread out the tent's floor covering. I don't think we'll need the top. Do you?"

"Only if it will make you feel safer," she teased.

The humanoids returned to the cave's entrance. Before revving up their engines to fly away, they decided to do one last thing to ensure the success of their mission. Together, they lifted a huge boulder and placed it at the entrance of the cave so no one could get in.

They pushed a button on their wrists, and their cloaking mechanism activated, rendering them nearly invisible and reflecting everything in their presence. Their electric rotatory engines began to hum, and they were lifted high above the cave's entrance. About two kilometers in the distance, they could see two men setting up camp too close to the Chaos Region. Both humanoids pointed their index fingers and fired killing rays, then quietly flew back to the military base on the far side of the planet.

◆ ◆ ◆

Morg's crew had followed his life signature to a hill in the western Chaos Region. Through their binoculars, they saw Morg communicating with two solders.

"Did you see that?" Mike said to his partner, Theodore.

"Yeah, man. That's military. What is military doing here on Mars? And why are they meeting with Morg?"

"You know he was trained by military."

"That still doesn't explain how they got here. We didn't bring them here. They weren't on our supply shipment."

"This is way out of our league, man. We need to head back to the Compound and share this with Admin Rittenhouse. Let her and the other administrators figure this out."

"What about the kids?"

"Look, they're going into the cave. Morg can return them to the Compound. He said he would."

"He has a lot of questions to answer."

Theodore and Mike set up their body-heat tent about two kilometers away from the cave. Suddenly a ray of light struck Theodore, and he dropped to the ground with a red mark on his forehead where a ray had penetrated his skull. Mike fell next to him, with a trail of smoke coming from his chest. As night fell, the cold air penetrated the two holes in their tent. Everything in it, including the men, was frozen solid.

CHAPTER 12

MORE THAN I WANT TO SEE

◆ ◆ ◆

CELINE AND ALEX SLEPT SOUNDLY through the night. It was the first time they felt safe and comfortable since leaving the Compound. The cave was warm and cozy, and neither the fear of freezing nor of wild animals disturbed their sleep.

Alex stretched and yawned. "What happened to the light?" He asked when he woke to find the cave totally dark.

Celine had awakened an hour ago. She sat silently thinking about her dad. Her head rested on the cool cave wall. Her simple plan to locate him proved not so simple.

"The light?" Alex said.

"I don't think I should turn it on. Morg and the soldiers might still be here."

"Well, we won't know for sure, sitting back here in the dark."

"You think the storm's gone yet?" Celine shifted so she faced Alex. "Can you see me?"

"I heard you move. Don't tell me you can see in the dark too."

"I'm just finding this out."

"I should have you on my show, Martian Girl. The headlines will be 'Freak with Insane Vision Can See Literally Everything.'"

"You just can't stop the insults, can you?"

"Lighten up. Where's your sense of humor?"

"The truth is I *can* see everything. Sometimes more than I want to."

"I was joking, but you sound serious."

"For a year now. I've been seeing things." Celine paused. "I—"

"I don't like the sound of that. You're not getting sick on me, are you?"

"It's not like that."

"Good. Then what are you trying to tell me?"

"Never mind. Let's go and see if Morg has left."

"Finally—sounds like progress. Let's go."

Alex patted the floor for his Navi.

"What are you trying to find?"

"My Navi and ray gun."

"They're against the wall to the right of you."

"I didn't put them there."

"I did. They were in my way."

Alex found the Navi. He tapped it, and it lit up. He quickly turned it away from the cave's opening. "I'll input this location.

That way we can leave our things here. But not this," he said, referring to the Navi. He then picked up his ray gun and attached it to the clamp on his suit. "And not this."

Celine, on her hands and knees, crawled to the cave's opening. She peeked out, looking for signs of Morg. She saw none. "Looks clear."

"Well, let's get out of here then. What are you waiting for? I need to stretch my legs."

Celine crawled through the tiny opening into the large cavern, and Alex crawled out behind her. The cave had served as a great hiding spot.

From their hiding place, they crept into the large centralized cavern. Five lava tubes expanded from it like arms from an octopus. The tubes were tall enough for a man to walk upright, but they were not inviting. They were dark and gloomy. Celine stopped where she had seen Morg's footprints.

Alex stopped in front of the tunnel where he had heard the running water. "I need my data recorder. I'm going in there."

Celine nodded. "I want to follow these prints."

Alex went back to their den and returned with their backpacks. He sat them on the ground next to his feet. Then he took out his data recorder and began collecting data from the tunnel.

"There *is* water in there!"

Celine came over to join him. "Shh—Morg might still be in here," she whispered.

"And there's water in there." Alex pointed to the tunnel. "And what did you say?"

"Look, Morg's been down there," Celine said. She pointed to a lava tube that headed away from the cave's entrance. "But the soldiers went back to the entrance."

"Why would they separate?" Alex inquired. "Do you think they're looking for us?"

Celine didn't answer. She noticed a green light coming from the ceiling of one of the lava tubes.

"That's strange." She stepped into the tube to get a better look, and instantly the tube became as bright as a Martian day. Celine tilted her head back in an attempt to find the light's source.

"Aah, disgusting," she said and nearly fell backward out of the lava tube.

Alex ran over to her. "What's wrong?" He widened his eyes and fell back from her. "Your eyes—they're glowing. What happened to you?"

"Nothing. I'm OK." Celine looked down at her ugly boots to avoid looking at Alex.

"You're not," Alex whispered. "Celine, what's going on?"

"Let me explain." Celine bit her lips, but she did not look at Alex. "I tried to tell you." Then she looked directly at Alex and stepped forward.

"Don't move." Alex placed his hand of his ray gun.

Celine stopped in her tracks. "You wouldn't."

"I might." Alex seemed frightened.

"I've tried telling you, but I was afraid."

"You were afraid. Right."

"I'm sorry Alex, but I was afraid you wouldn't help me if you knew."

"So this has happened before?"

Celine nodded.

"And you didn't tell me..."

"I told you I was afraid you wouldn't help me."

Alex swallowed. "Why does it happen? I won't catch it, will I?"

"No. I don't think so."

"Are you going to get sick? Cause I'm not carrying you back to the Compound."

"No, I won't get sick. Do you always put yourself first?"

"Yes. Don't you?"

"Not the way you do."

"Don't change the subject. Tell me about this condition. Why do your eyes look like my pet seal's?"

"Your pet seal ? Alex, you're awful. I thought you had changed."

"Looks like you're the one who's changed."

Celine sat on a large rock that was a meter from Alex. "I don't completely understand why my eyes change. It started last year, after I had my last Brain Booster."

"What's a Brain Booster?"

"You don't know about Brain Boosters? It's a brain booster injection."

"No, I don't. And judging by the sound of it, I'm glad I don't."

"I thought everyone had to get them until age twenty-five."

"Never heard of it."

"Oh." Celine was silent for a moment. "Maybe, it has another name."

"I don't know. Anyway, so it started with your last Brain Booster."

"Yes. It started with me noticing what appeared to be heat rising from my mom and dad."

"Why didn't you tell them?"

"It only lasted a few seconds, and I didn't feel sick."

"But it wasn't normal. You should have told them."

"Yes, I should have."

"Why didn't you? After a year? You and your parents seem close."

"We are, but no one's ever ill in the colony. I didn't know what was happening, and I didn't want to be the only one sick. Plus, I mean, I thought it would just go away."

"I heard you were ill when I arrived."

"Who told you?"

"Admin. Why does it matter?"

"Mom didn't want anyone to know. I needed light therapy."

"OK. So that's it?"

"Yes. But that was the first day my eyes changed. And I could see auras around everyone one—Chakra colors."

"I don't believe in Chakras."

"I do. That's how I knew those animals were irritated. Dark red was surrounding their bodies." *And I might have used mine to calm those animals. I better keep that to myself.*

"Like…auras?"

"Yes."

"Do you see other colors?"

"Yes, sometimes. I don't have any control over it."

"So, if I were angry, you would see red colors around me?"

"Maybe."

"What color is around me now?"

Celine stared at Alex for a few minutes. "Blue. There is always blue around you—" Celine paused. "Or red."

Alex looked away. Then he appeared thoughtful. "Interesting. You're a——" He searched for the right word. "A synesthesian. I've heard of people like you."

"You think I'm a synester?"

"Synesthesian, Celine. There're only a few people on Earth who can do what you do."

I don't think there's anyone anywhere like me.

"But don't get too excited," he continued. "There're only a few like you, and they're all in the military."

"Military?"

"Yes. They were drafted."

"Drafted. You mean they had no choice?"

"None."

Celine whispered, "My grandfather was in the military. Grandma said he hated it."

"I guess so. Who'd want to be treated like a humanoid?"

"My Enisi wanted me to keep my eyes a secret."

"But with those eyes—how are you going to hide it?"

"I don't know." Celine's eyes faded to normal.

"Your eyes are normal now. Darn, I wanted to get a picture."

"Don't say that." Celine turned her head from Alex.

"Lighten up, Celine."

"Promise you won't tell anyone about this."

"Why should I do that? You'd make a great story on my show: 'Alex Finds a Real Martian on Mars.'"

"You wouldn't dare!"

"I might." Alex chuckled, but then he got serious. "I wouldn't do that to you."

"Thank you, Alex…Something good is going to happen to you, I can feel it."

"Yeah, OK. What did you see in that lava tube?"

"I don't know what it was," Celine said nervously. "It looked like slimy animals dangling from the ceiling."

Alex unhooked his ray gun and readied it. He cautiously stepped into the lava tube. Instantly, the tube brightened. He looked overhead but did not flinch. Hanging from the ceiling were glowing worms.

"Worms! You're afraid of worms!" Alex reattached his ray gun to his clip. "Hand me my data recorder."

"Be careful, Alex." Celine searched the floor next to their backpacks. "I don't see it."

Alex walked over to his backpack where he had stored his recorder. "Your weird seal's eyes not working?"

"Shut up, Water Boy." Celine smiled.

"Good to see you smile."

Alex stepped back into the tube. Celine watched him as he recorded data. The worms moved back and forth as if blown in a gentle breeze. Then she saw a red haze radiating from them.

"Get out of there." Celine reached for Alex's arm. "You're irritating them."

Alex followed her from the tube. He shook his head. "You're way too dramatic."

"What are they?" Celine rubbed her arms as if she could feel the worms crawling over her.

"They look like the glowworms you see in the Amazons, but—"

"You've seen those kind of yucky things before ?"

"Not exactly." Alex continued to read the data. "Maybe they're not animals. They appear to be part metal." Alex pushed the replay icon on his data recorder. "There's also something in them listed as unknown on the recorder.

"How is that possible? Your recorder might be radiation defected."

"I kept it in my backpack. I only used it once on the surface. It's working fine. These creatures, whatever they are, contain some unknown element that enhances their bioelectric ability."

"You think they're manmade."

"No, I think they are alien-made."

"If there were intelligent life other than us on this planet, I would know it."

"I wouldn't be so sure of that," Alex said.

"Well, those things give off heat like they are alive. I can see that."

"So does a florescent light."

"But they look like they're responding to us."

"Built-in motion sensor?"

Suddenly, the Navi beeped wildly.

"Is Dad showing up?"

Alex looked down at the Navi and turned its volume off. "Possibly. Follow me." Alex placed his hand on his ray gun. Celine walked silently behind him.

They came out of the tube into another room-like cavern that also had four lava tubes extending from it. Alex's light dimmed, and he checked its charge. "Low. We can't afford to lose our lights in here. The Navi's low too. Let's go outside so we can recharge them."

"Dad might be in there. What if he leaves?"

Alex looked at the dark lava tubes. "Look, we don't want to get lost in here."

Reluctantly, Celine agreed. "Dad!" she yelled. Her only response was her own echo.

"Fine. Let's go, Alex," she said, crestfallen.

They headed cautiously toward the cave's entrance.

"Oh no!" Celine ran over to the huge boulder that blocked the entrance to the cave. She pounded the huge rock with her fists. "No!" She pushed on it until her heels began sliding. "I can't move it! Help me!" Celine and Alex leaned against the boulder and pushed, but it didn't move.

"Not even a millimeter," Alex said. They sat next to the large rock, exhausted.

"Alex, I think there's another way out."

"You think?"

"Remember Morg's footprints led down another lava tube. He never came back. It must be the other way out of here."

"What are you waiting for? Lead the way."

Celine started with Morg's footprints. She stepped into the lava tube, and it became bright.

"Spirit, they're everywhere."

"Keep walking. Don't look at them."

"Do you think they're dangerous?"

"If you're worried they'll eat us, don't be. There's no fecal matter in their system."

"Disgusting."

"Keep moving."

"Don't touch anything."

Suddenly Alex stopped in his tracks. "This could be a trap. Morg could be waiting for us." He unclamped his ray gun and laid his Navi on the floor.

Celine smirked. "What do you think you're going to do with that? If Morg's in there, we can outrun him, Alex. You won't need that."

Alex ignored her. He didn't see the puddle of slime in front of him. He lost his balance. As he slipped, he fired a laser beam into a patch of glowworms.

"Now you've done it." Celine rolled her eyes.

The worms shrilled so loudly that Celine and Alex were momentarily paralyzed.

Then the lights went out.

He crept from the floor. "Disgusting," he said. "Lead the way, Martian Girl."

He walked on Celine's heel. "Move faster."

Finally, they came out of the tube into another large area.

"Another cavern." The cavern was similar to the one they had left, almost dome-shaped with four lava tubes leading in the four directions.

"You want to put that ray gun away now?"

Alex didn't answer. He clamped his gun on his hip. "Celine, lead the way, please."

"Of course." Celine cautiously walked forward. She saw a faint heat residue coming from Morg's footprints. They glowed like directional signs. "Let's go this way," she said.

The prints led to the tube that went north. They stepped into the tube. The glowworms did not brighten their way, but Celine saw small green lights emitting from them. *At least they're not shrilling anymore. My eardrums still ache.* "Look, there's sunlight. I knew there had to be another way out."

They began to walk faster. "Careful!" Celine shouted.

Celine noticed the warm green glow from the worms change to a muddy red. "Run!" she shouted.

The worms began discharging electric shocks. "Ouch!" Celine said.

"Double that!" Alex said. He was shocked several times.

They ran to the end of the tube onto a ledge. "Stop! Stop!" Celine screamed.

Alex almost slid to a stop.

Both stood on the ledge waiting for their eyes to adjust to the sunlight. Celine wanted to chastise Alex for making the worms angry. Her body tingled. "Are you OK?" she asked. Then she noticed the magnetic field flickering around Alex's jumpsuit.

"Never felt better."

"Don't move, Alex. We're on a ledge." She looked at the narrow ledge. It was wide enough for a man to walk if he placed his back against the wall.

Both teens peered over the ledge at the large rust-colored rocks beneath it. "That could have been a nasty fall," said Alex. "At least thirty meters down."

The ledge curved around both sides of the hill. Celine could not see where either side led. "Which way?" She muttered.

"The Navi! I left it in the cave!"

CHAPTER 13

I SAW IT FLICKER

"I'M NOT GOING BACK IN there," Alex said. He folded his arms across his chest.

"We have to." Celine said. She didn't necessarily want to return to the cave either, but the Navi contained her dad's coordinates and needed to be retrieved.

"They were firing at me, not you. You go back and get it."

"Yes, they *were* firing at you, and they hit you too. They might have damaged your suit—I saw it flicker. You need to get out of this radiation," Celine said as she inspected his suit.

"All right, all right—enough with the lecture," Alex snapped as he slapped her hand away. "You go in first."

Celine was disappointed at Alex's immaturity, but she was not surprised. She had always admired him on his reality show. He seemed so brave and caring on the air, nothing like in real life. She was getting to know the real Alex, and it was a letdown. She reentered the cave.

"Alex," Celine said. She turned to look over her right shoulder at him.

"I'm coming." Alex followed Celine into the cave. He pouted and rolled his eyes.

When Celine entered the cave, she expected to see the Navi lying on the ground. "I don't see it," she said.

"That's because I left it in that tube." Alex pointed to the lava tube where the glowworms had shocked them.

Flashbacks of the shocks flooded Celine's head.

"Well, I don't see any signs of life in there now," Celine said with a hint of optimism. She cautiously walked toward the tube and took one step in. She peered up at the ceiling. "They're all black…Like they're burned."

Alex stepped in beside her. "Well, would you look at that? They burned themselves out."

Alex let out a prideful laugh then strutted down the tube to reclaim his Navi. "That'll teach you to mess with Alex Rittenhouse IV!" A swollen worm popped. Alex, startled, quickly grabbed his Navi and ran out of the tube.

"Let's get out of here," Alex said to Celine as he darted past her and led the way to the cave's opening.

"Wait, Alex! Your suit!"

Alex stopped at the opening of the cave. "Look over there," he said, ignoring Celine's remark. He pointed to flashing balls of light in the Martian deep red sky, then he drew back from the opening.

"You have to check your suit. Remember, I saw it flicker." Celine touched Alex's radiation suit.

Alex sighed and plopped down on to the cave's floor. He leaned against a wall. Celine could see the tension and sadness in his face. A dark blue aura outlined his body.

"I should've asked my dad for help," he said. He rested his elbows on his knees and entwined his fingers under his chin.

"We can't give up now. We're too close to finding my dad—and those coordinates you want."

Alex looked up at her. He gave a half-hearted smile.

Celine noticed the blue around Alex brighten a little.

"Sit down," he said. He patted the floor next to him. "Please."

Celine ignored him.

"Let me have the light and the Navi," she said. "They need to be charged."

Alex removed the light from his backpack. He handed it along with the Navi to Celine. She set them next to the cave's opening in the dim sunlight. Then she returned and plopped down next to him, pushing her back against the wall.

They sat together in silence for hours as they watched the storm in the distance.

"For once," Alex said, "I want to show him…I want to show him that I can do something great."

"Your dad?"

"Yeah. He's difficult to compete with."

"Why do you feel the need to compete with him?" Celine asked.

Alex paused as if racking his brain for an answer. "It's just the Rittenhouse way. We're competitors. We're winners."

"Does that mean someone has to lose?"

Alex looked surprised. "You're pretty naive, aren't you?" he said.

"I don't think so." She got up and walked toward the cave's opening to retrieve the Navi and the light. Suddenly, a loud scratching sound tore through the cave's silence. She stumbled back into the cave before the ball of lightning smashed to the ground a half a kilometer away.

"We won't be leaving this cave any time soon," she said. She slumped down next to Alex once again. "It's so quiet in here... kind of eerie." The wind howled. Celine swallowed and felt goose bumps rise on her arms.

"I guess I better check my suit."

"I can help if you want."

"No thanks. You go over there." Alex motioned to the opposite side of the cave. "No peeking."

Celine rolled her eyes. "I don't understand why you're acting so modest. I've seen your shows."

"Well, I'm used to privacy. I wasn't raised inside a can with a hundred people."

Celine sucked her teeth and walked to the other side of the cave.

Alex took off his suit to inspect it for damage. He saw a small hole burned on the left leg of his suit. "It's burned but not burned through the suit, thank goodness," he said.

Celine shuffled her feet back and forth. "But will it protect you when we're on the surface?"

"I hope so." Alex turned his suit's electromagnetic field off, and he slipped it back on. "OK, you can come out of the corner, if you'd like." He chuckled.

"Your suit," Celine said, "Why'd you turn it off?" She seemed stunned.

"We don't need it on in here. We don't need these helmets on either."

After doing another quick inspection of her surroundings, Celine turned off her suit as well. "Let's keep the helmets on. You wouldn't want a dead glowworm to fall into your hair or something."

"No, I wouldn't. Who would have thought something so inno-cent-looking could be so—I don't know—powerful."

"They didn't look innocent to me."

"Whatever. Let's go to the den. We can leave our gear there while we look for signs of your dad. Oh, and maybe I can find that water."

Alex turned on the Navi. "Fully charged! Good thing I saved the coordinates."

"You want me to lead the way again?"

"I got this." Alex strutted through the lava tube under the blackened ceiling.

"Wait, listen. It sounds like the running water."

"Which way?"

"I think it's coming from the tube where we saw the footprints."

"Let's check it out then."

Alex seemed excited. Then his expression changed. His eyes rolled around as if he were confused. "This place is actually awe-some!" he said.

"Yes, but no shouting. I don't want you to agitate the other glowworms."

"I am telling you, Celine, this cave is freaking awesome! I wouldn't mind staying here forever."

Celine stared at Alex, bewildered. His eyes and mouth were opened wide in awe. He almost looked like a different person. "Alex, have you lost your mind? You want to stay in this cave? Forever?"

"What are you talking about?" Alex replied.

"That's what you just said." Celine stood still. "Do you need more time to rest?"

"I don't need any rest. I need to find out where that water is. Water on Mars is more valuable than gold." He headed down the tube toward the gurgling sound.

"Wait for me." Celine followed Alex gingerly into the most beautiful cavern she could have ever imagined. There were columns of white and pink sandstone. What appeared to be water flowed in the center of the cave's floor. It was a light-pink puddle that bubbled up from the ground like a natural spring.

"There's your water." Celine smiled. "Still more valuable than gold?" She moved in to get a closer look. "I'd love to touch it. Have you ever seen anything like it? Pink water."

Alex pointed his data recorder at the spring. "It's acid," he said.

Celine gasped then fell back and scrambled away from the liquid.

"Relax," Alex said. He laughed. "It's a mild carbonic acid. The same thing that's used to flavor soda waters on Earth."

"So it's not dangerous."

"It could give you gas if you drink it." Alex took out his water bottle and scooped up some of the liquid for analysis. "This is amazing," he chuckled. "Pink water on Mars. There's got to be a source for the spring. Maybe an underground river."

"Aw, it's not pretty anymore."

"Celine, this stuff is safe enough to drink."

"Maybe, but I wouldn't do it if I were you."

"I'm not going to drink this. But if I were your dad and had run out of water, I definitely would."

Celine turned her head to one side "Quiet. I hear something?"

Alex stooped down next to her. "What?"

"Music. It sounds like a flute." Celine patted the outline of her flute in her backpack. "It's Dad! He's made a flute out of something. He's calling us! Come on, Alex. Follow me." She was ecstatic and quickly ran toward the sound. Suddenly, Celine stopped in her tracks.

"What did I just say?" Celine palmed her face. "Alex, what's happening to us? My dad wouldn't make a dumb flute. He'd be trying to find a way home."

Instinctively, she began to walk quietly, almost wolflike, cautiously, listening for movement. When she heard the sound directly above her, she looked up.

"It's the wind whistling through this tiny opening in the ceiling," Celine said, motioning upward. "Would you look at that? My goodness, there're hundreds of them!"

Alex looked up. "What kind of formation is that? I've never seen anything like it."

High up, around the walls of the cave, were perfect circular openings like those made by carpenter bees. However, these holes were large enough for a man to step through.

"They remind me of cliff apartments. You know, the kind Pueblos Indians lived in," Celine said. "But how would anyone get up there? The walls are pretty smooth." She further studied the surroundings. "No inclines either."

"Ladders. They would use ladders."

"Maybe it is just something natural, places where lava bubbled out. I just hope it wasn't made by some kind of animal." She looked for any sign of heat coming from the openings. "I can't tell if anything's in them."

"Do you think we should be in here?" Alex said.

Celine turned to face him. His eyes were glassy. He appeared to be in a trance.

"Alex, are you sick? How do you feel?"

"OK, I guess." He staggered.

"I don't want to go home without Dad. But maybe we need to go back." Suddenly, Celine noticed something shiny in the dirt. "Alex, may I use your data recorder?"

"No. Why do you need it? I can record."

Celine was surprised that Alex was acting so childish. But she didn't feel much like herself either.

"Alex, come over here...I think I found something. Look. Something's embedded in the soil.

"It looks like a chip." Alex pointed his data recorder at the metal. "It is—it's your dad's."

Celine took out her safety box and removed the tweezers. She used them to loosen the soil around the chip. She could see what appeared to be small bones in the dirt. The chip was caked with blood and dust. Finally she was able to pry it from the dirt. Celine picked it up and turned it over in her gloved hand. Her stomach tightened. "Here," she said. She handed it to Alex and then wrapped her arms around her stomach. "Is it still active?"

Alex looked at it. "Yes, it is."

"Is it possible the satellite picked up its signal?" Celine choked, but she held back the tears.

"I'm afraid so."

Celine felt woozy. She wanted to scream. She closed her eyes and shook her head.

"Celine, maybe your dad removed the chip. Maybe he doesn't want to be found."

Alex ran the data recorder over the area where Celine had found the chip. "There's animal DNA here."

"So you're saying my dad was eaten by an animal?" Celine began to cry.

"Don't cry, Celine...There's still hope. Plus, you'll need your O2 pill early if you cry. Stay calm, please."

Alex's comments went in one ear and out the other. Celine slumped to the ground and sobbed quietly.

Alex pointed the data recorder throughout the cave. He hoped he would locate Celine's father's gear. He found nothing.

He helped Celine up from the ground. "Let's go back to the den and get some rest. We'll leave in the morning." He guided her out; she sobbed even louder.

CHAPTER 14

RESTLESS SLEEP

AFTER RESTLESS NIGHT AND HOURS of crying, Celine decided to leave the den to look for her father one last time. Alex remained asleep. *Why is Alex snoring? He never snores.* She turned on the light and gasped. Alex's skin had a green tint to it.

"Alex!" Celine shouted. She quickly crawled over to him, nearly banging her head on the den's low ceiling. "Alex," she cried. There was no response.

Frantically, she searched his backpack for his first aid box. She examined it thoroughly. She hoped she could find something—anything—that could perhaps make him well. She found his O2 pillbox. She remembered her mom had told her that without enough oxygen, a person would turn green and suffocate. She opened the pillbox. *He should have three pills, not four. That's it.* "How could you have been so careless?" She took one of the blue pills from the box and forced it between his lips and onto his tongue.

"Chew it." She grabbed his face and moved his jaws up and down, mimicking a chewing motion. "Now swallow." Alex's eyes were closed, but he swallowed.

As the pill enriched his blood with oxygen, his complexion reddened, and his snoring ceased. But he still seemed out of it. *I don't know what else to do.* Celine felt so vulnerable and alone. Suddenly, an image of Morg's footprints flashed through her head. *I've got to find Morg.* At this point, she didn't care if he took them back to the Compound. Celine quickly made her way back into the cave and through the lava tube. Morg's tracks were still visible.

When she stepped into the cavern, she saw the sand mound blocking the exit. She let out a scream. "No! Not again, not again," she cried. She squeezed her lips together, tightened her fist, and charged into the hill of sand that blocked her way out. She began clawing her way to the top of the hill but failed to reach it. She could, however, see that it was dusk. She glanced at one of the lopsided moons as she slid back down to the cave floor.

"Why is this happening to us? We're too young to die." She went back to the den to check on Alex. He was unconscious. Celine sat next to him and crossed her legs, ready to meditate and ask the Universe for answers. She closed her eyes and began chanting, "I am mmm, I am mmm." No solutions to her dilemma came to mind. She held Alex's hand. "Alex, you've got to get well. You need those coordinates for your father! Come on, Alex! Please wake up!" Tears rolled down her cheeks as she squeezed and nervously massaged his hands.

Then she heard the explosion. Alex must have heard it too.

Alex opened his eyes and snatched his hands from hers. "What was that?"

"Alex, you're OK!" She wrapped her arms around his neck and cried loudly.

"Let go of me, Martian Girl," Alex said. He seemed confused. "Why are you crying?"

"You were—" Celine was too choked up to speak. "I couldn't wake you."

"What was that noise?"

"I don't know. How do you feel?"

"Really weak," he said. Then he stretched and laid back.

"Alex, you looked like you were dying. Why did you miss your O2 pill?"

Dodging her question, Alex asked, "Would you mind grabbing me the water bottle? I am so thirsty."

She snatched the water bottle from Alex's backpack and handed it to him. She watched him drink until the bottle was empty.

"You didn't take your pill." Celine reiterated firmly. "Why?"

"My pill. I've taken my pills." Alex massaged his forehead. "My head hurts. Let's talk about this later," he said. He closed his eyes and drifted into sleep.

"Alex, we're trapped in this cave." She sternly laid a hand upon his shoulder.

"Leave me alone," he mumbled, shoving her hand away.

Celine backed away from him and leaned against the wall of the den.

She wrapped her arms around her body and stared at Alex as he slept. Her heart pounded. *What am I going to do? I've got to find another way out.* She slipped out of the den. She found herself drawn to the cave where she had found her dad's signature chip. She walked quietly through the tube, no longer concerned about the glowworms. "They won't harm me if I don't harm them," she mumbled. She walked over to the area where she had scratched out the chip. She had been so emotional when she found the chip that she might have missed something. Celine shone her light and saw that, indeed, she had missed something. There was something green on the cave wall. It was not a color that would naturally occur on her planet. As she got a little closer, she realized that it was a drawing. She used her glove to brush aside the dust. She couldn't believe it. There was a drawing of a woman wearing a flowing green dress. She had a yellow aura painted around her body. A large yellow medallion hung from her neck and covered her chest like an armor plate. The woman's dark eyes had no white. There were paintings of other females too, but none stood out quite like the woman in green. *Who could have done this?* Suddenly, Celine felt a chill run through her body. *Someone's watching me.*

"Daddy, is that you?" There was no response. "Morg?"

She stood in silence. With her heart in her throat, she ran back to the den. As she crawled into the den, she heard a second explosion. This one shook the floor beneath her.

"Alex!"

"I heard it," he said. He seemed fully alert. "Volcano?"

Then they heard the crackling sound of water slapping the cave walls. Some crept into the den.

Alex grabbed his boots and shoved them into his backpack. He looked at Celine's backpack and then up at Celine. "Put your food and safety kit in mine." His jawline was tight, and his eyes moved quickly, acknowledging the seriousness of their situation. Celine obeyed without question. The tent floor was one of their most valuable possessions, and it was now covered in water. He rolled it into a lopsided ball and shoved it into his airtight backpack.

Celine rolled out of the den into knee-deep water. Alex pushed their backpacks and helmets out and slid out into the water next to her.

"Where is that water coming from?" he asked.

"The cave where Morg and the soldiers were," Celine said.

Alex's eyes widened. "That was an explosion!" Just as he said it, a wave of water rushed in over their heads. Alex came up first. "Celine!"

Celine could hear him, but she struggled to get afloat. "Alex, I'm here," she called.

"Stand up."

She struggled to stand. Now the water was in the middle of her thighs and pushing against her.

"Take off your suit," he said as he began stepping out of his. Then he placed it in a backpack pocket and zipped it closed. "The water might cause it to weigh you down."

Celine stepped out of her suit and shoved it into her back-pack pocket and zipped it. More of the rusty-red water gushed into their cave. It covered her bottom and dirtied her underwear. Celine's heart rate increased, and she felt completely discombob-ulated. Although it was a valuable resource, there was nothing appealing or comforting about this water. It jolted her. She had to fight it with great force in order to move in the direction she wanted to go.

"It feels strange. It's all over me, including my private parts. I don't like it."

Alex smirked. "Let's get out of here!"

Alex slung his dripping wet backpack onto his back and fas-tened its bottom belt around his waist. Celine slipped her arms through the straps of her bag; she was about to fasten the bottom strap when Alex stopped her, his eyes cast downward. He shook his head. "No."

Celine was too frightened to disobey. She looked down at the rising water. Her undershirt was covered in muddy red water. Though the water was warm, she shivered. It shoved her, and she nearly went under. The hairs on her arms rose.

"Just hold on to it if you can. Let it float."

More water burst into the cave. It slapped the walls as it rushed in. The glowworms shrilled, and some popped and flashed as water splashed them. Celine was lifted and tossed about. Alex grabbed her hand and pulled her toward him.

"Stick with me," he said. "And we're going to need your night vision." He began swimming toward the tube that led to the blocked exit.

"It's blocked! The exit is——." Suddenly a towering wave of water came crashing into the cave, sweeping Alex into another lava tube. The glowworms let out a high shrill and pulled themselves deep into the ceiling away from the water.

Celine covered her ears and squeezed her eyes closed. Her eardrums were in pain. When she opened her eyes, she noticed her light and backpack had floated away. She wanted to panic but used every fiber in her being to keep a clear head. Her eyes scanned the dark cave for Alex.

"Alex!" she screamed between mouthfuls of water and gags. She heard her voice echo. *Alex, where are you?* She fought the water until her arms ached. Then she thought she heard her grandma's voice say, "Stay calm, Granddaughter." Celine wanted to cry, but she felt a sense of encouragement and realized there was no time for tears. She flipped onto her back and allowed the water to take her with the current. She floated into the tube that led to the cave where she had seen the paintings on the wall.

CHAPTER 15

NO ONE WILL KNOW WE WERE HERE

CELINE SWIRLED INTO THE CAVERN where she had seen the paintings. The water here was calmer, but it was rising quickly. The entire floor was covered in the muddy red water; she sadly watched it rise until it covered the piercing eyes of the female on the painting. Soon the woman's head was covered, and the illustration was no longer visible.

"What a shame...No one will ever know you were here," she said solemnly. As the water rose higher, she noticed one of the "apartment" entrances was almost close enough to reach. She swam toward it and extended her arms in an attempt to reach the opening and pull herself up. Unfortunately, the water was not yet high enough.

A few more centimeters, that's all I need. The water level was rising, but not fast enough for Celine. Her muscles ached with exhaustion. She dove underwater to see if she could she find the entrance to the lava tube that she had come through. The water was too cloudy and turbulent to see anything. She came up and flipped on her back. She floated calmly as she waited for the water to rise a few more centimeters. *Somehow I'll find a way out of this place and head back home…Oh who am I kidding? The body-heat tent is gone. Alex has my O2 pills; where is Alex?*

Celine's head gently tapped the wall next to the opening, interrupting her thoughts before she might have slipped into a deep depression. She could hear music coming from the opening. *It sounded like her flute! This must be a way out,* she thought. *If only Alex was here with me.* She braced her feet against the cliff wall and pushed off. She bounced close to the opening, but she couldn't get a grip on the ledge of the apartment doorway. She tried again, this time putting one foot in front of the other as if she was running up the side of the wall. She pushed off and grabbed the bottom of the circular opening, banging her elbow in the process but refusing to let go of the ledge. Like wall climbing, her fingers gripped and inched into the opening until her hands were in deep enough to pull herself upward.

The music stopped just as she entered the apartment. The walls were lined by beautiful silk pillows in various hues of pinks and reds; some looked as though they had been encrusted with rubies and diamonds. A white fluffy rug covered the floor, and sitting cross-legged in the middle of the room was the beautiful smiling lady from the painting, the lady in the green dress.

"Can you see me?" Celine heard the question in her head. The lady's lips never moved but continued a gentle smile.

"Yes," Celine thought in reply.

Their conversation continued. Neither moved their lips, but each knew the other's thoughts instantly.

"Why are you here? You don't belong here. This is my home."

Celine thought, "Who are you?"

"I am the guard. This is my home."

Confusion ran high, and images of the colony flashed through Celine's mind.

"I know of it."

"No one knows you're here," Celine continued.

"Your military knows."

"Military?"

"I am the guard. This is my home."

Celine wondered if she was speaking to a hologram. *No, a hologram wouldn't have an aura around it,* Celine thought as she took notice of the woman's white aura that seemed to expand as they continued their silent conversation. Celine didn't feel threatened. The closer the white aura came to touching hers, the more relaxed she felt. The lady's energy continued to glow and expand. Celine closed her eyes and was totally engulfed in the white aura until her own aura was no longer orange. She felt a sense of peace like never before. She had neither fear nor worry, and the strenuous thoughts regarding finding her father and Alex ceased. Nothing mattered. Even before her dad was lost in the storm, she had never experienced such a high degree of internal serenity. Celine opened her eyes. She watched as the white aura retracted from her until it surrounded the lady once again.

"What just happened to me?"

"I shared my light with you as you have shared yours. Are you the one?"

"The one? I need to find Alex. I need to find my dad."

"You do not protect your thoughts," the lady said. She disappeared, and the beautiful illusions of the room with soft silk pillows and a fluffy rug vanished with her.

Celine heaved and puked. She had felt calm and almost worry-free in the presence of the lady, but now she felt ill. Her muscles ached and cramped. Again, the fear of not being able to find her father and Alex consumed her. All the unpleasantness she had initially felt came rushing back to her in an instant.

As she sat on the dusty floor, she wondered if she had simply hallucinated: *Was I dreaming? Perhaps she was an illusion...But I could smell the fragrance coming from her skin. Can dreams have scents?*

There was only one way in and out of the apartment, and that was through the circular opening. Celine looked through the opening for the lady and was surprised to see the water was gone. The beautiful lady was nowhere insight.

Celine swallowed. *How am I going to get down there?* The apartment hole was at least sixty-six meters above the ground; without the water, this was nearly a twenty-story drop. Celine had no time for rest though. She needed to find Alex and get out of this place.

The apartment was bare now; nothing remained except some old dusty object lying next to the opening. She used her hand to wipe away the dust. The hairs on the back of her neck stood up. It was a dusty ladder made of knotted silk cords.

So this is how they get in and out of these apartments, she thought. *Wait until I show Alex!*

She noticed two rusty hooks next to the apartment's opening. *This must be where I should hang the ladder.* The thought of using the long ladder made her nervous. The cords looked extremely old. As she stepped on to the ladder, she heard what sounded like an old woman speaking. "Careful," the old female's voice said.

"Who said that?" Celine paused for a moment. Her eyes searched the small room. There was nothing but dirt and dust. Then she heard laughter. She scurried down the ladder so quickly that she felt a sensation on her hands similar to rope burn. *I've got to find Alex and get out of here.*

Alex was a powerful swimmer. Much of his life had been spent in Earth's oceans with his pet seal. The current of the water was so strong, however, that it had taken him off course. *Now that the water is calm, I'll find Celine. We need to head back to the Compound.* We only have six O2 pills left. Alex floated in the dark and allowed the water to carry him back toward their den.

"Celine! Celine, where are you?" He could see nothing but heard a continuous thump against the cave wall. He bit his lip as he waded toward the sound, praying it would not be Celine's lifeless body. As he got closer to the sound, he could see light emitting from another cave. Then he saw what was thumping the wall: Celine's backpack. He waded over to her backpack and dragged it along with him until he was in the largest cavern he had ever seen.

"This place is awesome!" he said. "It's big enough for the entire colony to live down here." He noticed how warm it was. The ceiling was very high, and the glowworms shined brightly above the flowing water. Alex looked back at the entrance. It was completely dark. *Celine must be in here with the light,* he hoped. He looked around. *There are plenty of safe, dry places in here*. He pulled himself out of the water and began his quest for Celine.

He didn't see any footprints or signs of her. *She's never swum in real water. She probably needs me.* He began swimming reluctantly into the darkened lava tube. It was so dark that he could not see his own hands. He banged his fingers on the wall. He heard a click and felt a sharp pain in his index finger. He wailed in pain. *I'll have to wait until Celine makes her way over here...or until the glowworms in the tubes feel safe enough to come out. It's too dark to look for her. She has a better chance of finding me anyway...if she's still alive.*

He swam to the shore where he had left their backpacks. He stretched out, lying on his back and looking up at the ceiling. *This place is truly beautiful.* Glowworms lined the uneven ceiling. As he watched them, he experienced an odd sensation: he felt them getting closer and closer until it felt like they were just centimeters above his face. He blinked and sat up. "I've got to find a way out of here."

Thump! Something jumped on Alex's back and wrapped a filthy arm around his neck.

"Who are you?" the thing said. It held Alex around his throat.

"I am Alex. Alex Rittenhouse. Stop. You're hurting me," he cried.

"You're a boy!" the thing said as he flung Alex to the ground and stepped back.

Alex stared wide-eyed. Before him was a skeleton of a man covered in red mud. He had long, dirty hair that appeared to be reddish brown and curly like Celine's.

"Are you...Celine's father?"

The dirty man cautiously looked around at the walls and ceilings as if he expected something to jump on him. His bushy, unkempt facial hair and uncut fingernails made him look like some kind of wild animal.

"You know Celine?"

"Yes, she's my friend."

"Liar! Celine doesn't have any friends! You're in my head again, aren't you?"

The dirty man cautiously walked over to Alex and twisted and pinched his cheek.

"Let go of me! You old fool!" Alex snapped harshly.

"Fool? Yes, I am a fool. I am a fool," he sang as he skipped away.

"Wait!" Alex shouted. "Let me explain." This is not what Alex had envisioned when he set out to find Celine's father.

"Mr. Red Cloud, wait."

"He's not home," Mr. Red Cloud replied. "Get out of my head." He vigorously rubbed his disheveled hair.

CHAPTER 16

TASTES LIKE CHICKEN

◆ ◆ ◆

ALEX FOLLOWED MR. RED CLOUD to his den and was surprised to see Mr. Red Cloud sitting on the ground between two helmets. The helmets were used like bowls. One contained the pink water, and the other was filled with what appeared to be laser-roasted glowworms.

"Eat," Mr. Red Cloud said. He smiled, revealing his grimy orange teeth. He cocked his head to the side and licked his lips as he rolled one worm between his fingers before popping it into his mouth.

"See. Good. Tastes like chicken. When have you had fresh meat?" He patted the ground next to him. "Sit. Enjoy."

"I don't want any," Alex said. He backed away. "We need to find Celine."

"Celine is with her mother," Mr. Red Cloud said. He slurped liquid from the helmet and belched.

"No sir. She's here. The flood separated us. We came to the surface to find you."

"Celine is here?" Mr. Red Cloud smiled and gazed upward as if being warmed by the sun. "That's my girl. She's a go-getter."

"Yes, she is, sir. Quite a girl."

Mr. Red Cloud jerked his head up and stared at Alex for a while. "You're Alex Rittenhouse's son. I've seen you on the news with your dad. Why are you out here?"

"Celine and I came to look for you, sir."

Mr. Red Cloud's lips turned downward as he fingered and rubbed his dirty beard. "What's in it for you?"

Alex smirked. *The old fool isn't such a fool after all.* "The annual report, sir. It said you have coordinates for some minerals."

Mr. Red Cloud shrilled. The sound reminded Alex of a screaming chimpanzee. "You came for the coordinates?" He was overcome with laughter.

"Yes, sir," Alex said, confused as to what was so funny.

"There are no coordinates. There are no precious minerals."

"But the report said…" Alex trailed off then felt an overwhelming rush of nausea.

"What report? There is no report. Your dad was going to leave us here without food and supplies if we didn't find *something* he wanted!

So we dangled the 'golden carrot'—the coordinates—and here you are." Mr. Red Cloud leaned back and continued his wild laughter between coughing and spitting. Alex took a few steps away from him.

"My dad wouldn't do that!" Alex shouted. But even as he spoke, he realized that idea was not too far-fetched. "Look, this colony has drained my family since my grandfather started it; we're almost bankrupt because of it!" Alex couldn't believe he sounded so much like his father.

"Bankrupt?" Mr. Red Cloud said. "You know of the Trail of Tears?"

Alex nodded. "What does that have to do with anything?"

"Your family ordered it and then stole my family's land. I have a wife who hates it here, but we can't leave because of your father's life contract. I have a child who's never seen much life outside of the can we live in. And I was left in this cave to die. *I* am bankrupt!" He screamed and ran toward Alex and shook his fist in Alex's face.

Alex backed away. He had never thought about his family's history nor had he considered how much his family had benefitted from their lurid past. He had never known a Cherokee. He assumed they were all dead. He did not expect such rage and had no idea how to respond to it. "We have to find Celine, sir."

Mr. Red Cloud face softened when he heard his daughter's name.

"Celine is missing, Mr. Red Cloud. Can you help me?" Alex reiterated.

Mr. Red Cloud rubbed his beard and smiled as if fondly reminiscing.

"We were separated in the flood." Noticing how calm Mr. Red Cloud was upon hearing about Celine, Alex decided to continue. "Celine is very special. She's *different*."

"What do you mean?" Mr. Red Cloud raised an eyebrow.

Alex wasn't sure if he should say more. After all, Celine had confided in him with her secret.

"What do you know about Celine?" Mr. Red Cloud sounded threatening. "Tell me what you know."

"Celine said it was a secret, but she can see auras around living things," Alex blurted.

Mr. Red Cloud looked as if he had been slapped in the face. His cheeks were red, and his teeth clenched. He dropped to the ground as if his legs had given way. "She knows." Mr. Red Cloud looked down at his hands in his lap. Alex thought he looked defeated. "We didn't want her to know."

"She's probably looking for me now, sir…Do you have your miner's light?"

"It's the Eugenics Project," Mr. Red Cloud mumbled. "I came here to get away from it. My family has been a part of this project for over three hundred years. Why can't they just let us be?" he whined.

"Sir, you must be mistaken. *That* kind of stuff is illegal."

Mr. Red Cloud laced his fingers tightly in prayer and held them in his lap. With his head bowed and his eyes closed, he exhaled softly.

"I see you still have your backpack and your assistant's," Alex said, referring to the bags on the floor against the cave wall.

"The soldiers killed him. They tried to kill me too. I cut my chip out and hid in the mud pond." Mr. Red Cloud looked down at the scar on his forearm.

"Celine and I saw the soldiers, but they've left. They blocked the front entrance with a boulder, but we found another way out."

Mr. Red Cloud crawled over to his assistant's backpack. He sat next to it and stared. He had tears in his eyes. "He was a good man."

"I am sure he was, sir…OK, I really need your miner's lamp," Alex repeated with an increasing sense of urgency. "Do you have any idea where it might be?"

Mr. Red Cloud didn't answer.

Alex rolled his eyes and headed for Mr. Red Cloud's backpack.

Mr. Red Cloud looked up in anguish.

"Mr. Red Cloud, we need your miner's light to find Celine," Alex said, attempting to remain claim.

"That's my stuff!" Mr. Red Cloud ran toward Alex with the miner's light in his hand and tried to clobber Alex over the head with it. Alex ducked in time to avoid Mr. Red Cloud's swing.

"Give me that," Alex said. He snatched the light from Mr. Red Cloud and began backing out of the den. Mr. Red Cloud ran toward his two helmets of water and roasted worms. He held one helmet in each arm. Then he wrapped his arms around them as if they were dear to him. "Mine," he said. "Mine."

Alex backed out of the cave with the miner's light cradled in his arms. He couldn't believe he had traveled this far to meet a lunatic. *And damn it! No precious minerals!*

"What a day," he muttered under his breath. "What a day."

Celine wondered how the water could have possibly disappeared so quickly. The only sign that the water had been in the cave was the dry waterline on the cave's walls. She headed toward the tube that had brought her into the cave, passing the wall where the paintings had washed away. Some indistinguishable colors remained, but they blended much too well with the walls' natural colors.

She looked into the tube and noticed that the glowworms were back; the lava tube was now as bright as a Martian day. Celine also noticed that the worms were humming. It reminded her of the hum she heard when the florescent lights in the Compound were on the verge of burning out.

There are so many glowworms. I don't remember seeing this many. She looked backward into the cave in hopes of spotting another way out. Nothing. *Why are they so noisy now?* She looked for red auras around them but saw no colors. *This is one time I wish I could see auras.* A few dead-looking glowworms lay on the floor of the lava tube. When Celine actually entered the tube, the worms gave no response. She made her way through the tube, maneuvering around the dead ones on the floor.

"Where now?" she said out loud.

The water had changed the caves. A rush of relief came over her when she realized she had reached what she considered the entrance. She quickly made her way to the den where she and Alex had rested before the flood. There were no signs of Alex.

When stepping into the entry cave, she heard low voices coming from the tube she thought Alex had been swept into. *Concentrate. Focus.* After a moment, she concluded that the voices were familiar.

"That's Alex! He's talking to someone...Dad! He's talking to Dad!"

Celine started to run, but she decided walking quickly would be a much safer option considering how slick the cave floors were. She found herself in a cavern large enough for the entire colony. The ceiling was tall, and rocks of all sizes hung from it like icicles. There were cream-colored columns that extended so high from the ground that they almost touched the ceiling. She could see the columns reflected in ponds of clear water. Trickling water could be heard in the distance. The voices, however, had ceased.

Upon investigating, she found three streams of water that cascaded over three large boulders before joining and becoming one small waterfall. Though the water looked inviting, she was not thirsty enough to try it. *Where is all of the water coming from? Why is it so warm in here?* She wondered if she was near an active volcano. *I don't have time to find out. I've got to find Alex and Dad!*

She had no idea that nearly thirteen kilometers into the cavern, the beautiful smiling lady in the green dress had literally *sung* calmness into the raging waters and watched patiently as a trickle of lava had wormed its way down to patch up an exploded hole.

After walking for what appeared to be three kilometers, with no end in sight, she noticed a clear structure hidden in the shadows.

"Our tent!" Alex had draped the tent floor across two tall rocks, and it was now covered in dust and dead glowworms.

"Alex," she called, but he was nowhere in sight. She was horrified by what she saw in the middle of the dirt floor—her and Alex's helmets set up like bowls. Hers, the smaller one, was full of pink water, and Alex's was full of what appeared to be laser-roasted glowworms. *What's this? What's going on?*

CHAPTER 17

LIVE HERE FOREVER

"Alex!" she yelled as she backed out from under the tent. Little did she know that Alex was peering out from behind a stalagmite, watching her. Celine was too disturbed by what she saw to notice Alex's body heat radiating from behind the pillow of limestone. After a moment of dazed frustration, she returned to the den. The den served as a safe space for some reason; perhaps because it was where Celine and Alex had had their first actual rest since leaving the Compound.

Something didn't feel right. The tent seemed old and dusty. And why would Alex put up the tent as if he wanted to "live here forever?" Celine asked herself as she recalled Alex's statement. She sat in the den and pondered. She couldn't believe Alex would be so silly as to drink or eat what she saw in those grimy helmets. *Alex wouldn't dare drink that water or eat those disgusting glowworms unless he was out of his right mind.* She remembered how he had acted before the flood and shuddered. The idea that Alex might, in fact, be insane was frightening.

Celine decided to return once again to the cavern. This time she would ignore its beauty and enormity and, instead, utilize her senses to find Alex and her father. Upon entering the cavern, she noticed the scent of unwashed bodies in the air. *How could I have missed this before?* She saw a fresh set of large footprints behind a tower of limestone, still warm and glowing. The thing that intrigued her most, however, was the strange sloshing sound she could hear coming from a mud pond across the river.

Her hair and clothing were nearly dry from the soaking she had received during the flood. She was not eager to get back into the water, but she knew that she had to in order to reach the mud pond. Quietly, she waded into the water across the shallow end. It was warm and rather soothing unlike the rough handling she had received from the roaring waters of the flood. She probably would have enjoyed it, had she had felt safe. But she didn't feel safe in the slightest. She just wanted to find Alex and her dad and head back home.

It didn't take long for her to reach the other side of the river and to walk onto the shore. As she looked back across the river, she saw a boy sprint into the tent she had searched. He reminded her of Alex, but something about him was different…maybe taller?

Before she could call out to him, a dirty wild creature arose from out of the mud. Wet soil dripped from its unkempt hair. It appeared to be wearing Compound-issued outdoor wear, but it was caked with so much dirt and mud she could not tell for sure. Something about the creature looked familiar, but before she could manage a second glance, it slung her over its shoulder and carried her off like a sack of supplies.

"Alex!" She screamed.

Alex ran from the tent, looked across the river, and stood there, rolling his eyes at the creature.

"Put me down!" she screamed and began clawing at the creature's head. It began swatting at her as if she was some kind of pest. She fell from its shoulder onto the ground, but it continued swatting at the air. As she watched the bizarre thing dance, she realized she was looking at her dad.

"Daddy? Is that you, Daddy?"

Mr. Red Cloud stopped his jerky movements and looked upon her face with confused eyes. Then he pointed to Alex and said, "Thief!" He reached down and grabbed her by the hand. "I found you," he said.

She allowed him to lead her, almost dragging her. He seemed eager to show her something.

"Home," he said as he presented the cave he had lived in for months. She looked around the den-like area, his makeshift home. He had folded his body-heat tent, much smaller than the one she and Alex had used, into a sleeping palette. He was using both his and his assistant's helmets as bowls, like what she had seen in the other tent. In a corner on the ground sat two dust-covered back-packs. A pile of small rocks was built in a corner; his microscope sat on top of them.

He stood there smiling yet uneasy as if uncertain about his next move. His teeth were unclean, orange instead of their natural pearly white. His nails were so long that they curled under. He smelled awful; she found it difficult to imagine anyone could produce such an odor.

Tears swelled up in Celine's eyes—both tears of joy and tears of sorrow. Thoughts of her father as he had been in the Compound flashed through her mind. She remembered how he had always been so neat and organized...So much for that! She also remembered how he would occasionally let her help him with work. They would sit at his station outside the Compound examining buckets of rocks and minerals. He had taught her how to classify them. He would examine the rocks through his electron microscope. Then she would record the entries into a chart on his computer. She'd enter data regarding the rocks' colors, shapes, and hardness. They'd also shine different types of lights on the rocks to see how the lights would reflect. *Dad said he used the lights to determine the rock's luster*, she reminisced. He'd streak the rocks across a ceramic tile, creating rock powder; she had found it fascinating that the "streak" or rock powder color of a mineral never changed despite the fluctuation in color of the rock itself. They would study buckets full of rocks for hours, but not once did Celine ever see her father get dirty or sweaty, let alone produce any kind of foul odor. She looked up at him with tears in her eyes. He seemed so confused, nothing like the man she had called her dad. Tears streamed down her cheeks.

"Oh no. Oh no," he said nervously. He looked back and forth from her face to the doorway of his den.

She ran to him and wrapped her arms around his waist and held him tightly.

"Daddy," she cried. The tears flowed like a limitless waterfall. She sobbed shamelessly.

Alex stood outside of the den watching. "Girls, so emotional," he mumbled.

"I am taking you home, Dad," she cried.

"I can't go back," he replied.

"Yes, you can. I'll get help."

"No. He wants to kill me. You can't go back." He seemed terrified.

Celine had never seen fear in her father's eyes before. She wondered for a moment if it was legitimate fear she saw or insanity.

Speaking with her dad was getting nowhere. He would not back down from impending doom. She hoped she'd get better results from a talk with Alex.

She stepped out of her father's den and found Alex standing nearby.

Her father followed. When he saw Alex, he began shouting, "Thief! He's a thief! He's a thief! He's a thief!" The words went around and around and played on his tongue as if he was going into a seizure.

"Dad. Dad. Dad." After hearing Celine call him a third time, he was finally able to stop his rant.

"Celine." He smiled and looked at her as if he was seeing her for the first time. All of the anger had left his face. "I'm so glad you're here."

"Wait here, Dad. I need to go with Alex and get my things. Don't worry. I know how to take care of myself."

Mr. Red Cloud shook his fist at Alex before going into his den. Alex turned up his lips and rolled his eyes.

"Come with me," Celine said to Alex as she quickly left the area. She waded into the water without hesitation, not waiting for Alex. She was afraid to talk with him, afraid of what she might hear. *Is he insane too? Will I go insane? Am I sane?*

Celine walked into the tent and grabbed Alex's backpack to see if her O2 pills and food were still in place. Only her empty pill container and empty food wrappers were present. She checked her backpack but found no food or O2 pills. Her heart raced, and her stomach knotted up.

Alex had come into the tent behind her. He watched her as she searched the backpacks.

"Celine?" He finally said. "You haven't changed."

"Why should I? Where are my pills? My food? What did you do with it?"

Alex shrugged. "What did you expect me to do with them?"

I am alone, Celine thought. She slung her bag over her shoulder and left the tent without looking back. She needed to get away from Alex and her dad. She headed back to her den in the entry cave to regroup. As she stepped into the cave, she noticed that the boulder no longer blocked the cave's entryway. She listened carefully and heard the humming sound of the soldiers' mechanical hearts. The sound came from the cave where she had seen the paintings. She chastised herself for not hearing them enter. She knew she had to go back and warn her father and Alex. She frantically sprinted through the lava tube. The worms around her responded to her emotions. They moved in flowing waves as they leaned in her direction and followed her movements. *Thanks Spirit they aren't making noise.*

She entered Alex's tent. "The soldiers are here." She didn't know if she said it aloud or just moved her lips. Nonetheless, Alex understood and ran past her and headed to the mud pond. She dropped her pack in his tent and ran after him. They both swam quickly toward the pond.

"Dad," Celine called. He stood on a boulder and watched Alex and Celine. "Dad, please," she said as loudly as she dared.

Her father did not move. He seemed angry. Celine mouthed the word, "Soldiers." Finally, he understood what was happening. He ran toward the pond. Celine had never seen him move so quickly.

He arrived there just as they did. Holding her nose to keep mud out her nostrils and mouth, she immersed herself completely in the mud. So did Alex and her father.

Inside the cave where the paintings had been washed away, the soldiers' eyes were being used as cameras, scanning and sending back the images. The commander had not heard from Morg and needed to see if he had completed the job. Satisfied that the paintings were unrecognizable, the commander ordered the soldiers to return to the "box." Like mindless drones, they left the cave to return to the military base deep in the hills, one hundred kilometers away from the Chaos Region.

Celine heard them leave. She rose up out of the mud, followed by Alex and her father. She trembled as she climbed from the pond. She decided she would spend the night in her dad's den—with family and close to the mud pond.

CHAPTER 18

THIS ONE'S MINE

◆ ◆ ◆

CELINE REENTERED HER FATHER'S DEN. She didn't bother to wipe the mud from her face. Not in her wildest dreams would she have imagined herself or her dad in such substandard conditions. She sat on the dirt floor and crossed her legs as if to meditate, but she couldn't calm herself. Endless thoughts raced through her mind. *Why is Dad acting like this? Why are the soldiers after us? Is Mom OK?* Her father sat in front of her, his legs in a crossed position as well. His puffy red eyes studied her face as if he were an inquisitive toddler. He seemed frightened, and his eyes suddenly welled up with tears. She wanted to say, "Don't cry, Daddy," but she didn't know if she could keep herself from crying.

As she sat in front of him, she looked around and studied the place her dad so proudly called his home. *There's dust and dirt on everything in here, even on Dad's folded tent where he sleeps.* She was appalled. Her eyes rested on the two backpacks lying against the back wall.

Her dad interrupted her thoughts.

"You should eat," he said. He offered her roasted worms.

"No thanks." She got up and quickly moved over to the backpacks. She wondered if there would be anything in either pack that she could use. Her heart raced with anticipation. With trembling hands, she opened one of the backpacks. Before she looked into it, her dad jumped up and sprinted over to her. He lifted his assistant's backpack from the ground and handed it to her.

"You may have this one," he said as he gently took the one she was holding. "This one's mine." He wrapped his arms around his backpack and stepped out of arm's reach.

"Dad, I need to search it. Trust me. I promise I'll put it back." She found herself speaking to him in the tone he had used with her when she was younger—with love and simplicity.

"Mine," was all he said as he held the pack tightly.

"OK, Dad. Fine." Celine decided she would wait for the opportunity to search it.

She sat on the ground and opened Mr. Takei's backpack. The Universe must have smiled upon her because the backpack contained everything she needed for a four-day trek! There was a small folded body-heat tent, four O2 pills, and four packages of synthetic food. *Poor Mr. Takei must have been ready to leave for the Compound when he was killed.* She didn't remember much about him, but he always had a wide happy smile. He and his wife looked like they could have been related. *Mom said that tends to happen to people who love each other deeply. Funny she'd say that considering she and Dad look nothing alike.*

Her dad had not touched the contents of his assistant's backpack since Mr. Takei's death. Everything was neatly packed in its place and ready for use. Judging by the dust on the pack, Celine concluded that it had lain in that spot for months. She looked at her dad sitting in the dirt, rocking back and forth with his arms wrapped around his backpack. She knew the doctors could fix him if he had a broken arm, but she wasn't so sure what they'd do to fix insanity. She dared not call him insane aloud. Her grandmother had always told her to never say bad things aloud because it's like telling the Universe to bring it into your world. She tried to imagine how it would feel to live in a cave for months, constantly paranoid and running from soldiers as you lose your mind. *No!* She mentally rebelled against those thoughts.

Celine stared at the contents of the bag. She had not had an O2 pill in what felt like nearly twenty-four hours. And though there was enough oxygen in the cave, she was afraid to depend on it. She remembered how sick Alex was when he forgot to take his pill.

Celine gulped down one of the O2 pills and greedily slurped a water gel pack flat. She had no intentions of eating the glowworms or drinking the Martian water. With fidgety fingers, she tore open a packaged synthetic meal of textured meat and creamy potatoes. She gobbled it down in a matter of minutes. She turned the food packaging inside out to lick the meat juices and the remnants of the potatoes in a corner of the package. Now she only had enough provisions for a three-night trek home. This didn't concern her as much as having to travel alone. She'd have to cross the canyon and climb the gullet where she fell. Alex wouldn't be there to assist her. He had eaten all of her rations and his. His clothing appeared old and worn, unable to protect him from the sun's radiation. She looked down at her clothing. It wasn't clean, but it didn't look as abused as Alex's. She squeezed her eyes shut. *Think positive thoughts. You're going home. You're getting help. No one can say Dad's dead now. Morg is going to get what he deserves.*

Celine opened her eyes. Her dad had been silently watching her. He resumed munching on his glowworms. It was difficult for Celine to look at him. His eyes showed internal confusion. He began to doze off, and a sense of relief rushed over Celine. She wondered if eating the worms had caused him to fall asleep so suddenly.

She moved slowly and quietly toward her father's bag. She watched him for any signs of alertness. Normally her dad would wake with the slightest sound, but he was curled in a fetal position and completely unaware of her movements. She opened his backpack; inside she found a cloth wrapped around something. She prayed it would be something useful. Quickly she unraveled the cloth to see what her dad had wrapped so carefully. *Rocks!* She smiled. *At least a part of him is still there.* Next, she patted the side pockets of his backpack; she felt something solid. She opened the pocket and saw a small case, only a few centimeters long. She opened the case and was surprised to see brown colored contact lenses. She had no idea her dad wore contacts. She shoved the case back into the pocket. For a moment, she wondered if her dad might be a synesthesian like her. *No. If Dad had eyes like mine, I would know it.* Suddenly, her dad snored.

Celine placed the bag neatly against the wall. "I'll be back, Daddy. With help," she whispered. She slipped quietly out of the den with Mr. Takei's backpack. *Oh, the cloth.* Once outside, Celine realized she had not rewrapped her dad's rocks; she still held the cloth in her hand. She stuffed the cloth into her pocket and zipped it shut. Then she waded into the shallow end of the river, holding Mr. Takei's backpack high above her head. She didn't trust Compound-issued bags to be waterproof. She had left her pack in Alex's tent earlier. Now she realized she needed it, as it contained her climbing gear and her outdoor wear. She made her way back to the area where the tent was set up; she hoped Alex would not be inside, but he was, and he was awake. He sat behind their backpacks. His elbows rested on each one.

"Why are you here?" he said with authority. Celine thought he seemed rather silly.

"I need my backpack, Alex." Celine found herself standing more erect, ready to deal with a confrontation.

"It's going to cost you," he said. He chewed on a cooked worm as if it were meat jerky. "What's in the bag?"

"Nothing," she said. She wrapped her arms around the backpack. "It's mine."

He chuckled. He watched her every move. Celine felt as if she was being watched by a predator ready to pounce, rather than a friend. Not to mention, the aura around him was red, and that made her uneasy. Celine's mind worked overtime. She wasn't sure how to deal with this new irrational Alex. She noticed his ray gun on the floor. "I have credits," she lied. "In my backpack."

Alex smiled with delight. "Credits?"

"Yes, open my backpack. You'll see."

Alex took his eyes off of Celine for a moment and eagerly opened her backpack as if he were unwrapping a gift. Celine needed only that moment to race over to the ray gun and snatch it from the ground.

"Alex, get away from my backpack," she said sternly. She pointed the gun toward the ceiling.

Alex looked up at Celine and then at the ray gun. "Oh really, Martian girl?" he said with a grin. He paused to yawn twice before lumbering toward Celine. She fired and burned a black spot on the ceiling of his makeshift tent.

"Stay back, Alex. Please stay back." Celine wondered if Alex could sense her extreme reluctance to use the ray gun. The idea of hurting anyone or anything was painful for her.

"I'm not letting you leave here!" he said. He looked angry but also heavy eyed.

Celine looked at the ray gun's setting; it was still on high. She quickly reset it to low. She took her eyes off Alex for a moment, and he was upon her in seconds. He snatched her hand, and the gun fired. Celine looked at his face. His mouth was frozen wide open in surprise. A tear ran down his cheeks, and he slumped to the ground. "I'm so sorry, Alex," Celine moaned. Alex rolled his eyes. He was very angry and in control of his facial expressions, but he was immobile from his neck down. Celine didn't want to face Alex's rage when he regained his mobility. She quickly grabbed her backpack and helmet. She poured the pink water from her helmet and shook it dry. A metallic stench rose from it. She took the cloth from her pocket and dumped a heap of glowworms from Alex's helmet into it. Then she tied the cloth like a little bag and placed it in the outside pocket of her backpack.

"These might come in handy," she said. *Where's the Navi?* It didn't take her long to find it inside Alex's backpack. The battery was low. For a moment she wondered if it still worked. She looked at Alex who was still lying in the dirt. "He'll be OK," she mumbled. "I have to get help." She ran out of the tent and headed for her den. She felt as though she was in a bad dream. Her heroes, Alex and her dad, could not save her. She'd have to save them and herself.

On the way to the den, her thoughts were interrupted by the eerie sound of a man moaning softly. It didn't sound like Alex or her dad. It was a pathetic yet familiar voice. The quiet sobbing was coming from an area further into the cavern, past her father's den.

Her normal instinct would be to locate and help someone in need, but she was afraid. *Could it be someone else from the Compound who has gone mad in this place?* She wanted to help, but more than anything, she wanted to leave for home in the morning. She couldn't jeopardize her chances of getting out. She left the cavern and headed to the entry cave where she would hide in her den.

She was surprised yet glad to see the soldiers had not replaced the boulders in front of the cave's entrance. She could see the dark violet night sky from the opening. She could see only one of the moons, Phobios. Its lopsidedness fit her nightmarish mood.

The only good thing about the cave was its warmth. She could see fog rising from the frozen surface. Soon she would have to face it alone. Her fear of freezing to death in a Compound-issued body tent reared in the back of her mind. She'd preferred Alex's tent, but he had damaged it; it was spread wide between two stalagmites.

Thoughts of her normal dad resurfaced. When she was a youngster, he had taught her how to swim in the holographic pool. She remembered being afraid of lying on her back and floating in the pool; she thought she might bump her head on the surrounding walls. But her dad told her courage was like regular exercise: the more you practice courage, the more courageous you become. He wouldn't let her give up. She was soon one the bravest and most skilled swimmers in the Compound. *Thanks, Dad. I'll need to draw from that pool of courage right about now.*

She once again thought about the climb she would have to make without Alex's help. *I won't worry about that now. I'll have to climb on my second day out. I need to take one day at a time. I can do this."* She almost made a song of the words. "I can do this," she chanted.

She crawled into her small den. *It's too cold on the surface, even for the soldiers.* She slept seated with her back against the wall of her den and with Alex's ray gun resting in her lap. After drifting in and out of sleep for a while, she decided get up and go back to the entry cave to see if the sun had come up. A part of her wanted to start her journey, and a part of her wanted to wait for someone from the Compound to rescue her. At this point, even Morg's help would have been welcomed. She eased out of the den and headed to the entry cave. Once there, she peered up through the opening.

The sky shone hues of reds and pinks, no clouds in sight. She could even see the small bluish dot, Earth, among the stars. Normally, she would have called this a beautiful sky, but not today. Today, it would be her partner and provide her with some sense of comfort. Thankfully, there was no storm coming; she was safe—at least for now. *Can't sleep. The sun will rise soon. I might as well stay awake.*

She hoped her father and Alex would not wake until she left. Having to use Alex's ray gun again didn't appeal to her. She would never forget that look of agony in Alex's eyes. She didn't want to inflict pain like that on anyone ever again.

I have to leave this place while I'm still sane. Remembering the beautiful lady from the painting made her wonder if she even still had her sanity. *Maybe I am not sane. But one thing's for sure, I don't belong here. I've got to get back to the Compound.*

She looked over at the lava tube that led to the cave paintings. All of the tubes were silent. The glowworms seemed dormant. She was glad they showed no reaction to her when she walked through the tube to the cave where she thought she had seen the lady. She had to see if a ladder was there. It would be concrete proof that she had experienced something extraordinary. Her eyes searched rows of apartment openings for the ladder. There was nothing. Celine's throat tightened. "I've got to get out of here," she whimpered.

Celine moped back to the entry cave and from the cave's opening, she saw the sun-brightened sky. She went back to her den to retrieve her backpack. She unsealed it and took out her radiation suit and boots. Tears streamed down her cheeks. She removed the armband that had blocked her life signature. Now, she desperately wanted to be found. She put on her outdoor wear and boots. She pulled her helmet over her head and fastened it to her suit. Slowly, she put on her gloves. *Well, this is it. No one's coming for me.*

She noticed the soldiers' large boot prints in the dirt as she stepped outside into the light, but they were nowhere in sight. Celine looked up at the sky. "Clear day," she said quietly. "What a great partner." She squinted as she faced the east. She thought about her Cherokee ancestors who traveled westward toward a desert on Earth. She imagined hundreds of them traveling to their death. "Just me," she whispered, "but I'm going to survive."

With her head bent toward her chest, she walked out into the cold windy gales and began her journey back home. "I can do this. I can do this," she whispered over and over as if she could will her success. "Three days to the Compound. I can do this."

CHAPTER 19

CHAOS

CELINE LOOKED BACK AT THE Chaos Region before beginning her descent into the canyon. It didn't seem beautiful anymore; it almost seemed like a large scab on top of the Martian surface. Ripples of angry red hills with dark volcanic ash in their folds nestled between deflated and lopsided volcanoes. The terrain lived up to its name—and so had the experiences she had endured while inside those hills.

She patted her backpack pocket where she had placed some of the cooked worms. *I hope I don't end up needing these.* She turned and faced the eastern horizon. The brightness of the sun made her squint; it was not that the sun was any brighter than usual, but after spending days in the dimly lit caves, her eyes needed time to adjust. The sun unfortunately did not provide her with the warmth she had experienced while in the caves. *There are things more comforting than warmth*, she thought, *like family and the familiarity of home.* She shivered as she realized it was time for her to get moving. Now that she was back on the surface, she could feel the usual chill in the air—a harsh farewell to the warm, dark, underground world. The sun was still low in the sky, peeking through coral-colored haze, with a salmon-colored backdrop. As she gazed out over the terrain, she had mixed emotions. She loved Mars, but she was afraid of it. After all, its terrain could be the death of her.

She had crossed miles of inhospitable terrain to find her dad and had expected a joyous reunion after completing her mission. She would've never imagined that she'd find him sick and incapable of traveling with her. She assumed he'd be strong and wise and able to solve all of the problems that lay ahead of them. Then she realized...Even if he had been well, she and Alex hadn't brought any provisions for him whatsoever: no climbing gear, no extra food rations—nothing. *How could he have made it back with us anyway? What were we thinking?*

She studied the landscape and noticed the shifted dunes. *After two days inside the caves, the terrain seems different.* From her position, she could see long vertical scratches from a sandstorm along the eastern side of the canyon. She thought about how she would navigate around the immense amount of sand. The gullies, the place where she fell, would have to be climbed tomorrow morning if she wanted to keep to her schedule. From afar, she could see the shiny hooks she and Alex had used during their climb, still embedded in its wall. *Having this ridiculously good vision isn't half bad.*

Other than the scratches on its eastern side, the canyon looked scooped out and perfectly concave. Celine remembered the cluster of small hills in the center of the canyon. Now she noticed a small opening in one of the hills. It looked like an animal had tunneled into it. She studied the opening but saw no movements or heat signatures. She reached in her backpack and removed the bag of worms. After examining its contents, she placed it in the hip pocket of her radiation suit. "They're holding up nicely," she mumbled.

She traveled at a steady pace. She would reach the gullies before the gales. At the bottom of the gullies, she would set up camp, have her meal, and rest. She began her descent, which she found to be surprisingly easy, despite the fact that some of the slopes were so steep that she had to run downward rather than walk. As she got closer to the floor of the canyon, she could feel its warmth, and she appreciated it wholeheartedly.

Moving across the canyon floor would be a breeze. *Finally out of the Chaos Region and on my way home!* She found herself racing toward the eastern ridge, jumping over rocks and moving like someone on a mission (which she was).

She sprinted past the small hills in the center of the canyon floor and felt great. She had made it to the halfway mark across the canyon floor! As she passed the opening in the hill, she heard underground movements. She had heard these same sounds when she and Alex were together. She continued at a fast pace, hoping whatever she heard would remain underground.

Racing toward the eastern wall, she did not bother to look back until she heard something moving very quickly on the surface, coming in her direction. Though unlikely, she hoped to turn back and see Morg or his crew. She paused. Cupping her gloved hands to block the sunlight, she turned around and squinted her eyes to get a better look through the trail of dust behind her. In the midst of a large cloud of red dust, three large doglike creatures were gaining on her. With their long thick fur and leather-covered noses, they reminded her of the large wolves on Earth she had seen in photos. She could see their long canine teeth and yellow eyes. She wasn't far from the eastern ridge where she had planned to camp. Now, hopes of a quiet reprieve were null. She would have to climb the gullies today, without rest, and she'd have to do it fast.

She began sprinting. By the time she reached the wall, she was exhausted and gasping for breath. She had taken her O2 pill for the day, but the chase and the fear caused her to use up much more oxygen than normal. She found herself feeling light-headed and weak. She could barely see the shiny hooks embedded in the cliff's wall. She took out her rope; it felt much heavier than usual. After making a loop in one end, she threw the loop several times before it caught over the closest shiny hook.

It was here where she had fallen but been saved by her harness. Now she didn't have time to take out any safety gear. She simply wrapped the rope around her waist twice and began climbing. Her arms trembled as she strained to lift herself upward. She could hear the animals racing toward her. They were getting closer.

Their long teeth and large drooling mouths could be seen through the clouds of dust that surrounded them as they neared her. Every cell in her body was heightened with fear. She was only six feet above the pack when they reached her and one began snapping at her boot. She screamed and drew her legs up toward her chest. She began fumbling with her backpack pocket. *Where is it?* Her elbow banged against the wall as she struggled. She was in pain, but she maintained a tight grip on the rope. Feeling woozy, she found it difficult to think. She wrapped the rope twice around her wrist and with her free hand reached into her hip pocket where she felt the wrapped worms.

Glancing down she could see the three large beasts clawing and trying to reach her. Their large red auras extended from their woolly bodies into Celine's orange aura. Their yellow eyes showed hunger, but Celine was determined to *not* be their meal. She slung the pack of worms as hard as she could at the leathery nose of the lead dog. It yapped, but it was the first to gobble a mouth full of worms.

Straining her muscles to hold on with one hand, she grabbed the end of her rope, made another loop, and threw it to the next hook. She unhooked the first loop and climbed up just as the beasts could find no more worms on the ground to eat. They were too late, and now she was out of their reach. She couldn't rest where she hung though, as she knew she might faint and fall into the pack. She continued to climb slowly and methodically. She was too fearful to look back until she had reached the rim of the eastern ridge and had flung herself over it. The two larger animals were lying still. A smaller one and a young pup she had initially not noticed were nudging the still animals. She had guessed correctly that eating the worms caused sleepiness. She hoped the animals would sleep for a while, or at least until she could get far away from them.

The gale winds began to blow. She knew that the gales meant the sun would be going down shortly, and the temperature would be dropping below zero immediately after. She felt too weak to walk, and she was still light-headed. She rolled away from the ledge and slipped off her backpack. She fumbled with the zipper until she could get it opened completely. She could not risk getting a tear in her folded tent, so, despite how overwhelmingly tired she was, she pulled it out with care. After what felt like an eternity, she smoothed it on the ground, pulled its tab, and watched it pop up like a small turtle shell. On her arms and elbows, she dragged her body and backpack into her tent. With her last ounce of strength, she pressed down the magnetic flap for a complete seal. There wasn't much room to move around, but she didn't need it. She lay on her side in a fetal position waiting for her heart to stop racing. She listened to the sad howls of the dog and pup in the distance. Night was falling. She knew even wild dogs wouldn't travel at night. With that in mind, she drifted to sleep.

During the night, a sense of being watched caused her to awaken. She rolled over and looked into the yellow eyes of a hairy animal. It wasn't the beast that had chased her. This creature seemed almost human. She screamed, and so did the animal. It sounded like an alternation of piercing screams and insane laughter. Finally, the animal seemed to calm down. It moved a few feet farther from her, then sat on its haunches and continued to watch her. *What kind of animal could tolerate such cold?*

Celine could not sleep. She and the animal watched each other all night. It had an orange aura around it like hers. A few times she'd doze off and awake quickly to the yellow eyes peering through the orange glow. She kept her hands on her ray gun, set high though she knew using it would destroy her tent and cause a disaster for her. Celine's stomach knotted up.

Finally, the sun rose. The temperature rose to a comfortable three degrees Celsius. It was bright enough to get a good look at the animal and warm enough for Celine to break camp. However, fearing she might agitate the animal, she was in no hurry to break camp. She studied the animal, and it appeared to study her. It moved its wide lips into a grin, exposing long fangs, nearly five centimeters long. Celine immediately looked down. She didn't want it to see the fear in her eyes.

Celine noticed its reddish-brown humanlike hands were sticking out from what appeared to be thick and tightly matted fur. Its barrel chest expanded, and its gills pulsated beneath large ears. *It's some kind of engineered monkey.* For some reason, maybe because the animal was alone, it didn't frighten her as much as the pack of wild dogs did. She hoped she could shoo it away.

She put on her helmet while watching the animal. Then she slipped her feet into her boots. The animal tilted its head right then left, curiously watching her every move. Celine took her tent down and stuffed it into her backpack.

Suddenly, the animal stood up. It was as tall as Celine. Long arms dangled from its broad shoulders. It walked upright toward Celine.

"Leave me alone!" Celine yelled. The monkey stopped and seemed confused. Celine reached down in the dirt and wrapped her fingers around a small volcanic rock. She hurled it at the animal. She thought she might frighten it away. The animal caught the rock and flung it back at her, barely missing her fragile helmet.

"Dang!" Celine threw her backpack over her shoulders and ran down the hill. She heard one of the wild dogs howl. She turned back and saw the monkey creature run to the ledge and look down to where the dogs lay at the bottom of the cliff. It bared its fangs and growled.

"My God! Great Spirit, help me get home alive." Celine continued down the hill. She was relieved the monkey creature did not follow.

Celine hadn't noticed the ape make its way down to the two dead dogs; they had remained unconscious throughout the night and had frozen to death. The ape dragged the two frozen creatures into its underground den.

Celine moved quickly. She wanted to put as much distance between her and the animals as possible. She continued eastward.

She looked for signs of body heat and auras radiating on the horizon but saw nothing. She hung the Navi on the clip outside of her radiation suit. *Maybe it'll charge in the sunlight.* She felt her forearm. *I really hope Mom or even Morg will see my body signature on the Watch Computer.*

She started her journey eastward with strong winds out of the west blowing forcefully and pushing her forward. *It's extremely windy for the second week of May. There's even more of a chill in the air than usual.* She stopped to observe a dust devil in the distance and was relieved to see that it was headed south.

Suddenly she found herself lifted by a gust of wind and slammed a few yards forward. She landed on her buttocks. While she wasn't actually injured, she was a little shaken. Brushing the dust from her bottom, she decided to change the setting on her graviton boots to Earth's gravitational pull. It would make her heavier and less likely to be lifted by the wind, but it would also make walking more challenging. When she stood up and began walking forward, she found it harder to lift her feet. She decided she had to make do with the slower pace. When it came down to it, she'd rather carry a little bit of extra weight rather than encounter another gust of wind that might not be so forgiving.

When the gale winds returned, as they always did at dusk, Celine was disappointed with the distance she had covered. Having the boots set for Earth's gravity had slowed her down significantly. There were no signs of the Compound when she decided to set camp. There was no buzzing chatter, no rising heat waves, just Celine and the silence. She had never felt so alone.

She set up camp next to a large cropping of rocks. The rocks seemed familiar, and this gave her some sense of comfort. Inside the small tent, she lay cramped on her back with her knees bent. She took her flute from her bag. She blew in it once and was relieved to find that it was not damaged. She wanted to play an old Cherokee melody her father had taught her, but she decided to hum it instead. She couldn't afford to waste precious oxygen.

She continued to hum and gazed at the blue planet until one of the dog creatures howled in the distance. She peered in the direction of the howl. She could not see anything, but she knew there were at least two of them out there, a large one and a puppy. Hours ago, when she was a few kilometers from the canyon she noticed the larger one coming in her direction. However, the animal went back for the puppy, and she assumed that, together, they went after slower prey. *Maybe I am the slow prey.*

Suddenly she saw a shooting star streak across the sky. "I wish I was home in my compartment," she said in the tradition of wishing upon a star. Then a barrage of shooting stars brightened the sky. Celine's heart began racing. Though she was not cold, she shivered. She stared at the meteor shower in disbelief. *It's the second week of November! Nearly half a Martian year has passed!*

CHAPTER 20

METEORS

HOW COULD THIS HAVE HAPPENED? Celine chuckled. She had gotten so worked up over nothing. *The comet must have moved a little closer to the planet. Yes, that's it. That's why the meteor shower came early.* It was the only thing that made sense to her. The thought of not being able to account for half a year was unthinkable. After all, she'd been in the cave for four days. Once she had made sense of seeing the meteor shower, she was able to rest.

The next morning, Celine felt refreshed. She looked out over the terrain and saw no signs of the dogs. Even though she saw no signs of the Compound, she was confident she would come across something soon. *I'm sleeping in my bed tonight if it's the last thing I do. Wild dogs, you'll have to find something else to eat.*

The wind wasn't boisterous, but the air was still chilly. She reset her boots to Martian gravity. *I've got to make up for lost time.* She took a few practice steps. *Now that's more like it.* The airiness of her steps was soothing to say the least.

The extra burst of physical strength courtesy of the Martian setting on her boots made Celine feel more energized than ever. She checked the Navi. It still wasn't charged, and she thought it might have been damaged during the flood. She looked toward the rising sun and began her journey home, headed eastward with much more bounce in her steps.

Chanting a rhythmic beat kept her moving forward at a relatively quick pace. "I can do this, I can do this, I can do this," she chanted as she maneuvered over rocks. She chanted tirelessly for nearly two hours until finally she saw a small low cloud.

Heat waves were rising above the Compound. They were invisible to others, but to Celine they appeared as a foggy mist. She couldn't see the Compound yet; most of it was underground. The radiating heat waves gave her an overwhelming sense of accomplishment and comfort. "Home," she sighed. Her journey was not over though. Although she could see the heat waves, there was still distance she needed to cover before the evening gales came. She was determined to make it home before she needed another O2 pill. She wondered if Morg would be a part of her aid team when she arrived.

Regardless, she would say nothing about finding her dad until she could speak with Mr. Rittenhouse. *Mom will be so happy. Now she won't have to marry Morg. I can't believe I did it. I found Dad.* Celine paused for a moment and wondered if her dad would ever be the same. *I won't ever be the same, but that might not be so bad.* Then her thoughts shifted. *And I'm never taking another Brain Booster either. Why did I even need them in the first place? Mom, you have a lot of explaining to do.*

Celine then thought about the beautiful smiling alien from the cave. The time she had spent with her was so calm and peaceful. She felt like she had been in some kind of utopia or dream world. *Come to think of it, she looked like Mom. Maybe it was just a dream...Or a nightmare—who knows?* Recalling her supernatural experience in the caves made her think of her father and Alex. *They'll be home soon, recovering from this awful ordeal. Dad will be safe with Mom and me, and Alex's dad will take care of him. Everything's going to be all right.*

The drone flew above the half-buried Compound and as far as twenty kilometers from its perimeters. It collected data that fed to the Monitored Computer. While no colonist had to endure time on the cold surface guarding the Compound from dangers, some unlucky soul had to monitor the computer inside a small room next to Morg's quarters. In the event that something out of the ordinary was discovered, a human, rather than a drone, was preferred to make the necessary decisions.

The data from the drone was usually monitored by one of the protectors: Morg or one of his crewmembers. Morg had reported that wild dogs had killed two members of his crew. Also, he had been unable to find the teens, and he didn't return to the Compound after his search for them. So since the protection crew was shorthanded, one of Mr. Rittenhouse's private protectors, Stan, was now manning the computer. He despised sitting in front of a computer, watching and waiting like an uneducated guard; he was a trained protector. He had been through years of training in both karate and jujitsu. He cringed at the thought of his beautiful, defined muscles wasting away while he spent his time monitoring the computer. So Stan devised a plan. He would check the computer several times a day but spend the majority of his time in the exercise room doing what he loved.

As he did several push-ups, he mumbled about his boss leaving him on Mars. "How could anyone volunteer to live on such a boring planet? Rittenhouse better get a replacement soon, or I'm quitting. I didn't sign on for this. Now, if he wants me to work on the moon, I might consider it. The nightlife there is out of this world."

After finishing his daily routine, he made his way to the commons for his weekly salad. On Earth, he could have a salad anytime, but with the small greenhouse on Mars, fresh vegetables were limited. He wanted something cold to drink, but there was nothing of the sort, only water gel packs to quench his thirst. After a leisurely lunch and an hour of watching those "busybody scientists" work, Stan decided it was time to return to that cabinet of a room to monitor the computer. *Don't these colonists know that people on Earth don't work like that anymore?* he thought as he made his way down the corridor.

He had been in the exercise room when the drone relayed Celine's life signature and a view of her walking on the surface. Stan sat down on the hard cold bench to review the computer's data, and he noticed something different on the screen. The name of the girl who went missing back in May flashed in the upper right corner. He had no idea what that meant. He then saw the visual feedback. "There's someone on the surface," he cried.

"Admin Rittenhouse," Stan said into his Com. "There's something you need to see."

Celine wasn't close enough to hear the busy chatter of the Compound, but she began to think about the constant noise that pervaded her home day and night. Aside from the humming glowworms, the caves, she recalled, had been very quiet. She'd miss that. She remembered all of the talkative people in the Compound who gossiped nonstop, especially Ms. Armbruster. *What would she say if she saw my glowing eyes? Is there such a thing as hide-the-glow contacts?* She sighed.

Then something with more relevance crossed her mind; she wondered what had caused Alex's and her father's illnesses. She noted that both Alex and her father's behaviors were similar. Most of the time, they seemed sleepy and confused, but on top of that, her dad's calm intellect and Alex's ability to reason seemed to have been compromised. Thoughts of the sobbing male she heard in the cavern made her stomach tense. *Who was that tortured soul?* Something about the voice had sounded familiar, but then again, she had never heard a male cry before.

Rarely did the colonists show overt emotions. Lack of emotions was one out of numerous criteria for being chosen as a Martian colonist. The fact that the man in the cavern was sobbing meant that he, if from Earth, was under extreme mental duress—probably much like Alex and her father. She would report all of this to Admin Rittenhouse and Alex's dad once she reached the Compound.

Analyzing the surface between her and the Compound, Celine wondered why she hadn't yet spotted a rescue team of some sort. *They should have seen my signature by now.* She touched her left forearm. *I hope nothing's wrong with it.* After taking a moment to recollect all of her incidents—the fall she had from the gullies, the wind lifting her, banging her elbow while fleeing from the dogs—, she came to the conclusion that nothing should have actually damaged her life signature chip. The fact that there was no team of colonists rushing toward her gave her a tinge of discomfort.

Finally, after a mild rush of anxiety, Celine saw two colonists heading toward her. She could tell by the smaller size and confident walk of one of the colonists that it was Dr. Baylor. She did not recognize the other person. He was big and muscular, which was rather unusual considering that the males in the colony, besides Morg, were lean. *And why isn't Morg with them?* she thought. A part of her wanted him there so she could taunt him with a grin. *Yes. I did it. I found Dad.* There was another part of her, however, that didn't know if she could control her anger. Celine breathed a small sigh of relief. *Maybe it's best he's not there.*

Suddenly, Celine heard movement behind her and turned to see the dog creature and puppy only a few kilometers in the distance. They would catch her before she could reach the rescue team.

She put down her backpack, unfastened her ray gun, and aimed it at the big dog. The big dog's aurora was as green as the puppy's that tried to keep pace with it. *Green. They fear me as much as I fear them. I don't want to hurt them.* The large dog began to run toward her. Its long fangs were exposed, and drool dripped from its mouth. Its aura flashed red. *Can I change its aura? No, it's coming too fast!*

All of sudden, the big dog lay yapping in the dirt. Sparks and rocks went flying in all directions. Celine crouched down. She looked behind her. A few meters above her was the guard drone. The drone burned a hole through the wild dog's chest. It was stretched out, and smoke was emitting from the hole in its body. Celine dropped to her knees and sat back on her heels. Her head was spinning. The puppy finally caught up with what appeared to be its mother. Its aura was bright green. It stood by its mother and whimpered.

"You didn't have to kill it," she yelled to the drone in anger. "I could have ch——." She bit her tongue. The wild dog *would* have eaten her. The aura around it was powerful, almost dense. It lay there with a hole in its chest. Even dead, it looked ferocious. The puppy nudged its unmoving body. The puppy reminded Celine of a baby wolf. It didn't look scary whatsoever; it looked vulnerable, as a matter of fact. Celine wanted to comfort it, but she could hear Dr. Baylor warning her to get away from the animal, as "it might bite."

Poor thing…it's frightened. Celine took out her last packaged meal. She was basically home now and knew that she did not need it. "Come here," she said in a gentle voice. The puppy did not move. Celine slid the food toward the dog and walked away. As Celine continued toward the rescue team, she heard the puppy gobble up the meal, including the plastic wrap that covered it.

CHAPTER 21

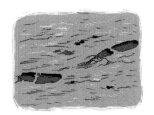

FOOTPRINTS IN THE SAND

◆ ◆ ◆

BY THE TIME CELINE REACHED the rescue team, she was barely able to lift her feet. She dragged them across the sand, leaving behind two very long footprints. Her oxygen level was dangerously low.

"Don't move!" She heard Dr. Baylor shout through her audio Com in her helmet. Celine stopped in her tracks and flopped to the ground, relieved that she didn't have to trudge on any further. She watched silently as Doctor Baylor took a data recorder from her backpack and began scanning her with it from a distance, testing for harmful microbes. She was on the verge of toppling over when she realized Dr. Baylor had sat behind her and was holding her up. She grabbed onto Dr. Baylor's arms and allowed herself to be cradled.

"I found Dad," she said in a voice barely above a whisper.

"Save your breath," Dr. Baylor said. Dr. Baylor took an O2 pill and a water gel packet from her medical bag. Flipping back the mouth flap on Celine's suit, she pushed the half-wrapped oxygen pill against Celine's dry, cracked lips. Celine opened her mouth slightly and felt the pill fizz on the tip of her tongue. She smiled in satisfaction and leaned back into Dr. Baylor's arms. Dr. Baylor then placed the thin water gel tube up to Celine's lips and squeezed the gel into her mouth. Celine wrapped her fingers around the doctor's hand and sucked the nourishing gel from the tube. At last, she knew she would be OK. Celine kept her eyes closed, and Dr. Baylor's attentiveness caused her mind to drift to thoughts of her mother. She hadn't thought much about her mom since she had left the Compound, but the gravity of the situation dawned on her: she had just run away from home and risked her life on the surface—with a boy! While she figured her mother's top concern would be her safety and the fact that she made it home alive, she also knew that there was a strong possibility she'd be furious. *But how could she be angry though? I found Dad. The only one who has a reason to be angry is Morg...* She opened her eyes and looked up at Dr. Baylor's beaming face.

"I'm...I'm OK," Celine said weakly, as she tried to sit up. Dr. Baylor put her hand behind Celine's back for support.

Celine turned to face the doctor. "I found my dad, Dr. Baylor. He's alive."

"Are you certain, Celine?" Dr. Baylor appeared quite worried.

"There's something wrong with him. He really needs your help, Doctor." The words came gushing out.

"What about Alex? Is he with your father? Is he OK?"

"He's OK. I mean he's alive. He's with Dad, but something is wrong with him too."

"Where are they?"

"They're in this big cave in the Chaos Region."

"A cave? The Chaos Region? Do they still have O2 pills?" Dr. Baylor's confusion was obvious.

"No, but there's oxygen in the cave." Celine could tell Dr. Baylor was in utter disbelief by the look on her face.

"I'm telling the truth. Why don't you believe me?"

Dr. Baylor seemed surprised by Celine's outburst. "What else did you see there?" she asked.

Celine detected a change in Dr. Baylor's voice. She had been so anxious to share her story that she hadn't noticed that Dr. Baylor's facial expressions had soured. *Moments ago, a bright yellow aura had surrounded her, but now she glowed a bright red. She's angry!* Celine was confused. She did not know what she could have said to possibly make Dr. Baylor angry.

"I am not certain," she replied. "I-I'm not sure if what I saw was real or if I...imagined it all." The fine hairs on Celine arms rose as she stammered her answer.

"And this cave is in the Chaos Region? You're sure of that?"

"Yes, ma'am, I'm positive."

Celine's experiences in the Chaos Region were etched in her mind. She didn't think she could ever forget them, even if she tried.

Dr. Baylor stood up from the ground and walked over to Stan, who should have been setting up the tents for the night but instead was yawning. Celine remembered hearing Dr. Baylor say that Stan was a celebrity's bodyguard on Earth and didn't belong here.

Dr. Baylor shot him a cold look. Stan shamefully looked down at his boots.

"You do know how to set up the tents, don't you?

Stan didn't reply but began fumbling through his backpack for the tent.

Dr. Baylor stumped away. "Idiot," she mumbled. She took out her Com to call Admin Rittenhouse. "Rittenhouse, this is Baylor. I have Celine. She appears to be in good health. She says she's found her father…She left both Mr. Red Cloud and Alex in a cave in the Chaos Region…Great. No problem…Thanks." Dr. Baylor placed her Com into her backpack and returned to Celine who was resting on the ground.

"Admin Rittenhouse has ordered a satellite scan of the area. We should have their exact location by the time we reach the Compound."

"Thank you," Celine said. She felt like a weight had been lifted from her shoulders. She had found her dad, and now she would have help getting him home. She watched Stan set up the tent.

Suddenly it dawned on her that the usual protectors were missing.

"Where's Morg?" she asked Dr. Baylor. *Surely he'd want to be here to bring me back into the Compound and impress my mom.* Celine rolled her eyes.

"Does my mom know I'm here?"

"I'll answer all of your questions when we are back at the Compound. Don't think about anything right now. Just rest."

Months earlier:

Morg was extremely satisfied with himself. He had gotten rid of the mess the humanoid soldiers had made of his crew and had sent the rescue team to look for Alex and Celine. Little did they know, they were headed in the wrong direction. He was on his way to the Compound, planning to remain safe and sound, when he received a message from his commander.

"A thunderstorm is headed toward your coordinates," the commander said. "Take cover."

Dang. He was almost out of the Chaos Region. He glanced back toward the hills and caves he had just left behind. That's when he saw her, the most perfect woman he'd ever laid eyes on. She was singing, and the sweetness of her voice glided across the wind like the sound of a delicate flute. She stood there in the opening of the hill, not too far away, in a cave close enough to safely run into for cover. He felt compelled to follow her, so he did just that. Her sweet laughter rang in his ears.

"Catch me if you can." He heard a playful voice call out—or was it what he *wished* he had heard. Somehow, it didn't matter. Morg made his way to the cave, but when he reached it, he did not see the woman. He did, however, see the glowworms giving off an unusually bright light. He made his way deeper into the cave, because for some mystically unusual reason he felt comfortable pursuing the illusory woman. *How great would it be if there were more of them in the cave? I mean, they might need my help, after all.* He remembered he had encountered the beautiful wall paintings of lovely ladies. When he finally reached the end of the lava tube, he found himself in a large cavern with several tubes extending from it.

"Which way?" he mumbled.

"This way," he thought he heard. He turned to the right and saw the end of her flowing green silklike dress. The scent of warm vanilla and cinnamon lingered in the tube as he followed her. Morg followed her until he thought he might be going in circles. After a while, he couldn't tell if he were. *I'd better get back to the entrance. Maybe the storm has passed. Besides, I'm tired of this silly game.*

Morg turned to leave. Suddenly, he heard something that reminded him of a compulsion engine: a powerful force coming straight toward him. In a matter of seconds, this invisible force slammed into him with such power that he keeled over, landing on his back. For moments, Morg lay there unconscious. When he awakened, his entire body tingled. Morg compared the power that had just struck him to what putting two moist hands on the Compound's generator would feel like. *I'm alive.*

He tried to stand, but his legs were wobbly. He was not in any pain, but he could not control his legs. They were like rubber. He took out his Com and attempted to call his commander, but, unfortunately, there was no signal. He opened up his Com. The wiring was somehow melded together. *Maybe Celine and Alex are still in here.* He cried out for help, but there was no response. He dragged himself to the lava tube that he thought would lead to the exit, but the glowworms did not brighten the tube like before. He would turn away, and they would glow, but when he dragged himself to any of the lit lava tubes, it would go dark.

Morg opened up his backpack. His light was missing, so he took some food from it and began eating. Eating always made him feel better. *Surely Abbie will send someone out to look for me.* Then he remembered his two crewmen who had been murdered by the soldiers. Samuel was the only one left on his team of protectors. *Sam follows orders well, but can he organize a rescue team? I doubt it. I'm my best chance of getting out of here.* Morg took out a second meal and gobbled it so quickly he didn't even know what he had eaten.

In a matter of days, Morg had run out food. He noticed a few dead glowworms had fallen near him. He heated them with his ray gun; it didn't take much convincing before he popped a couple in his mouth and found them to be very tasty. "Pretty good," he said, wiping his mouth with the back of his hands. "Tastes like chicken."

In between eating and sleeping, Morg had some time to reflect on his life. He remembered when he was a child, he had been the only one in his apartment building who was overweight. Though the children he grew up with were decently nice to him, he wasn't nice to himself. First off, he hated his name—Milton—and he despised the way he looked. His self-worth was at an all-time low, but then he decided to join the military. In the military, he changed his name to Morg and used his size to bully others. He was fearless. No one got in Morg's way. Slowly, he moved up in ranks and was offered the position of First Protector of the Martian colony. He felt like he was at the top of his game until he arrived on Mars and met his new commander—a pint-size, but extremely stern, woman.

Dr. Baylor wanted to start treating Celine with pure oxygen immediately, but because Celine's lungs were in the pill-induced dormancy state, she would have to wait until they arrived at the Compound. She was concerned that Celine had been on the O2 pill for so long. At this point, she thought, it might take longer than usual to get her lungs acclimated to inhaling and exhaling the normal level of oxygen her body needs.

She had many questions for Celine, but they would have to wait. Her temper had calmed down since hearing about Morg's incompetence. Morg had failed in his mission and lied about the whereabouts of the teens. No one was supposed to be in those caves, but now she had to send a rescue team there. It was a good thing Morg was missing at that moment, or she would have had him demoted and shipped back to Earth immediately. She had no tolerance for anyone who would lie to his commander.

Celine was on the brink of sleep when she heard whimpering sounds coming from the puppy. It was sitting outside of her tent. The gales had just begun, so she figured she would have a few minutes to set up a tent and get the puppy into it before the sunset.

"Do you have another tent?" she asked Dr. Baylor.

"Yes, but not for an animal." Dr. Baylor rolled her eyes.

Just as the gales started to blow harder, the puppy began digging and burrowing into the ground.

"You see," Dr. Baylor said. "Wild things can take care of themselves."

Celine was relieved and nodded off to sleep.

When she awakened, the puppy was prancing around her tent.

"I don't have any food for you," Celine said in a stern voice as if the animal could understand her. After they had packed their tents, Doctor Baylor gave Celine a morning ration: a sweet protein bar. Celine broke off a piece and laid it on the ground for the puppy. The puppy gave it one lick and swallowed it whole. She patted its head and touched its fur. She was surprised at how small the animal's body was.

"You're just a ball of fur." The animal appeared to be listening. "You poor thing. You lost your family, just as I found mine." Celine thought about Alex and his pet seal. While there were no pets whatsoever on her planet, she could see how a person could get attached to an animal.

"May I keep it?" She asked, even though she knew the answer before she opened her mouth. Food in the Compound was rationed, and there would be nothing for it to eat.

Dr. Baylor was furious. "Don't feed it!" She said. "If you didn't want your ration, I'm sure Stan would have taken it."

"Yes, ma'am," Stan said. Celine thought he had a silly grin.

"Besides," Dr. Baylor continued, "when it's grown up, *you* might become its meal."

Celine hadn't thought about that. Although she didn't want to admit it, the doctor had a good point. Celine began putting on her backpack and ignoring the puppy. Nonetheless, it ran back and forth to her, as if it wanted to be chased.

Even after they began their short trek home, Celine could hear the puppy following them. She had no idea how to discourage it. *Maybe when it's hungry enough it will go search for food.* Just as she thought it, Celine saw a mole-like mound off in the distance. The puppy saw it too and ran toward it. When the puppy reached the mound, it began digging and kicking dirt, moving its feet in a blur. Moments later, it wiggled its way out of the tunnel with a mole-like rodent between its teeth.

"Wow!" she said. Then she smiled with pride.

"What?" Dr. Baylor asked. Then she looked back at the puppy toying with its food.

"What a survivor!" Celine said.

"What a pity," Dr. Baylor responded.

When they arrived at the Compound at midday, they went through the quarantine entrance. They were thoroughly vacuumed of the red dust that covered their helmets, suits, and especially boots. After they were vacuumed, they each stepped into the privacy booth where they removed their clothing and placed each garment into the extractor that removed all dirt particles and stains. Next, each person went into a cubicle for a blue light shower. Finally, they stood in front of the imager that showed their bodies were normal inside and out—no parasites. Then they put on their sanitized underwear, leaving their outerwear to be inspected by the electronic repair team.

Celine was not her usual self. Her lungs were still dormant, and her O2 pill was wearing off. She leaned on Dr. Baylor for help to the isolation chamber. After Celine was helped to the bed, Dr. Baylor began setting up the oxygen facilitator.

Celine expected to see her mom and Morg waiting outside of the isolation room. Only her sitter, Hannah, was there with a smile on her face and sadness in her eyes.

"Where is my mom?" She asked Hannah. "Is she OK?"

Hannah looked at the doctor who nodded her head, "Yes."

"We're trying to get in touch with your mother."

"What do you mean?" Celine lifted up from her bed.

"Celine…your mom is back on Earth. You've been missing for so long."

Celine's heart dropped. "I-I don't understand…Is she with Morg?"

"No." Hannah looked at Dr. Baylor. Dr. Baylor watched Celine.

"Why did my mom leave Mars?" Celine began to bawl. Tears streamed down her face. "Is Morg here? I want to speak to him." Celine sniffled.

"We don't know where he is. Morg went missing months ago. He was lost in the sandstorm when you went missing back in May." Hannah continued, "Mr. Rittenhouse let your mom out of her contract."

Celine didn't hear much after the words "back in May."

"Back in May? I know I've only been gone a week at the most," Celine said between sniffles.

"No, Celine——" Hannah was about to say more, but Dr. Baylor hushed her.

"What's today's date? I want to see a calendar." Celine sat up completely.

Dr. Baylor didn't say anything. She pulled up her calendar on her computer. She handed it to Celine. It showed: November 16, 2123.

"Is this some kind of joke? Nothing about this is funny."

Hannah and Dr. Baylor looked at Celine with bewilderment.

"No. We wouldn't joke with you about this," Hannah said. "You've been gone for five Martian months."

"How could you not know this?" Dr. Baylor asked. She studied Celine's face intently.

Celine didn't answer. Thoughts were rushing through her mind, making her feel faint.

Five Martian months—that's nearly ten Earth months. Celine swallowed. "I need to rest now," she said and closed her eyes.

CHAPTER 22

ISOLATION CHAMBER

◆ ◆ ◆

CELINE LAY IN BED INSIDE the isolation chamber. She had not spoken or eaten since learning her mother had left Mars. When the doctor told Celine she had been missing for five months, she didn't think things could get much worse, but they definitely did.

I found Dad, and now Mom's gone. When will I ever get my family back together?

Celine opened her eyes. *It's not a bad dream.* She noticed Hannah as she sheepishly peeked over her pillow. Hannah's sad eyes were watching her.

"You've got to eat something," said Hannah. "Admin is doing everything she can to locate your mom."

Celine did not answer. She stared blankly. When Hannah left, Celine cried softly. She didn't care about anything anymore.

A month before Celine returned to the Compound, Abbie had boarded Mr. Rittenhouse's ship. She was tired. She felt empty. As the ship pulled out of Mars's atmosphere, Abbie looked out the porthole and stared back at the red planet.

Mars has cost me everything: my husband, my only child... Abbie sniffled. *And Morg.* Mr. Rittenhouse had released her from her contract. *It's ironic how things turned out; I've wanted to return to Earth for years, but never this way—not without Celine.* Abbie moaned and wrapped her arms around her chest as if a hug could make the pain go away. *I should be taking Celine home to meet her cousins.* Abbie sobbed.

"May I get something for you, Ms. Voltaire?" asked Mr. Rittenhouse. He looked down at Abbie. He appeared tired, and his eyes were moist. "Before the ship stabilizes the wormhole?"

"No, thanks. I'm OK," Abbie replied. She shifted in her chair to sit up.

"Mr. Rittenhouse," she started just as he was turning away. "I want you to know that I really appreciate all you are doing for me," she said. She gave a soft smile.

"It's the least I could do," he said sadly. His lower lip quivered.

Abbie had been so hopeful of finding the children in August when Mr. Rittenhouse brought a floater to Mars. He had flown it over the Cydonia Region, where Morg said he had seen the children. Mr. Rittenhouse had searched the area several times, but he always returned without them, emotionally drained.

The ship's captain entered the cabin. "We're ready to launch, sir," he said.

Mr. Rittenhouse sighed, "Thank you, Doolittle." He slumped into one of the four empty chairs across from Abbie.

"We'll be on Earth in thirty-three hours. I want you to think about where you'd like to vacation. Take as long as you need. Heck, take a month, and then you can join us at Earth Base in Florida."

Abbie nodded. "Thank you." She placed both hands over her face and sobbed.

Mr. Rittenhouse turned his face toward the porthole. A tear slithered down his cheek.

"Launching sequence has begun," the captain announced on the intercom. "Launching in sixty seconds."

The cylinders from the ceiling, above the seated passengers, slid down, encasing them in a sea of fluffy shock absorbers and circulating oxygen and heat. The captain released his control of the ship to the computer command and activated his cylinder. The ship vibrated violently, slipped into the wormhole, and headed to Earth.

◆ ◆ ◆

"I have Celine's computer," Hannah told Dr. Baylor. "I want to contact her grandmother, but I don't know Celine's password." Hannah placed the computer on Dr. Baylor's desk. "I'm sure Celine's grand-mother could cheer her up a little."

"Leave it here," Dr. Baylor said. "I will give it to her when she's wakes up."

As soon as Hannah had left the infirmary, Dr. Baylor typed in Celine's password and checked her Com log. Dr. Baylor had been monitoring everyone's calls and watching them with cameras hidden throughout the Compound. She looked through Celine's log until she saw the word: Enisi. "Grandma," Dr. Baylor said. She tapped the link.

Twenty minutes later, she heard the excited voice of Celine's grandmother.

"Celine?"

Dr. Baylor leaned into the monitor. "This is Dr. Baylor, Ms. Red Cloud."

"Oh," she sighed.

"We found Celine, Ms. Red Cloud."

Enisi was silent for a moment. "Is she all right? May I speak with her?"

"Not now, she's resting. When she wakes, I will have her call you if we can get through."

"I'm surprised you were able to link. I've been watching the Martian weather reports."

"I need to locate Celine's mother."

"Abbie's missing now?"

"Technically, yes. She's back on Earth, and we haven't been able to locate her."

"She's here? I'll try to get in touch with Abbie's mother. I don't have her Com link, but I remember the name of the company where she works. I'm almost positive she has an apartment there. It's time I give her a visit."

"Thank you, Ms. Red Cloud. Celine needs to hear from her mother as soon as possible."

◆ ◆ ◆

As Celine lay in bed, her thoughts raced over the events that took place while she was in the caves. Nothing about her experiences allowed her to believe she could've possibly been in there more than a few days. She retraced her steps. *When I left the cave apartment, all of the water was gone. And there were so many more glowworms.* She remembered that there was something different about Alex's appearance. She wasn't quite sure. He seemed taller and his face dirty and...different. Suddenly, Celine realized what it was that made Alex's appearance distinct. *Whoa, Water Boy had hairs over his lip*...Celine began to sob. She startled Dr. Baylor and Dr. Duke, who were discussing her scans and blood samples.

"Celine, I've spoken with your grandmother, Ms. Red Cloud," Dr. Baylor said.

Celine stopped crying to listen.

"She's going to your *other* grandmother's apartment to converse with her about your mother."

Celine sniffled but took slower breaths.

"Are you OK? May I get something for you? Water pack? Nourishment?"

Celine inhaled deeply and shook her head.

Dr. Baylor handed Celine a buzzer. "Call me if you need me. I'll be in my office."

Celine nodded.

Dr. Baylor closed the door to her office where she and Dr. Duke continued a heated discussion. Celine strained to listen. *They're talking about me.* Celine quietly rolled from her bed and crept toward the voices.

"There's nothing wrong with her test results," Dr. Baylor continued. "In fact, her body hasn't aged more than a few days. There's been no cellular damage. It's like she's been put on ice."

"I'm not talking about cellular damage," Dr. Duke said. "And you know I'm not!"

"So you have never seen tapetum lucidum in a human's eyes before?

"No, I haven't." Dr. Duke paused. "Should I have?" he asked sarcastically.

"Well, I have. These people are special. Extraordinary actually. They shouldn't need drugs to be made normal."

"Look at this," Dr. Baylor said. She showed Dr. Duke a photo of Celine's grandfather, who had glowing eyes as well. "This is Red Cloud's father. This family has been part of the Eugenics Project for three hundred years. They've been bred for the military! You have no right to interfere!"

"You talk about them like they're animals, Baylor! Bred?"

"OK, so I used the wrong term. But they are special. I wish I had their abilities. You shouldn't drug them with some fake Brain Booster to dull down their abilities! They're the saviors of humanity, Duke. We have enemies you know nothing of!"

"I don't care about that! Her mother requested it. She wanted to raise a normal child."

Celine could hardly believe her ears. *Mom had Dr. Duke drug me to keep me normal. The Brain Booster is all a lie? I'm not normal? No, none of this can be true.* Celine's chest tightened from her sore lungs to her throat. She swallowed in a fruitless effort to stifle a cough. She had to hear more. She rolled her lips over her teeth and clamped down, but she still felt a tickle in her throat. *Oh no! Not now!* Suddenly she began what seemed like a nonstop coughing fit. She lowered her head and wrapped her arms around her chest. Tears ran down her cheeks, and the coughing continued.

Dr. Baylor opened the door. "Celine, what are you doing up?"

Celine continued coughing as Dr. Duke opened a water gel packet and shoved it into her hand. Celine sucked the water gel from the packet in between bouts of coughing. Gradually the coughing subsided, and Dr. Baylor walked Celine back to her bed.

"Why were you up?" Dr. Baylor asked.

Dr. Duke stood next to the door observing and listening. Celine noticed Dr. Duke had a fearful greenish blue aura around him, but Dr. Baylor's aura was her normal light blue.

"I heard you talking about me," Celine replied.

Dr. Baylor rolled her eyes at Dr. Duke.

"I heard what you were saying. You were talking about my dad's family and something about...a Eugenics Project." Celine looked at Dr. Duke. "You said my mom wants me to be normal. What did you mean by that? I am normal." But as the word "normal" rolled from her lips, she knew she was something far from normal. "Answer me!"

"I'm not the one to explain it to you," said Dr. Duke. "It's a family matter. Talk with your mother about it."

"I would...if she were here!" she exclaimed. Her aura beamed red.

Abbie had not had a vacation in fourteen years. While resting in her little cottage near the ocean shore, she was disturbed by a knock at the door. It was the resort manager; he came with a message in hand, courtesy of Abbie's mother.

"Thanks," she said in a soft voice as she closed the door and unsealed the letter. "Return home immediately," it read. *Thye must have found the children.* She didn't want to hear the bad news but prepared herself for the worst. She gathered her things and made her way to her mother's apartment where she was surprised to see her mother, Ms. Red Cloud, and Mr. Musk, one of Mr. Rittenhouse's representatives, waiting for her.

"Abbie, sit down," Mr. Musk said. "I have good news for you."

"Oh, good news?" Abbie crossed her arms in front of her chest and sat on the edge of a chair next to the window. She began to feel mocked by Mr. Musk's radiant smile.

Mr. Musk continued grinning. "Your daughter is alive, and she located your husband! He's alive as well!"

Abbie's eyes widened; she fell back into the chair. Her jaw dropped, but she was speechless.

CHAPTER 23

ON THE COM

"YOUR MOTHER HAS BEEN LOCATED," Dr. Baylor said to Celine in a neutral tone.

Celine sat up in her disheveled bed. The covers and sheets were twisted around her body, and her hair was a mess of tangled curls.

"She'd like to speak with you. She's on the Com now." Dr. Baylor placed Celine's computer on the bed next to her hand.

"Mom, when are you coming home?" Celine cried out.

"Celine, how are you feeling?" Abbie replied.

"I-I'm fine." Celine responded in a raspy voice. "I found Dad, Mom. You need to come home quick. He needs your help."

"Your dad can take care of himself. I'm not worried about him. I'm worried about you."

"He's not well," Celine emphasized.

"I've been told. I'm sure Dr. Duke will be able to handle him just fine."

Flashes of Dr. Duke's conversation with Dr. Baylor pierced Celine's thoughts. She turned to look at Dr. Baylor. "Has the rescue team found Dad and Alex yet?"

"Celine, your mother is right. You need to rest."

"Why is no one answering my questions?"

"Ms. Voltaire, I think Celine's had enough excitement for today. You may call her tomorrow," said Dr. Baylor.

"No! We can talk now," Abbie said.

For a moment, Dr. Baylor seemed a bit taken aback. She then softened her face and cracked a smile at Celine.

"I'll be in my office. Buzz me if you need anything." Dr. Baylor made her way to her office, closed the door behind her, and turned on an intercom so that she could monitor the conversation silently.

"Celine, I want you to come to Earth. I want you to live here with me."

"Live on Earth? Mom!" Celine was frustrated with the unnecessary complexity of the situation, but she was also utterly confused.

Abbie squeezed her lips together and looked down at her hands resting in her lap.

"What about Dad?" she continued. "I want us—I want us to be a family again."

"Celine, it's not that simple. And you don't always get what you want—you know that." Abbie spoke in a motherly tone.

Celine felt like her world was falling apart. She wanted to tell her mother what she had overheard between the doctors, but she realized it wouldn't be the best time given the distance between them.

Abbie softened her voice. "Darling, promise me you'll think about it. You could have a wonderful life here."

Celine sniffled. She turned her head away from the computer screen.

Abbie sobbed. "I love you, Celine. You belong here with me."

"I love you too—and I love Daddy, and I love Mars," Celine sobbed. "And…" Celine didn't know what else to say. *I'm not normal anymore like you wanted. Will you even love the real me?*

Abbie rubbed her pale knuckles. "You don't have to decide right now."

Dr. Baylor entered the room. She took Celine's computer from her lifeless hands.

"Ms. Voltaire, it's time for Celine to rest now."

"I will call you tomorrow, my love," Abbie said, with sadness in her eyes.

Celine noticed that her mom did not acknowledge Dr. Baylor.

Celine reached for Dr. Baylor's hand. "I am so confused."

"Life can be that way," Dr. Baylor said. "Everything is not always black and white."

Celine rolled her eyes and inhaled deeply. "Can I have something to eat now? I'm hungry."

Dr. Baylor smiled. "Why, of course! I'm glad you've changed your mind..." Dr. Baylor paused for a moment. "You know you're very special, Celine. And don't let anyone tell you otherwise."

◆ ◆ ◆

Later that day, Dr. Duke returned to the infirmary.

"It's time for her to go back to her own compartment," Dr. Duke said to Dr. Baylor. "There's no longer a need for isolation. Plus I need to get that room ready for Mr. Rittenhouse."

"Sure. I'll put her with Hannah for now."

"What about her father?" Dr. Duke inquired.

"I don't know yet. We'll have to diagnose his condition before we make any further decisions."

"Noted."

"So, Rittenhouse and his entourage are coming in today. Can't wait."

"He's already announced that he's going out tomorrow in that floater."

Dr. Baylor groaned. "That old thing's nothing but a glorified helicopter without propellers. But anyway, he's bringing in our shipment."

"Great. Glad to know he can actually help us with something."

"I ordered contact lenses for Celine. The refractions should hide any glowing issues so to speak."

"Are you sure we can't reverse it? Her mother——"

"She's gone too long without that so-called 'Brain Booster.' Fortunately, it can't be reversed at this point."

"Her mom won't be happy about this."

"She has no choice but to accept it," Dr. Baylor muttered.

Mr. Rittenhouse's ship docked outside of the isolation chamber. He had brought along a shipment of equipment for enlarging the colony's greenhouse, as well as a large supply of dried meats, berries, and nuts. His assistants took the supplies to the decontamination dock.

Mr. Rittenhouse quickly strode into the isolation suite with his head held high and his chest puffed out. *My cousin will be happy with some decent food for a change. And that little Celine—should I thank her or punish her? Alex wouldn't have been out there in some cave if it weren't for her.*

He began firing questions at Dr. Duke the moment he laid eyes on him.

"I need to speak with Celine. Where is she? Why'd she leave Alex?"

"Calm down," Dr. Duke said gently to Mr. Rittenhouse.

"I'll calm down when I am calm. Where is my boy? Lost in some cave?"

"Mr. Rittenhouse, the Administrative team will be here shortly to discuss the rescue efforts."

"Why hasn't anyone left here already?"

"Sir, you did hear about the storm, right? The lightning? It took Celine three days on foot to get here…I understand we'll be using your floater?"

"Indeed—where is the thing? I didn't see it when we were landing."

"It's covered, sir. You know," Dr. Duke cleared his throat, "the weather."

"It appears you've gotten much smarter since the last time I saw you."

Dr. Duke ignored the backhanded compliment. "We're still making good time despite the storm, Mr. Rittenhouse. You did bring energy packs for the floater, right? And our medical supplies, sir?"

Mr. Rittenhouse rolled his eyes and twisted his mouth to one side. He turned to his entourage and began barking orders about the supplies.

Later, the administrative team, Celine, and Mr. Musk, a geologist, came down to the isolation chamber.

Mr. Rittenhouse looked back and forth between the digital timer on the wall and Mr. Musk, who was setting up a table and a three-dimensional model of the Chaos Region.

"It's about time," Mr. Rittenhouse said when Mr. Musk finally completed the model.

Admin Rittenhouse commenced the meeting. "This model was created from satellite images of the region. We have completed an electromagnetic sweep of the Chaos Region for life signatures and were unable to pick up any. We've taken heat image of the region, but the hills and caves are impenetrable... We've come up cold."

"They're in the mud," Celine chimed in.

"Elaborate, Celine," Mr. Rittenhouse said in an encouraging manner.

"There's a mud pond in the cavern, and it blocks life signatures."

"Mud?" Mr. Rittenhouse said. "So, you mean my boy found water?"

"There's lots of water in the cavern, sir. But it's not safe there." Celine looked down. "They're sick."

Mr. Rittenhouse's eyes widened.

Dr. Baylor continued where Celine stopped. "Dr. Duke and I speculate there might be some kind of neurotoxins in the air."

"But Celine." Mr. Rittenhouse gestured at the girl. "She's OK, right?"

"Celine did not breathe the air. Her lungs were dormant the entire time she was in the cave. The toxins we found, we found in her hair."

Mr. Rittenhouse squinted.

"I'll give you the data later," Dr. Baylor said.

Admin Rittenhouse interposed. "Celine, can you just show us the cave where you left your dad and Alex?"

Celine looked at the model for a few minutes. "I'm sorry. I can't tell." She paused and looked at Mr. Musk. "Where is the canyon?" she asked.

"There's no canyon in the Chaos Region," the technician said. "Wait a minute! There is a canyon just east of the Chaos. Right here." He pointed to the model. Celine bent over to get a closer look.

"That's it! That's it! That's the cave," she shouted, pointing to the model.

Mr. Musk began entering the cave's coordinates into his computer.

"Give the coordinates to my captain," Mr. Rittenhouse told Mr. Musk.

With the mood lightened ever so slightly, Admin Rittenhouse addressed Mr. Rittenhouse. "So cuz, did you bring some of the good food with you this time?" Everyone laughed. "And the energy packs for your reconditioned helicopter?" she added.

"It's a floater," he replied. "My captain has already installed the energy packs and is taking it for a test run. We'll be on our way to the cave at first light."

"We?" Admin Rittenhouse said. "You, Dr. Baylor, your man Stan, and Celine will comprise the rescue party." Mr. Rittenhouse started to say something and then shook his head in agreement.

"OK," Admin Rittenhouse confirmed. "Now have your people hurry up and bring in some of that food. I'm famished."

CHAPTER 24

ON THE FLOATER

CELINE SAT IN A FIRM yet comfortable chair while on board the floater. She was amazed at how quickly it sped. She had never ridden above ground before, and it made her slightly nauseous and dizzy. She closed her eyes and leaned back in her seat.

"What the heck is that?" Mr. Rittenhouse called out when he saw the wild puppy chasing the floater's shadow. Stan moved quickly to the other side of the vehicle to record the animal.

"This may be good material for a commercial," Stan said in a giddy, juvenile manner.

Mr. Rittenhouse chuckled. "You're a good man, Stan. I appreciate your loyalty." Stan raised an eyebrow and smiled.

Celine opened her eyes just in time to see the puppy. "The puppy!" she squealed in excitement.

"Look at it go." She laughed.

Mr. Rittenhouse shot Dr. Baylor a questioning glance.

"Puppy?" Mr. Rittenhouse asked Celine.

"I want it," she said. "The drone killed its mother. Now it's alone."

"Celine, we've had this discussion," said Dr. Baylor.

"What discussion?" Mr. Rittenhouse interjected.

"She said I can't have a wild animal as a pet." Celine ignored Dr. Baylor's smirk.

"Nonsense! Alex has a pet seal for crying out loud."

"Well, Alex's pet seal won't have him for dinner," Dr. Baylor fired back, defending her stance.

Celine looked out the window and waved at the wild dog.

"If you had a pet, Celine, how could you even take care of it?" Mr. Rittenhouse asked.

Dr. Baylor sucked in air and turned her head to look out of the window.

"I wouldn't have to take care of it. It can take care of itself!"

Mr. Rittenhouse snickered, and Dr. Baylor rolled her eyes at Celine.

"Tell us about the cavern where you left your father and Alex," Dr. Baylor said.

Before answering, Celine looked at Mr. Rittenhouse in hopes he would override Dr. Baylor's authority.

"We'll continue this conversation later. Let's save my boy," Mr. Rittenhouse said.

"Celine," Dr. Baylor said, calling her attention back to the matter at hand.

"Well, it's huge, and there're lots of lava tubes. We will have to go through one of them to get to the cavern where I left them."

"You said there were glowworms in the lava tubes that provided light," Dr. Baylor said.

"Yes ma'am. They're actually really creepy. Sometimes they watch—no, they sense your movements."

"Did you ever feel threatened by them?" Mr. Rittenhouse asked.

"Once, but that's only because Alex shot some with a ray gun. They shot bolts of electricity back at us."

"I don't like the sound of that," Mr. Rittenhouse said. "Why didn't you mention this back when we were in the Compound?"

"I did. I told Dr. Baylor that Dad and Alex have eaten some of them."

Mr. Rittenhouse looked at Dr. Baylor and shook his head in disgust. "Oh, Alex."

Moments later, the floater circled around the cave in the Chaos Region. The captain could not find a flat area near the cave that was large enough to land the vehicle.

"I'll release the ladder for you," he said to Mr. Rittenhouse. "I'll wait for you in the canyon. Call me when you are ready to leave."

"Roger that. Let's suit up," Mr. Rittenhouse said.

Celine put on her helmet and attached a small oxygen canister to its hose. After everyone was suited, Stan climbed down to the surface first; Dr. Baylor, then Celine, and finally Mr. Rittenhouse followed.

As Celine climbed down the ladder, she was reminded of her climb from the cave apartment. She wondered if she'd have a chance to see it one last time.

As they waited for Mr. Rittenhouse to finish his descent, Celine remembered there were quite a few things she hadn't mentioned. She had not told anyone about her visions in the cave, or the soldiers she had encountered, or the moaning she had heard. *It kind of sounded like Morg now that I think about it.* Suddenly, Celine noticed a shiny cap on Dr. Baylor's head.

"When did you put that on?" Celine asked Dr. Baylor. The cap appeared to have been made of a metal mesh.

"Just a moment ago, on the floater. Only a few colonists have caps like these."

"Why is that so?"

"I'll tell you later."

Celine didn't expect that answer. Dr. Baylor always seemed secretive.

Celine's chest tightened as she began piecing together Morg's whereabouts in her mind. *Morg's in the cave too. That moaning I heard—I know it was him…He left my dad in there to die. He doesn't deserve to come back to the Compound.*

"What's the matter?" Dr. Baylor asked as she noticed Celine's sour facial expression.

"Nothing. I want to hurry and get Dad and Alex and leave this place."

"I agree. Lead the way."

As Mr. Rittenhouse joined them, Stan took his ray gun from his backpack. Celine sighed with relief when she saw it.

"This is incredible!" Mr. Rittenhouse said as they walked in the entry cave.

Dr. Baylor had her data recorder in her hand. "The air is twenty-two percent oxygen, and the temperature is twenty-five degrees Celsius," she said.

"Is that good?" Mr. Rittenhouse asked.

"It would be the perfect place to set up a colony if it wasn't for the organophosphates. The level is way too high: ten percent."

"What?" Mr. Rittenhouse asked Dr. Baylor.

"There are toxins in the air."

Mr. Rittenhouse nodded. "What's the source?" he asked as he gazed at the ceiling of the cave.

"I'm not sure. It appears to be a byproduct of the glowworms," Dr. Baylor replied as she entered a lava tube and stood beneath the quietly observing glowworms.

"Why is it so warm?" Stan asked no one in particular.

"Judging by these lava tubes, I would say we are uncomfortably close to a volcano," Dr. Baylor replied.

"Why are we standing around *lollygagging*? Let's go get my boy," said Mr. Rittenhouse firmly.

"This way!" Celine said. She pointed to one of the lava tubes. Six days had passed since she had last seen them. Images of two very old men flashed through her mind. *I hope they're still here, only six days older.*

Stan and Mr. Rittenhouse followed her through the lava tube. Dr. Baylor continued to collect data from the glowworms inside the lava tube.

"They won't hurt you if you don't hurt them," Celine said.

"I'll be the judge of that," said Dr. Baylor. Using the spear end of her data collector, she picked up a dead worm from the floor.

"Look at these cute little lightning bugs," Stan said. He reached for a glowworm on the lower part of the ceiling as they traveled through the tube. The instant he touched one, he appeared to be frozen. It seemed as if his finger was glued to the glowworm for a moment. He shook but said nothing. Then he dropped to the floor and rolled back and forth.

"Don't touch him," Dr. Baylor said. "Theses glowworms pack the punch of an electric eel. Nearly sixty percent of their bodies are…well…in layman's terms, it's like an electric battery." She looked at Celine.

Mr. Rittenhouse stood a few feet from Stan and asked if he was OK.

Stan opened his eyes after a few moments.

"What the heck happened?" he asked. He looked at Dr. Baylor.

"You touched one of those cute little lighting bugs. And the next thing we knew you were rolling around in the dirt," Dr. Baylor said.

"It starts like this…" Celine said with fear in her voice. "Alex started doing dumb things—things out of character. Then before you knew it, he just…" Celine trailed off.

"I don't think Stan is acting out of character," Dr. Baylor said. Stan sat up and rubbed his helmet as if he were rubbing his own head. Dr. Baylor pointed her data recorder at him. "He'll live," she said.

"Don't touch anything else in here. Understood?"

"Absolutely." Stan attempted to stand, his legs still trembling.

"I'm still not picking up their life signatures," Dr. Baylor said as she entered the cavern.

"My dad removed his. I'm not sure about Alex. They might be in the mud pond, over here." Celine stood beside the mud pond. She turned on the speaker in her helmet.

"Dad, Alex!" Celine called. "Come out! It's Celine!"

No one came out of the pond.

Mr. Rittenhouse and Dr. Baylor looked at each other.

"Dad, I'm stealing your backpack! Alex, I'm taking your tent!"

Suddenly, her father and Alex rose from the mud pit. Mud caked their hair and dripped from their faces. It was apparent they had not washed since she left them.

"Celine." Her father smiled. One of his teeth was missing.

"I brought help," she said, "Dr. Baylor and Mr. Rittenhouse—and Stan."

"Dad, you came for me," Alex squawked.

Mr. Rittenhouse glanced at Dr. Baylor, who was taking injectors filled with sedatives from her medical bag.

"Don't worry," she said. "It'll go back to normal once he's been in the Compound for a few days."

Alex rose from the pond and took giants steps toward his father.

"My boy!" said Mr. Rittenhouse. He opened his arms wide. Alex ran to his dad's arms and sobbed unabashedly.

Dr. Baylor used that moment to swab Alex's neck and give him an injection.

Alex slapped his neck as if stung by an insect. Then he collapsed in his dad's arms.

When Mr. Red Cloud saw Alex collapse, he backed away from Dr. Baylor, right into Stan's waiting arms.

Stan easily held the weakened man until Dr. Baylor gave Mr. Red Cloud the injection as well. Then Stan helped the doctor wrap her patients in radiation protection bags connected to canisters of oxygen.

"Why didn't they bathe? You'd think with all of this water, they'd use some of it to clean themselves," Stan muttered.

"Who knows what they were thinking," Dr. Baylor replied. "It seems they've only used it for drinking."

"This is a gold mine," Mr. Rittenhouse said. "My son struck water! I need to borrow Stan from you, Doc," Mr. Rittenhouse said.

"Here, Stan." Mr. Rittenhouse held his arms out like he was a king appraising his land. "Get busy videotaping that river and the pond. Don't miss these pillars."

"Mr. Rittenhouse, I'd like to get the patients back to the Compound before the sedatives wear off," Dr. Baylor stated.

"Oh, of course," Mr. Rittenhouse replied. "Just a few pictures," he told Stan.

Celine was so relieved that her father and Alex were finally getting the help they needed, but a wave of guilt rushed over her knowing that she had told no one about Morg. She hated what Morg had done, but she couldn't stoop to his level.

"Dr. Baylor," she said. "I think Morg might be in here. Before I left this place, I heard someone crying. It sounded like Morg." Celine pointed past Alex's tent. "Down there," she said.

"Stan and I will check on it," Dr. Baylor said to Mr. Rittenhouse. "You and Celine can wait here with the patients."

"Captain, bring the floater," Mr. Rittenhouse said into the Com. He turned to address Dr. Baylor. "You have ten minutes. Then we're out of here."

With his ray gun in hand, Stan and Dr. Baylor began a cautious trek further into the cavern. Dr. Baylor was first to notice Morg; he looked like a pile of muddy clothing on the floor of the cavern, next to a pond of clear water. He appeared to be asleep.

"Morg," Dr. Baylor said. Morg didn't answer. As she got closer, she could tell that Morg was dead. His shattered helmet lay next to his ash gray body. She waved her data recorder over him.

"He's been dead for at least forty-eight hours…He was a good soldier."

Stan stood in silence as he stared at Morg's lifeless body.

"Give me your gun. You go back and help get my patients onto the floater. I'll download his life signature data and dispose of his body." Dr. Baylor nodded toward Morg's body.

"Yes, ma'am," Stan replied solemnly as he turned away.

Dr. Baylor studied the bruises on Morg's body. "Massive trauma," she whispered. "Rest in peace, my comrade." She set the body ablaze with Stan's laser gun. "One day, your commander will avenge your death."

Stan and Mr. Rittenhouse helped lift Alex and Mr. Red Cloud onto the floater. When Dr. Baylor noticed that everyone was on the floater waiting for her, she decided to complete one last task before leaving the cave. From a hidden compartment in her medical bag, she took out a rapid-firing atom disrupter. She entered the cave where the paintings had been washed away; she had seen it through the cameras in the eyes of the soldiers.

"We don't want any trouble from you and your people," she said, though she neither saw nor heard anyone inside the cave.

"But if we get any," she continued, "we're ready for you." She backed out of the cave, her thoughts protected by her lead cap beneath her helmet.

At the cave's entrance, she folded her weapon and placed it back in her medical bag.

"We're not leaving this planet," Dr. Baylor said before climbing the ladder into the floater. She did not notice the hot lava bubble up from the ground where she had stood nor did she catch Celine watching her through the window of the floater.

Celine watched as Dr. Baylor boarded the floater. She could see lots of heat coming from Dr. Baylor's boots; there was also an abnormally large red aura surrounding her when she entered the floater and took her seat.

Though Celine wanted to ask Dr. Baylor to whom was she speaking, she didn't. That large red aura meant trouble. She watched as

Dr. Baylor's red aura expanded to Stan, and he rolled his eyes at Mr. Rittenhouse. Then it expanded to Mr. Rittenhouse.

"Your irresponsibility and ignorance caused me so much grief," Mr. Rittenhouse said in Alex's direction even though he was asleep and could not hear the comment.

Celine recalled how the red aura had spread from one animal to the other when she and Alex were being chased and how they eventually became angry. She was witnessing the same thing happen right in front of her. She shut her eyes and thought only of the Great Spirit. You are Love. You are Peace. You are Joy. She chanted silently over and over until she felt extremely calm. She opened her eyes and saw her aura had become white and was expanding. The red aura that had been spreading from Dr. Baylor faded pink. She continued to chant; this time she chanted aloud.

"What are you doing, child?" Mr. Rittenhouse asked.

"She's chanting," Stan said. "Let her chant. I feel better already."

Mr. Red Cloud let out a loud snort, causing everyone to turn toward the area where he and Alex lay asleep.

"That's a good sign," Dr. Baylor said. Her darkened eyes brightened. She looked at Celine with what appeared to be pride. "You've done well," she said to Celine. "You saved your father and Alex. You're the kind of hero we need."

Celine looked at all of the pink auras that surrounded everyone on board. Everyone appeared calm and relaxed. She smiled with gratification. "Thank you, Dr. Baylor," she said.

THE EPILOGUE

❖ ❖ ❖

CELINE SAT IN HER QUARTERS, patiently awaiting a call from her grandmother. Her mom's room replacement, Ms. McAndrew, had moved out and was living with Hannah. Celine was finally beginning to settle back into her daily routine; nothing was normal though. Her dad would be released from the infirmary soon, although he still was not quite himself. The doctor said it would take more time—a few months, maybe—for him to adjust. Her mother filed for divorce and said she would never return to Mars. Celine constantly wondered if any of this was her fault. Maybe things would have turned out better if she had just stayed home and taken her fake Brain Booster. *I'm not sure of anything anymore.*

An electronic female voice cut through the pondering silence. "You have a call from Enisi," Uji said. "But you have five months of lectures and assignments to make up. No calls for you."

"I missed you, Uji, but I don't really need a sitter anymore."

Celine typed in the override code her father had given her.

"Overridden," she said. Uji disappeared. "I'll call you when I get bored and start playing Dad's flute."

"Greetings, Granddaughter," said Enisi.

"Good day, Enisi. Grandma, you were right. Everything you said was true." Celine burst into tears.

"Tears, Granddaughter? You have done the impossible."

"Nothing turned out the way I expected." Celine sobbed.

"You found your dad. It is because of you he is safe."

"But I want my family."

"Things don't always turn out the way you want, Celine."

"Why do adults always say that?"

"It's because you cannot control what others do, but you can control your reaction to it."

There was a long silence. "I thought I had done everything right. Things shouldn't be this way."

"Little one, you must look inside your heart, not your circumstances, to find true happiness. You have much to be grateful for. You have a father and mother who love you. I love you."

"I know that, but Mom wants me to move to Earth and live with her. I can't leave Dad."

"Well, you don't necessarily have to move to Earth, but you could always visit."

"I haven't told her I've changed, and I don't think she wants me to."

"This is true. But you are Waya now. And you are her daughter. She will love you regardless."

"Yes, I am Waya. Dr. Baylor said nothing could change that."

"So Dr. Baylor knows?"

"Yes, Enisi. And I think she is military."

"Military? Even on Mars...I told your dad he could not hide from them. What are you going to do?"

"I don't know, Enisi. I like Dr. Baylor. I think she likes me."

"She is manipulating you, Celine. Don't be fooled by her."

"Grandmother! Stop!" She paused for a moment. "We might need the military, Enisi. Maybe I can help. Maybe I *should* help. Maybe, somehow, I can change things."

"I do not understand your thought process, but you are young. You have plenty of time to decide."

"Yes, I do. Do you know that Morg died?"

Enisi's white aura turned pale blue. "I've heard. It is his karma. The energy he sent out returned to him."

Later that day, Celine visited Admin's quarters to say goodbye to Alex.

Their friendship had developed far beyond Celine's dreams.

"Celine, you're a star!" Alex blurted out when he noticed her. "You're in all the media! They are calling you the Sacajawea of Mars!"

"Sacajawea? Why?"

"Because you are a Cherokee, and you led the Rittenhouses to water!"

"Sacajawea was a Shoshone, not Cherokee."

"Does it matter? You're famous!"

"Yes, it does actually." Celine noticed the disappointment on Alex's face when she didn't share his excitement. "I guess I can see the similarities," she said.

"Definitely. On Mars, water is so much more valuable than any ores! Dad said he's about to prepare the next hundred colonists!"

"Really?" Celine was excited to hear this. "Will there be any children?"

"I'm not sure."

"Oh." Celine exhaled. Her lungs were no longer sore.

"I thought you were moving to Earth," he ventured. "You know, to live with your mom?"

"No, I'll visit when I'm caught up on my lessons."

"Got it. Well, anyway, I'm starting a new reality show, and I really want you to costar." Alex said. "We could call it *The First Martian*, hosted by Martian Girl and Alex Rittenhouse."

Celine snickered. "I have five months of lectures and assignments to finish."

"Oh, you'll never finish," Alex responded jokingly.

"I'll get caught up. You have my Com link, and I have yours." Celine stared at Alex. He had grown at least six inches. She reached for him to give him a hug. Surprisingly, he didn't recoil but held out his arms to embrace her. "You're my hero," she said. "You're the friend I've always wanted."

"No, Celine, you're my hero. And honestly, you're more than a friend."

"Good day to you, Alex Rittenhouse," Celine said proudly.

"And so it is, my *best* friend. Good day to you, Martian Girl."

ABOUT THE AUTHOR

JACKIE HUNTER GREW UP IN Richmond, Virginia, and worked as a school administrator and a middle school math/science teacher in the Richmond area. She is a lifetime member of the National Parent Teacher Association. Ms. Hunter holds a master of education from Virginia Commonwealth University. She divides her time between Richmond and Suwanee, Georgia, where her daughter, Ramirra, and son-in-law, Jerry Stackhouse, maintain a home.

Made in the USA
Columbia, SC
06 February 2020

87602221R00174